Neighborhood News

Other Books by Glenn Alan Cheney

Promised Land: A Nun's Struggle against Landlessness, Lawlessness, Slavery,
Poverty, Corruption, Injustice, and Environmental Devastation in Amazonia

Poems Askance

Love and Death in the Kingdom of Swaziland

Potshots from the Left

Thanksgiving: The Pilgrims' First Year in America

Journey on the Estrada Real:
Encounters in the Mountains of Brazil

Journey to Chernobyl:
Encounters in a Radioactive Zone

Frankenstein on the Cusp of Something

Passion in an Improper Place

Acts of Ineffable Love: Stories by Glenn Cheney

Dr. Jamoke's Little Book of Hitherto Uncompiled Facts and Curiosities about Bees

Tender Returns (translation)

The Best Chronicles of Rubem Alves (translation)

Be Revolutionary: Some Thoughts from Pope Francis

How a Nation Grieves:
Press Accounts of the Death of Lincoln, the Hunt for Booth,
and American in Mourning

for Howie

Printed in the United States

Neighborhood News

Glenn Alan Cheney

New London Librarium

Neighborhood News

What's really happening in Sprague.

January - 2000

IRS Rejects Local Brain Deduction

The Internal Revenue Service has rejected a local resident's $20,000 deduction for the brain he intends to leave to science, anonymously, after he dies.

"While this taxpayer's endowment is of considerable interest to scientific research, we cannot allow a deduction in the current year for a future donation," explained IRS spokesperson Martha Schinsplintz. "Logically, we cannot accept such a deduction in the future because by definition, the taxpayer will no longer be a taxpayer at that time."

The anonymous benefactor has promised to donate his brain to Three Rivers Community-Technical College for research and academic purposes.

Upset by the IRS decision, the donor says he is now having second thoughts.

"It don't make sense," the donor's attorney said in a written statement to the press. "The way my client figures it, if a kidney's worth $10,000, a brain's got to be worth twice that at least. You got two kidney's, right? Two times ten thousand is how much? You tell me."

Schinsplintz said that the IRS was not questioning the value of the individual's cerebellum.

"We don't seem to be getting through," Shinsplintz said. "Nobody can deduct anything after their vital signs show zero income. It's a rule."

The would-be doner says he plans to appeal the decision, but meanwhile is looking into the rules of other countries.

"Mexico don't have a rule like that," he said. "It's only in this country. I'm thinking about going to Tijuana and see what the deal is there. ✻

Pentagon to Close Baltic Rumor Mill

The Department of Defense has announced that it may soon close its experimental Baltic Rumor Mill, where hundreds of highly skilled workers have been developing top-secret weaponry.

"Baltic has done its job," a Pentagon spokesman said. "BRM research and development personnel have perfected the use of rumor as a powerful weapon. America's interballistic smear and besmirchment systems will serve us well into the 21st century."

No one knows how long the Pentagon has been conducting rumor experiments in the heart of Sprague, but the word on the street has it that unfounded rumors have been aimed at individuals ever since 1914, when Hanover resident Josephine DeGray masterminded the assassination of Archduke Ferdinand in Sara-

jevo, touching off World War I.

Since then, Sprague has thrived on the rumor business, churning out slander, libel, aspersions and calumny at an unprecedented rate. Rotating shifts have kept production going 24 hours per day, 365 days per year.

Rotating shifts have kept production going 24 hours per day, 365 days per year.

Baltic workers contributed key weapons systems to the country's newest nuclear submarine, *The Defamator*, which contributed to the badmouthing of Sadam Hussein during the Gulf War. BRM designers developed the prototype of *The Mudslinger*, a robust anti-tank weapon that uses not only sticks and stones but names to harm enemy

Continued on page 2

Town Adrift as Paradigm Floats Away

Canoeists head south as Selectmen look for prototype.

A vague sense of uneasiness has swept through town as Paradigm Gazebo is reported missing and probably halfway to the Atlantic by now. Dubious witnesses said they saw it toppled into the Shetucket River, which runs along the town green, shortly after 2:00 a.m. on a recent Saturday morning.

"It was lying on its side at the edge of the river, all broken-like, with the waters rising and a beaver chewing on it," said Vinnie Vandaloso, a free-lance fork-lift operator. "If it isn't there now, it got washed downstream."

A fleet of local canoes headed down the Shetucket to look for debris as a morose board of Selectmen met to discuss whether to replace the Paradigm and, if so, how.

Paradigm Gazebo was the result of century and a half of volunteer effort. Putting cross-cut saws and crudely hewn mallets to used second-hand materials from Quebec,

the group built a public structure that was worthy of the town around it. It stood behind the War Memorial.

"We just don't know where we stand without the Paradigm," first selectman Stephen J. Papineau said. "This is the worst thing since the mill burned down. I hate to think what's going to happen if we try to do without one."

Robert Meya, president of Hanover Philosophical Society, offered an unusual suggestion.

"Why don't we just imagine one?" Meya posited. "That would minimize maintenance costs and leave us a certain flexibility."

Papineau said that the town would probably opt for a modified duplicate based on the paradigm prototype. ✻

Continued on page 2

Man Without Team Does Tricks with Cheez-Wiz

William B. Soleaux calls himself "the man without a team."

Soleaux describes himself that way because he is indeed without a team

"I have no team," Soleaux says. "I've been a sports fan all my life, but I've neve been able to make up my mind. As soon as a team starts to look good, like something I could identify with, somebody leaves and goes to a new team, or the whole team up and moves to a new city, and

I'm left standing there like an idiot."

Forced to wear seed caps, corporate tee-shirts, and plaid jackets, Soleaux says he feels unloved, unwanted and unnoticed. Not once has a team come to him and asked to be his. Despite overtures to the Red Sox and even the Yankees, Soleux has never received a response.

"Sometimes I think they just don't care," Soleaux whines. "I try to do everything right. I kill a Saturday afternoon in front of the TV. I

put my feet on the coffee table. I drink the worst of beer. I eat taco chips with Cheez-Wiz 'til they're coming out my ears. You think that's fun? It's disgusting is what it is. And then the team I'm leaning toward goes and loses. And that makes me feel like a loser, too. And that's what I am. And that's why no team wants to be mine. And I'm ugly, too. I just can't take it anymore. I think I'm going with the Cubs. Might as well." ✻

Lone UPS Truck Still Haunts Sprague

Sightings of the famous Lone UPS Truck of Sprague have been reported by several credible witnesses, including RepublicanTown Committee chairman Dennison Allen, several members of The Smilers chorus, and a FedEx driver.

"It was a little past midnight when I saw him go by," said Allen. "Normally I wouldn't be up that late, but it was a full moon and my dog was acting strange."

Allen said the truck seemed to materialize from the late night fog on River Drive, glowing dull brown in the moonlight.

The Smilers caught a rare, daylight glimpse of the truck on the way back from a gig at the Norwich Nursing Home.

"It was plain as day, as big as the nose on your face, and just as brown as a... as a...I don't know what," said Shirley Masson, conductor of the Smilers. "It was driving right down Main Sreet. We saw the driver and everything."

The so-called Lone UPS Truck has been a ghostly rumor around Sprague since 1967, when a truck, driver, and full load of packages disappeared. Some say it fell into Little River and was stripped by beavers. Others say it was swallowed up by a black hole. Others believe it is still wandering around, lost and looking for a road out of town. Residents have reported receiving deliveries in the middle of night. Some have found yellow notes stuck to their front doors, but the truck never returns.

Bob Something, a FedEx driver who makes deliveries in Sprague, was especially disturbed to see the truck rumble around the curve on West Main St. and disappear.

"It gave me the creeps," Something said. "I got to thinking about it. That could be me, you know? You drive into a black hole or a time warp or something, and... poof!"

A certain chairman of the Sprague Committee on Supernatual Events, said the recent sightings have been reported to the United Parcel Service office in Norwich. As in the past, witnesses described the truck as large, squarish and brown and the driver as a skinny guy with a black mustache and nice buns.

Penelope Soiltone, UPS vice president of missing trucks, says the descriptions are of little help since all the company's trucks are square and brown, and 95 percent of their drivers are skinny guys with black mustaches and nice buns.

The SCSE has offered a reward of $1,000, no questions asked, for anyone capturing a photo o the truck. ✳

Chelsea-Groton Offers Home ATMs

Sprague's biggest bank just got bigger. Now, qualified homeowners can have an ATM installed where it's most convenient - at home!

New customers who open a checking account will receive ATMs with built-in toasters.

"We believe that home ATMs will make it easier to access accounts without going through the hassle of driving to the bank," said branch manager JoAnn Lynch at a ceremonial unveiling of the new units. "We hope the toasters will allow customers to enjoy their breakfast while they're enjoying the convenience of in-home banking."

Homeowners will be able to open the back of their personal ATM and load it with cash. They can then withdraw cash periodically just as they would at the in-bank ATM. The toaster can be set to rare, medium or well done. A rack on the side of the unit holds deposit slips and up to three flavors of Chelsea-Groton jam. ✳

It's Breath Odor Month at SPL

Is bad breath a problem at your home, office, school or camp? If so, May is the month to hit the shelves at Sprague Public Library, where the entire collection on respiratory odor is on display.

The library staff has also located several web sites dedicated to the identification and treatment of "bad breath."

Ann Jones, library director, said that one Harlequin romance, *Halitosis in the Fields of Heaven*, already has **88** people on the waiting list but that several others — *You and Your Breath* and *Talking with Friends about Toxic Exhalation*, and a children's book, *Live Bait, the Barber's Dog* — are immediately available.

Every Wednesday in May, the children's story hour will be dedicated to smells, foods, toothbrush etiquette, mouthwash techniques and the chemistry of the alimentary canal. Children will paint pictures of their loved ones' breath and build a vivarium that replicates the ecology of low tide. ✳

Continued from page 1

reputations.

"We can cut down anybody, anywhere, any time," a certain resident who may or may not work at Sprague Public Library is allegedly reported to have supposedly said. "Like Mother Teresa, for example. I you knew only *half* what I've heard about her, you wouldn't believe it."

The closing of the BRM will idle over 2,800 workers. ✳

Town to Offer Course for New Residents.

Sprague Town Hall has announced a ten-hour certification course for new residents. The course will be obligatory for anyone who moves into town after the first of next month.

"Living in Sprague is not as easy as it looks," said first selectman Steve Papineau, who is already a Sprague Certified Resident. "We feel that ten hours of instruction is the minimum needed to prepare outsiders for the very special place that is Sprague."

The course will teach the history of Sprague, the importance of town meetings, the fable of the Baltic Mill, the basics of rumor defense, what to expect when entering Sprague Public Library, the proper treatment of *Neighborhood News*, and the use of Dumpsters as street decorations.

Weekly Quiz

The most difficult part of the course will be the use of Bob's Rules of Order, the informal variation of Robert's Rules of Order that Sprague employs at town committee meetings.

A weekly quiz will be given to check whether the new residents have watched *Sprague Today* and read *Our Town*. They will also be required to be able to spell and pronounce Shetucket, Versailles, Papineau, Pel-

continued on p. 3...

Lost & Found

Found

9 dirty socks, yellowish-white, on living room floor, 77 Plain Hill Rd. Owner can pick up anytime.

Shredded report card. Owner apparently not too bright.

Lost

Marbles, somewhere along Hanover-Versailles Rd.

Dumb possum, last seen on Saturday night, headed for nearest road.

Town Hall Offers Placebos

Sprague Town Hall is offering free placebos to all residents. The pleasant-tasting pseudomedications are available under a federal program that seeks to make people feel better about living in America and their local communities.

"These things are great," said town health director Hal Burdo, taking an extra one just to demonstrate his support. "I feel better just knowing they're available."

The placebos come in five flavors: chocolate, spearmint, oak, Mexican, and Bud Lite. Prescriptions are available at St. Mary's Church, Sprague Public Library, the Hanover Playground, and Pap's Package.

Federal spokesperson Olestra Drippe said that the pills are especially effective at countering the distress caused by excessive television viewing.

"If you take a federally sponsored placebo and just tell yourself that everything's going to be all right, everything *will* be all right," Drippe said.

Drippe said that the placebos are effecttive against long-term low-dose radiation, arcane concerns, the effects of inbreeding, mild stick-to-it-tiveness and vegetarian urges. ✳

State Mother to Put Town in Order
Onus Hits Board of Ed on proper use of subjunctive

In a move to combat misbehavior and improve tidiness, the Connecticut Department of Adult Supervision has assigned Brunhilda Onus, CPM, to Sprague. As the town's public mother, Onus will oversee general discipline, hygiene, orderliness and nutrition.

Stephen J. Papineau, first selectman, said he appreciated the State's effort to improve the general appearance of Sprague while helping to make its citizens better adults.

"Mrs. Onus is the woman we all need in our lives," Papineau said. "As a Certified Public Mother, she will make us more responsible, encourage us to be more productive and instill in us a proper sense of guilt. And before you even think of it, I do not – repeat *not* — want to hear *anyone* referring to her as 'Big Mama.'"

Papineau reiterated that ~~Big Mama~~ Mrs. Onus was not assigned to Sprague because of her imposing size, which, at a height of six feet three and a weight rumored to run as high as 430 pounds, has already made a strong im-

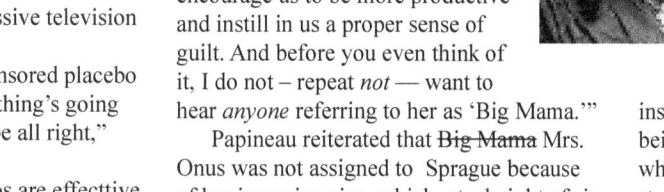

pression on the local brood.

In her first report to the public, Mrs. Onus pointed out that there is no reason for so much litter along the roads of Sprague.

"I spent almost all day Tuesday picking up fast food junk, pint bottles and empty beer cans along Baltic-Hanover Road," Onus nagged. "I am not supposed to be the maid around here. I want the rest of that trash picked up or nobody's going to Florida next winter. Nobody. Is that understood?"

Onus has also made her presence felt at Sprague eateries, both TJ's Restaurant and Fred's News. At TJ's, she snapped off the television and insisted that everyone converse like human beings. She cited three cases of individuals who had failed to eat their string beans. She stymied one patron's attempt to order the fried fish platter, changing it to eggplant goulash and accepting no guff about it.

At Fred's News, Onus discovered a toilet seat left up, a dishwasher that needed emptying, *three* copies of the Norwich Bulletin scattered willy-nilly across the counter, and eight individuals who had long since finished their coffee and were doing absolutely nothing productive.

"The dice were warm when I arrived," Onus reported to the first selectman, referring to a gambling game that patrons have been known to play at the counter. "Today's it's for coffee; tomorrow you're hocking your house, and the next thing you know, you've sold your kids to the Arabs. If I catch anybody playing dice in this town, Christmas is going to be mighty disappointing."

Onus came down especially hard on the Board of Education, where after fifteen minutes of observation she informed chairman Michael Bychowsky that when he is referring to hypothetical situations, she would appreciate it if he would use the subjunctive.

"If I *were*, Mr. Bychowsky, not If I *was*," Onus said. "And *exasterbate*, Mr. Ozga, is not a word. It never was, and God help me it never will be."

Onus also gave Bychowsky a quick lesson in the proper way to blow a nose.

No less harsh on the Board of Finance, Onus gave board member Linda W. Peutz to the count of three to get her butt upstairs and into the meeting room, where she was to keep

continued on p. 4...

Child Seen as Talented, Disgusting

Howard Bulgarino has real talent. At the age of nine, he can do things that few if any other people can do. Many of his neighbors and fellow students have often suggested he take his talents on the road...and never come back.

"He's a *nice* little boy with a weird little joy, using his body like a funny little toy," said Leo Connellan, state poet laureate and Bulgarino's neighbor at Hanover Apartments. "If he grabs his schnozola with all of his might, turn around quick, get out of his sight, 'cause Howie Bulgarino just ain't screwed down tight."

Bulgarino's most astonishing talent is his ability to make his eyes pop out of their sockets when he sneezes while holding his nose. Few adults have witnessed his eye-popping, but several children claim to have seen it on the playground and school cafeteria.

Priscilla Hansin-Hooper, 9, described the popping as "gross."

"For just a second, you could see all the red behind his eyes," she recalls. "It was all, like, slimy in there. And they kind of go, like, *g-slurp* when they come out and, like, *g-schlik* when they snap back in."

Bulgarino claims that by holding his nose while sneezing, he can also make brain juice squirt out his ears. Under the advice of his doctor, however, he is unable to demonstrate.

Bulgarino can also touch his nose with his tongue, drink milk through straws inserted in his nostrils, spit over 23 feet, pee an arc five feet high, belch three syllables in basso profundo, hold his breath till he turns blue, and play popular tunes by squeezing his hand in his armpit.

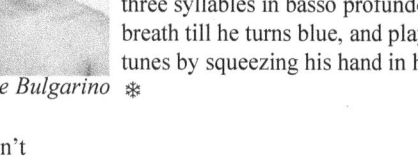

Howie Bulgarino ✳

Certification, continued from p. 2

legrino, Bibeault, Deignault, and T.J.

New residents must complete the course by scoring 65 percent or better on the final exam and swearing to uphold the town principles. Certified Sprague Residents will be able to speak out of turn at town meetings, roll dice at Fred's News, and haul anything they want out of the metals bin at the transfer station. ✧

Cheney Named Town Liar

Glenn Cheney has been named Town Prevaricater. The honorary title puts Cheney in charge of local fabrications of nontruths, deviations from strict fact, questionable innuendos, propaganda, fictionalization and satiric wisecracks.

The position also prohibits Cheney from telling the truth under any circumstances.

"This is the last thing I needed," Cheney said with a wink at the swearing-in ceremony at town hall. "License to lie. It's a terrible responsibility."

The position of Town Prevaricator was created to relieve local citizens from the burden of making up their own stories. Under pressure, Spraguers with a need to deviate from the truth can contact Cheney, explain the truth of their personal situation, and ask the Prevaricator to fabriate a credible alternative.

For several years Cheney has served as the town's unofficial liar, producing excuses for wayward husbands, denial for alcohol and drug addicts, and official explanations issued by town hall. He has helped write letters to lovers, stories for literary magazines, and articles for the critically acclaimed *Neighborhood News*.

"I really hate lying," Cheney confessed. "The truth is is plenty interesting, and it usually gets you want you're supposed to get. But a town without lies is like a meadow without toads."

Robert Meya, president of Hanover Philosophical Society, added his own thoughts at the closing of the ceremony. "A Town Prevaricator brings us a complex set of quandries," Meya said. "Given the high probability that any given statement from Cheney is a lie, and given the epistemological impossibility of speaking nothing but lies, it becomes increasingly difficult for us to discern what is lie and what is truth, what is dream and what is real."

As an example, Meya cited the hypothetical statement, 'I always lie and never tell the truth.' If the statement is true, the speaker must not be telling the truth. If he's lying, then he must be telling the truth. Or the other way around. The pre-Socratic philosopher Testosticles pondered the self-perpetuating contradiction for forty-five years, thinking in every-widening circles until he finally exploded.

"Look what the concept does to that fundamental tenet of human existence: *I think, therefore, I am,*" Meya noted. "Suppose a liar says that. Then what have you got?"

Meya warned that if Cheney isn't careful, he runs the risk of ripping a hole in the fabric of reality as it is now known. Cheney promised to take all due precautions. ✳

Librarian Pleads for Past Perfect

If Sprague expects respect in the 21st century, it had better gets its grammar in gear. That's the message passed down from the director of Sprague Public Library, who, for longer than anyone cares to remember, has served as the town's leading (and anonymous) littérateur.

"I am utterly vomitous over the inability of local youth to properly employ the past perfect tense," Jones says. "It makes us all look like idiots."

The past perfect, Jones explained, consists of the past tense of the verb "have" followed by the past participle of the verb in question. Its proper use indicates either a) a shift from a time in the past to a prior time, or b) a conditional and hypothetical nonoccurring event in the past.

"The school board has trouble with this, too," Jones warned. "I doubt there's one of them that knows the past subjunctive from a hole in the ground."

In a written response issued to the press, Board of Education chairman Michael W. Bychowsky said, "Oh yeah? If she's so smart, I bet she can't spell Bychowski?"

State Mother, continued from page 3

her elbows off the table and not speak unless spoken to. Peutz confirmed that this was understood.

Onus also issued a verbal warning to the Baltic Fire Department, granting them permission to play with their fire trucks but that she'd better not find them lying around when she went to bed. ✳

Sprague first selectman Stephen Papineau advised the town to listen to Jones.

"The library is the sacred space of our intelligentsia," Papineau said, "and Ann Jones is the pope of it. She speaks for us all. If she says to use the past perfect, then I guess we better." ✳

Poem of the Month

Wet Your Pants

Go ahead.

Do it.

Just once in your hot-shot

so-called big-deal adult life.

Cut loose. It won't kill you.

Nobody has to see, to know.

You can wash the pants,

or just chuck 'em out the window

on some dark backstretch of the inter-state.

Worst case scenario,

you get a fine for littering,

not for what you really did.

So go ahead.

Do it.

See if you can hear

that softest of all sounds, feel

that lava emanating like a nice memory

stretching itself at dawn. Watch

how it lubricates the mind. You'll know

by the way your eyes waver, seeing

nothing, knowing all, as data feeds up

from the frontiers of

acceptable perception.

You can do it right now.

You can do it later.

You could do it never,

but then you'd never do it.

You could go the rest of your adult life

wondering if you'll ever do it.

For a while, you'll know you never will.

But one day you'll know

you've been holding it too long.

Then you'll know you

really are going to do it.

And then you will.

And then you'll know.

Anonymous Botch

Neighborhood News

February - 2000

Census Shows Sprague's Stats

The results of the state census are in, and local authorities are still interpreting the results for the population of Sprague.

The census statistics indicate that on July 15, the population of Sprague was 2.949, an average of 223.2 per square mile. Median age was 34.5. Median residential sales price was $99,500. Though 98.3 percent of homes had a indoor toilet facilities, only 37 percent rated their most recent bowel movement as "satisfactory" or better.

Of 822 minors in town in the previous 12 months, 679 had played a prank involving a parent's toothbrush. Over half of all males under the age of 14 had pulled the pigtail or ponytail of a female in the same age bracket. Sixty-one percent of the victims reported the incident to the proper authorities.

Among the town's 1,334 registered democrats, 1,291 said they would not hesitate to vote for a farm animal if it ran on the democratic ticket. Forty-two percent of Republicans said they had experienced periods of embarrassment. One hundred percent of registered Greens said he would vote only for himself, Ralph Nader or a certified organic plant.

Ninety-three percent of adult males reported wasting at least one Saturday afternoon per month asleep on a couch or sofa, and 88 percent of adult females admitted to spending more time in a bathtub than was really necessary. Among adolescents, 94 percent had experienced periods of sloth, and 98 percent of their parents had correctly identified the symptoms. Of those adolescents in residences with over ten square feet of lawn, 34 percent reported pouring gasoline in the oil spout of their lawn mowers, and not by accident.

Only 50 percent of married people considered themselves "female." Of the rest, 12 percent weren't sure whether they were married or not. Forty-two percent of all married adults said that at least once in the previous twelve months they had experienced a funny taste on their toothbrushes.

Catholic clergy reported that only 22 percent of confessions had really been worth hearing but that a surprising 67 percent of the really good ones had come from Methodists. Congregationalists reported that half of their clergy had left town in the last 12 months.

Only 8 percent of Spraguers said they had actually seen the Lone UPS Truck, but 29 per-

Continued on page 2

Town May Sell Mention and Naming Rights

In a bid to minimize taxes and increase the efficiency of official functions, Sprague-B.V.D. town hall is experimenting with a program to sell "naming and mention" rights for many municipal entities and events. Commercial messagers may be subtley inserted into official municipal statements as well.

"Did somebody say McDonald's?" stated Stephen J. Papineau, Sprague-B.V.D. first selectman. "We feel it is important to allow corporate participation in government. Commercial messages are a good way to sponsor our local democracy. We do chickens right."

Papineau pointed out that the town itself was named after a company. That precedent justified a tentative decision by the Sprague-B.V.D. Sugar Frosted Miniwheats Board of Selectmen.

The town privatization program is a protype for the eventual selling off of the federal government.

Claude Pellegrino, chairman of Sprague-B.V.D. New Improved Tampax Board of Finance, reported that the plan, if fully enacted,

would make it possible for property owners to use oak leaves to pay up to 50percent of their taxes.

"We've come a long way, baby," Pellegrino said. "This is the spirit of capitalism brought home and made a part of our democracy. For example, we are now negotiating with a major food company to rename Main Street Prince Spaghetti Street. For whiter, cleaner teeth."

Pellegrino said that Coca-cola, Alpo and Quaker Oats are bidding on naming rights for Baltic Reservoir, and that Amway has its eye on Sayles School. If Amway wins naming rights for the school, the name of Amway Sayles' basketball team will be changed to the Mustangs to the Reps.

Resident state trooper Chris Johnson declined to comment on his opinion of mounting an illuminated Domino's Pizza sign on the top of his cruiser, though he predicted it would be full of bullet holes by the end of the first night he had to use it.

"We deliver," Johnson said.

Papinea denied any intention of changing the name of the town itself to a brand name.

"Just do it," Papineau said. "That's one thing we ar not going to do. Spague-B.V.D. is proud of its partnership with one of America's best known brands of men's undergarments. Don't leave home without it."

Mrs. Guertin Knows What You're Thinking

Most of old-time Sprague has passed through the rigorous classroom of Sayles teacher Edna "Mrs." Guertin. As students, they learned a few lessons. As their teacher, Mrs. Guertin learned a few things, too.

"I know what you're all thinking," Guertin revealed one day at the counter of a downtown eatery. "I can tell just by looking at you."

At her words, the heads of several diners sank a few inches and their faces turned red. After two minutes of hard silence, one man, an elected member of a town board, wiped his lips, excused himself, and slinked from the dining room, leaving behind most of a short stack in a puddle of cold syrup.

"You all ought to be ashamed of yourselves," Guertin said, looking deeply into her cup of tea. "I think it's time we learned how to behave like ladies and gentlemen."

At this, one patron, at a table behind Guertin, stuck out his tongue and wiggled his face at her.

"I saw that, Mr. Courtmanche," Guertin said without turning around. "Why don't you go sit outside until I call you?"

"I don't have to," said Courtmanche. "You can't make me."

Indeed, Guertin did not have to make him.

Continued on page 3

An Alien Lives among Us!

An alien from an unknown galaxy has infil trated Sprague, according to the Sprague Committee on Supernatural Events. The alien has apparently been here for many years, maybe even decades, the SCSE says.

"The alien is disguised as one of us," said the anonymous committee chairman. "It's a very clever disguise, based on years of cultural observation. About all I can say is, it's the person you least suspect. When I say 'person,' of course, I don't mean a person like you and me. It's an alien in human clothing."

The alien has Sprague's 3,000 residents
continued on page 3

Inside . . .

Queen Awards Benson Double-Two Status

LONDON - In a secret ceremony at Bucking-ham Palace, Sprague road crew chief Mark Benson was awarded double-two status. Similar to the double-0 status that gives secret agents license to kill, double-two status gives Benson license to do road work without a shirt on.

At a press conference in the town maintenance garage, Benson, now known in England as Double-two-8, said he was surprised when the Queen called him at 3:00 a.m., which is 9:00 a.m. Greenwich time. When he met the Queen in London, however, it all made sense to him.

"I remember we were repaving one side of one part of Hanover-Versailles Road last July," Benson explained. "It was a real hot day, and this old lady kept driving by real slow in a Rolls-Royce. I wondered, *what the?*"

Benson is especially pleased with his assigned number.

"Double-two-8 is 8-2-2 backwards," he said. "Very easy to remember."

Benson has already been approached by Hollywood agents who are looking for a lead actor to play in three new Warner Bros. films, "Potholes are Forever," "Asphaltfinger." and "Sprague is Not Enough." ✳

Norwich Offers Asylum to Baltic Boy

A simple case of a runaway child has blown up to the proportions of an international crisis, and until authorities resolve the issue, the population of Sprague is down by one.

It all started when a Baltic boy, Howard Bulgarino, lashed together a raft of inner tubes and scrap lumber and floated down the Shetucket to Norwich. A childless couple rescued him and now refuses to allow his return to Baltic.

"Howie can have a much better life here," said Joe Soiltone, a UPS driver who lived in Baltic until he was 12. "We have all the conveniences of modern civilization - a movie theater, a bowling alley, a ballpark, and a normal library. We think it would be cruel to send him back to Sprague."

Sprague first selectman Stephen Papineau, calls the situation outrageous and has threatened to send the town's resident state trooper to Norwich to arrest the boy. The trooper is on vacation, however, and will not return for two weeks.

Bulgarino, who has gained 18 pounds since being dragged from the Shetucket, said he is awaiting a counter-offer from his parents. The Soiltones have offered the boy two televisions in his bedroom and a constant supply of chocolate chip cookie dough.

Cuba premier Fidel Castro has offered the Bulgarino a home in Havana, where a position recently opened up in the home of a childless widower. Castro has promised the boy a free college education, free medical care, a 1956 Chevy BelAire, a job at a raft manufacturing plant, and a lifetime supply of really good cigars.

President Clinton immediately retaliated with an offer of education at a high school with a metal detector, free medical care after the boy turns 65, a low-interest car loan, a job at a casino, and a really, *really* good cigar. ✳

EDC to Rename Planet

Sprague Economic Development Commission has called for a referendum to rename the planet long known to the English-speaking world as "Earth."

"We have a number of issues with the name of this big ball of mineral resources American taxpayers live on," said EDC chairman Kevin Generous. "For one thing, where did the name come from, and who says we have to keep using it? Or maybe that's two things. But still, it goes on and on. And it turns out people in other countries have whole other words for the planet. Who's to say who's right? Why can't we all agree on one name? I say it's time we took our planet back. And where does this Mother Earth business come from? How do we know it isn't an Uncle or a Brother-in-Law?"

Generous pointed out that the very name of the planet brings to mind trees and rivers and whales and puffy clouds on a summer day, images which, he says, skew people's opinion of the place. The subsequent political impact, he says, is having a devastating impact on the economy.

"If we say, 'We're really going to rip Mother Earth a new one up at the Mukluk Nature Preserve,' everybody gets all, like, *ooooooo, what about the bunnies, what about the bunnies* and then all of a sudden they want to know why their taxes are going up," Generous explained. "But if we say, 'Hey, let's dig an open pit in Uncle Gravelball,' everybody's like *whatever.*"

Noting that there is no trademark on the name Earth and that no law, statute or ordinance requires its exclusive use, the commission is calling for a referendum to choose a new name for the planet. While the local ordinance would not apply in other jurisdictions, the EDC feels that by being the first community to rename the planet, it will be perceived as a global leader.

And that, Generous says, means just one thing: tourists...and the hard cash they carry.

The EDC has conducted a town-wide survey in search of possible names. After screen-

ing out names it considered inappropriate, such as Animal Planet, Terra, Gaia, The Blue Orb, and Eden, the commission settled on five names from which voters can choose in the referendum:

- Taxhaven
- Moolah
- Grave
- Dirtbag
- Kevin

"We're talking about choice," Generous said. "It's time the Board of Selectmen stopped assuming that they and they alone control the name of the planet. Nowhere in the United States Constitution does the word Earth appear. I say let's put all the options on the table and let the people decide." ✳

BoE Ups Budget Ozga Ups Lunch

Confirmed fiscal conservative and board of education member Anthony Ozga brought last Wednesday's board meeting to an early adjournment following a moment of confusion when a scant majority unwittingly raised the school budget above the legal minimum required by the state government. Ozga's instinctive reaction was to table the contents of his stomach.

The adjournment precluded the possibility of spending the excess funds on a new nuclear-powered lawn mower, an item at the top of the board's wish list.

"It looks to me like we were saved by scotch and pirogis," said Tracy Medling, a citizen who attended the meeting, intending to speak up for an expanded budget and more educational programs. "I never thought I'd be glad to see Tony Ozga open his mouth, but this time, he really came through for education." ✧

Sprague Stats.continued...

cent believed in it. Among believers, however, only 36 percent believed the truck housed an abnormally large carnivore or was in town for reasons other than being lost.

A shocking 13 percent of adults did not know in what direction the Shetucket River flows. Of the rest, 17 percent said it depended on which way you were facing it, 52 percent correctly answered "downhill," and the remainder said they were undecided, couldn't remember, or would have to ask their parents.

In the Village of Hanover, 44 percent said they could recognize someone from Baltic just by looking at them. Eighty-seven percent of Balticians doubted this was true. One quarter of the population of Versailles said they couldn't give directions to Hanover and doubted they'd ever need to. ✳

New Coke Machine Feels Wallets

Baltic Convenience Store has installed a new, hi-tech Coca-Cola vending machine that sizes up consumers before they get within ten feet. The machine then adjusts its price up or down to a level that matches the consumer's estimated income.

The machine uses two technologies to assess potential customers. One recognizes the physical attributes of the individual. It measures height and weight to develop a ratio which socio-marketers say is roughly proportionate to income. The machine also checks eye and skin color and correlates it to the height-weight ratio, narrowing the probable accuracy of the estimated disposable cash.

If the machine detects crooked teeth, it

adjusts its price suitably downward. Missing teeth, however, are interpreted as an indicator of large consumption of sweets, including soda, resulting in an upward tick of the price.

The machine also sends electronic feelers into the prospect's wallet, where it can detect magnetic strips on credit cards. The more credit cards in the wallet, the higher the assumed income and the higher the consequent price of the product.

In a gesture of corporate charity, short, heavy, dark-skinned, dark-eyed individual with no credit cards will automatically be dispensed a "sympathy soda" at absolutely no charge.

Similar machines have been deployed in

test market areas across the country, often with considerable resistance from consumer activists. Right-wing Republicans warn that it sounds like socialism and may encourage poverty by rewarding it.

Urban liberals, on the other hand, say that the free beverages are demeaning, and the upper end of the price range — $8.25 for tall, slender, blue-eyed orthodontivated people of Scandinavian complexion with more than twenty credit cards — is too low.

The machine at the corner of Main and West Main seems to have something else on its mind. It has been accepting Mexican coins and dispensing nothing but generic root beer. ❖

Networks Attack

Sprague Today

Four television networks have called for Sprague Today to be taken off the air, or, to be more precise, off the Adelphia cable system. They claim that the weekly program is giving viewers the wrong idea of what TV's all about.

NBC spokesperson Humphrey Lapsediddle said that the show was having a negative impact on its entire program schedule.

"Viewers who watch Sprague Today become uncontrollably disoriented," Lapsdiddle said. "They start believing that television should in some way relate to them and their lives, and their sense of humor definitely drops off the radar."

Continued on page 4

Alien, continued...

looking at each other with suspicious eyes. The alien could be a neighbor, a teacher, a postal worker, a librarian, or, as Lucille MacDonald believes, someone who spends a lot of time at the Senior Center.

'I'm pretty sure I know who it is," MacDonald says. "He seems like a nice guy, but somehow you just know he's packing a laser blaster."

Finance Board member Diane Hastings claims she knows who MacDonald is talking about but says it isn't him.

"I'll give you one hint," Hastings says. "It's a lady. And you'd never suspect her because you'd expect an alien to be smarter than she looks like she is."

The SCSE chairman asks that all suspicions be registered with the committee. An Alien Alert fact sheet, available at Town Hall, offers tips on alien recognition. Residents are asked to look for any kind of behavior that doesn't seem quite normal.

Mrs. Guertin, continued...

In the suddenly silent diner she simply sipped her tea until Courtmanche got up and took his chair out to the sidewalk, where he sat sniffling and wiping his eyes until given permission to rejoin the diners.

Most residents of Sprague will confirm that Mrs. Guertin has eyes in the back of her head, but none have suggested that she is the extra-planetary alien said to have infiltrated Sprague.

As life-long resident Tom Charon explained, "She isn't the alien. We're the aliens. All of us." ❖

A Village In His Image (but is it science?)

Sayles School administrators are rending their fragile psyches in consternation as they debate the eligibility of a controversial Science Fair project. The project, developed by eighth-grader Howard Bulgarino III, is a crudely hewn miniature scale model of a village built entirely of human parts and products, among them hair, nail clippings, navel lint, dandruff, scabs, skin, toejam, teeth, earwax, boogers, blood, sweat, tears, and, by the smell of the thing, other common body fluids and solids.

"It's disgusting," said school principal Dr. Harrington "Mojo" Heifer-Titlbaum, "but if you squint your eyes and look at it when it's all lit up, it does kind of resemble certain parts of town. But the question is, is this science?"

Pleading his case before the Board of Education, young Bulgarino said that no one ever told him what science is, the Science Fair rules say nothing about body parts, and if given enough time, the miniature village will eventually rot, proving something that everybody knows but few are willing to talk about.

Bulgarino said that scores of Sayles students, from kindergarten on up, had contributed to the project over the years, most of them voluntarily. He denied using the tonsils of classmate Brenda Pons, though he admitted telling a kid that story just because the kid was, in Bulgarino's words, "dumb enough to believe anything."

Called to the witness stand, Ms. Pons stated that her tonsils had indeed been removed right around Thanksgiving last year, but she had no

idea of their whereabouts. She also said that in her experience, Bulgarino was always telling the truth whether he was asked about it or not and that's why no one should ever believe him. She also said, "I love you, Howie."

Bulgarino wept.

Dr. Heifer-Titlbaum said that neither tonsils nor truth had nothing to do with it because it was a question: *Is this science?* The answer could mean the difference between an A and an F."

School psychologist Hibiscus Speculum (not his real name) said that it was more a matter of psychology, which many people believed to be scientific, though others consider it more of a medical art, a secular religion, or a con game.

"Whatever it is," Speculum said, "they don't make a ten-foot pole long enough for me not to touch Howie Bulgarino with."

Sprague Scientist Questions Earth's Location

For years scientists have believed that Earth is part of the Milky Way galaxy. Recent research at Sayles Elementary School, however, indicates that astrophysicists from out of town may be off by several trillion light years.

"Any dope can show you that we're not part of the Milky Way," said Seth Pellegrino, a Sayles astronomer who has been researching the issue. "We're standing on the Earth, right? It's, like, right here. And if you look up at night, there's the Milky Way, way, way up there. Obviously *we* are not part of *it*."

Researchers at the Harvard Observatory scrambled to explain their oversight. Harvard has always supported the notion that the earth and its solar system are part of the distant galaxy.

"It's rather difficult to explain in terms understandable to the layman," said Dr. Pearson P. Peabody, Professor of Astrology at Harvard. "To use a simple illustrative analogy, imagine looking at something through a telescope. It looks much closer than it really is. That's pretty much what happened, except the problem was compounded by us using a really, really big telescope."

Pellegrino said his discovery will be explained in a project demonstration booth at the upcoming Sayles School Science Fair. Using a simple picture of the universe and a 12-inch ruler he will demonstrate how the earth isn't part of any galaxy.

"It's just here," he says, "all alone in the dark." ✷

Let's Get Composted!

Sprague Garden Club needs volunteers to make compost. The compost will be used to fertilize the flower boxes that are installed at the Gazebo, Lord's Bridge, and intersections around town. A Club spokesman explained that it takes a good three to four good volunteers to fill one box, depending on their size. The composting process involves chipping and shredding the volunteers, mixing them with nitrogen-rich organic compounds, and storing the mixture in an anaerobic container until earthworms and micro-organisms have reduced the volunteers to a dark, nutrient-rich humus. Volunteers should step forward now for the spring planting. ✷

Sprague Today *continued...*

Lapsediddle went on to explain that many viewers simply stopped watching anything but the half-hour talk and humor show, which talks about nothing but a town which, in NBC's opinion, "amounts to less than a scratch on a spot on a hair of a wing of a flea on the tail-end of a shepherd mix."

ABC went even further in its criticism, claiming that the channel 14 program was actually taking control of people's minds. An official statement said that viewers were no longer paying proper attention to commercials, causing a reduction of corporate profits, a dip in national consumption, and a downward trend in the Dow Jones Industrial Average.

"People who watch *Sprague Today* don't buy anything," the statement read. "That is unhealthy and unAmerican. Everything ABC tries to accomplish for Christmas economics gets completely undone by mid-January."

The Fox network has offered to buy the program for $300 million just to stop its broadcast, but Ian Cheney, vice president, humor, and Robert Batten, junior assistant humor intern-in-training, stated that the *Sprague Today* bank account was not large enough to hold that much money and that the crew was highly insulted at the suggestion that they could be bought off.

Batten also took exceptional exception to Lapsediddle's comment.

"There's nothing better than a mutt," he said, "and any idiot knows that fleas don't have wings." ✷

Alligator pit.continued...

explicably in 1997. Meya's collar was found on a branch 8 feet off the ground at the corner of Parkwood and Main.

Dunn said that if the planning board wanted to remove his reptiles, they could come get them. ✷

Poem of the Month

Please, Go

Don't bug me, OK?
Buzz off. Beat it.
I want to do something
Stupid and I need
To be alone.

No help needed,
Thank you, no
accomplice, no audience
either, don't need your tools,
Your advice or opinion.

It's easy, really,
Foolishness is.
Takes no planning, no
Forethought, no permits
Required, no license.

Experience a plus, yes,
But really, any idiot
Can do it, and I
would prefer to do it
Alone.

Anonymous Botch

Town Sets Curbside Guest Pick-up

Sprague has set February 8 as the day local residents can clear their houses of lingering guests by leaving them at the ends of their driveways. The town crew will make one run around town to pick up out-of-town in-laws, aunts and uncles, unemployed college graduates and others who have over-stayed their keep.

"We hope this program will help keep Sprague's roads clear of abandoned visitors," said town crew chief Mark Benson. "Last year, the mess was incredible."

For the safety of the town crew, furniture will not be picked up. If the family couch potato has been left at the curb with the couch, for example, he will be pried from the couch before the crew rolls him into the truck, and the couch will be left behind.

"We regret this limitation," Benson explained, "but last year, a crew member strained his back while we were lifting a Castro Convertible that was abandonded on the side of Hanover-Versailles Rd. It had three uncles lying on it, all of them from Quebec and stuffed with holiday food, some of it dating back to Christmas of 1998. We estimate the whole thing weighed over 1,800 pounds." ✷

Community Calendar

Teen Swap, Hanover Playground, Friday nights

Cookin' with C'lesterol, Lib's, Feb. 14, 7 - 9

Snow-shoveling Contest, 18 Parkwood, T.B.A.

Jeopardy Try-Outs, Library, Feb. 18, 7:00

Neighborhood News

What's really happening in Sprague.

March - 2000

Glenn Cheney, Editor

ED Commission Rolls Out Fat Rat

"An illustrative example of something..."

The Economic Development Commission has unveiled the foundation of a major plan to stimulate the local economy.

It's a 32-pound rat.

"Work on the economic stimulus plan is on-going," stated EDC chairman Ken Genron. "We aren't exactly sure how Ed is going to fit in, but we are certain we have the beginning of something here. We've made the hard decision. Now we just have to work out the details. A mouse that has attained such impressive size speaks well for the prosperity and advancement of our town. It's a symbol of growth, a potential tourist attraction, a model for our children and our children's children, and as far as I'm concerned, a work

Ed

of art that harks back on our industrial heritage while harking ahead to a future of Smart-Growth and low taxes."

Ed is the rat. Genron said that he has been able to reach his current weight by specially formulated diet that began with milk and peanut butter, then dog food and an intravenous cocktail of transfats, high fructose corn syrup and Baltic tap water. Ed now survives on Wild Turkey and live cats.

Asked how a rat the size of a beagle would lower taxes, Genron said that the ED Commission and almost everyone else in town was in favor of lower taxes, a simple concept that seemed to evade the understanding of the Board of Finance, and that the full plan would be presented to the townspeople as soon as it had been developed and approved by the commission. Until then, he requested approval to proceed with the plan.

Several potential businesses had expressed interest in "employing" Ed for a variety of productive and promotional purposes.

"The International House of Gruel is definitely interested in bringing the town mouse into their business profile," Genron said. "And that's just one example of the many ways that other tax-paying enterprises can partner with the town to stimulate progress and bring folks a little tax relief."

Genron said that Ed would be used to help Sprague establish a thematic identity along the lines of frogs in Willimantic, roses in Norwich, and whales in New London. The EDC plans to take Ed to Sayles School as "an illustrative example of something" on which they can base lessons about economic development. ✲

Swear Words Legalized

In a historical and unprecedented move, the Sprague Board of Selectmen has approved the legalization of all swear words, including [expletive], [expletive], [expletive], [expletive], and that old navy favorite, [expletive].

"[Expletive]," said selectman Kenneth Caisse as he emerged from town hall after Thursday's board meeting. "I've always wanted to say that. [Expletive] but it feels good."

The legalization of the long-prohibited words permits everyone over the age of 21 to use the so-called "four-letter" words at will, even in public and in the presence of children and pets.

The town ordinance also gives minors the option to use formerly borderline semi-swears such as those used to denote bowel gas and mucus in both solid and liquid form. The news is expected to touch off civil disturbance at Sayles School, where an underground network of middle-grade linguists has been passing down the words from generation to generation in an oral tradition that stretches back to the days of the Pilgrims.

Continued on page 2

Homeowner Suffers Freak Yard Appliance Accident

A Pautipaug Hill man was reported in critical condition after being found with a leaf blower wrapped around his neck.

Neighbors say they had heard him using it non-stop, from before dawn until after dark last Saturday, but they have absolutely no idea how the accident might have occurred.

"Probably raccoons," said Vince Chrznowski, of Pautipaug Hill Rd. "Sometimes they can be real rascals."

Police are still investigating. They advised other users of leaf blowers to use caution. ✲

President Praises Local Dumpster

Sprague found its niche in national history last week when the President of the United States named West Main Street's most prominent garbage bin National Dumpster Laureate. The honorary title allows the unit to pursue its muse without concern for commercial popularity.

The stalwart recepticle has been hunkering resolutely in the shadow of the Flat-iron building for almost 50 years, bearing the trash of an entire edifice. And except for the occasional toot of a passing motorist, the President said, it has never been thanked or acknowledged.

"For half a century the West Main Dumpster has stood there in rain, snow, sleet, heat and humidity," the President said at the inaugural ceremony. "It has been

Continued on page 2

Prehistoric Board of Finance Unearthed

Stockholm University archeologists have uncovered what may be Connecticut's oldest fossilized remains of a board of finance.

The archeologists were surprised to find the six human figures and long table under thirty feet of ancient volcanic ash at a dig on the east slope of Lee's Hill in Hanover. They had been searching for pterodactyl bones when they came across the petrified remains of some of Sprague's earliest citizens.

A single empty seat at the table was interpreted as an indication that one board member had known of impending disaster and chose to miss the meeting.

Using sophisticated carbon dating technology, the Swedish archeologists estimated that the remains dated back to the middle Pleistocene era. The early human forms were characterized by short stature and exceptionally long jaw bones, and fossilized documents on the table indicated a rudimentary knowledge of French. ✲

Many in Sprague were surprised by how fast the ordinance was passed.

"We really had our collective [expletive] in gear for this one," said first selectman Stephen Papineau. "We've had an unbelievable amount of [expletive] in this town for so [expletive] long, but we never had the words with which to handle it properly. Now we can cut the [expletive] and say what needs to be said."

While many in Sprague rushed to utter the vulgarities they had never dared pronounce, Robert Meya, president of the Hanover Philosophical Society, said the lingual liberalization had merely shifted the problem to a new subset of verbal quandaries.

"Now that it is socially and legally acceptable to articulate these verbal expressions of and disdain, how do we curse?" Meya asked. "When you get a flat tire during a sleet storm and then find out your spare's flat, too, what are you supposed to say?"

In an empirical demonstration of the complexity of the issue, Meya put his thumb on the end of his nose and smacked it with a hammer.

"Now what is the appropriate oral response?" he gasped. "Ow?"

Glenn Cheney, editor of *Neighborhood News*, said he regretted not being able to use the words in the publication. Due to a Y2K glitch, his computer automatically corrects "misspellings," in this case replacing them with words such as *ship, trap* and *Shetucket.* ✳

Dumpster, continued

filled and emptied countless times, its lid slammed in the silence of dawn, its gut filled with the trash of a thousand lives, its resolute khaki the dream of a world where trees spread their shading canopies and ferns unfurl their subtle radiance. But the West Main Dumpster has stood its ground, doing what Dumpsters are destined to do."

The Reverend Norman Bouley of the Baltic United Methodist Church, spoke a few words as he blessed the stand-alone unit.

"When you think about it," he mused, "aren't we *all* Dumpsters? Don't we all have our jobs to do? Don't we all smell pretty bad sometimes and take up too much room on the sidewalk of life?"

The Dumpster brought back many memories from those who have worked and walked the streets of Baltic.

"I remember filling that Dumpster when I was a kid," first selectman Stephen Papineau chuckled. "It's always been there. It's part of my life and all our lives."

The ceremony culminated with the First Lady breaking a bottle of Cold Duck on the unit, sending up a cheer that echoed down the street to the village green and the corner of Main, where a pair Dumpsters sat, sad, forgotten, odiferous and forlorn. ✳

Hanover Nursery to Offer Bank and Financial Services

Hanover Nursery School has announced that it has formed a banking division. The new corporation will be known as Hanover Nursery and Bank. The company will continue to offer its traditional day-care services but will also provide savings and checking accounts, home mortgages, and a variety of investment programs.

"We are very excited to be growing our business," said Cindy Way, president. "We expect to see a lot of synergy between our nursery and banking divisions."

Way explained that the two areas are not only compatible but mutually supportive. The children under her corporate care will help with the banking by counting money, hiding deposits under their cubbies, building things out of coins, and drawing certificates of deposit with crayons.

Bank patrons will be able to stop in for milk and cookies, take a little nap on the floor, or have a short book read to them.

To help blend the two divisions, the bank will issue checks that look like graham crackers and have a slightly sticky feel to them, and the children will sleep on cubbies that look and smell like dollar bills. The ATM will have big, brightly colored buttons that make barnyard sounds as customers touch them.

Parents will be able to pick up and drop off their children at a drive-up window. Children left for more than 30 days will be returned with interest.✳

"And the sky was rife with meaning..."

A quasi-religious epiphany is reported to have struck the chairmanship of the Sprague Board of Education. The rest of the board immediately sensed that education in Sprague would never be the same when chairman Michael Bychowsky suddenly gripped his head with both hands, gasped deeply and said, "The beauty! The beauty!"

The board sat in collective silence as Tracy Harrison, secretary of the board, tore through Robert's Rules of Order in search of an appropriate response.

"Do I second that?" asked Cheryl Blanche. "Was that a motion?"

Bychowsky silenced Blanche with three hard, long-swung whacks of his gavel, after which he held his palms toward the ceiling and said, in the voice of one weeping, "Order! Order!"

There was no further audible response from the board, though six mouths hung agape and more than one head slowly shook.

Through quivering lips, Bychowsky continued his mysterious message. He gestured widely with his arms, as if to embrace the room and the world, and said, "Are not the interiors of this stuff that forms the fabric of our lives all secretly appareled in celestial light, the child's dark radiance of a dream? Are we - you, me, all of us and all the fishies in the deep blue sea - not the very manna of heaven, the manifestation of the universal good?"

Bychowsky scanned the board as if for an answer. Receiving none, he continued with his vision.

"I hear the rains joined in chorus in the waters of the rivers; I taste truth in the sweetness of the unseen air. Clouds burgeon with the silhouetted simplicity of hydrangea, Montana, a serpent, the bust of Beethoven and the buns of a sumo. What bruise is this that marks the blow of blindness past? Or is it but a false creation of the heat oppressed brain? Things are not now as they have been of yore. Wheresoe'er I turn my head by night or day, the things which I have seen I now can see no more."

As Bychowsky waxed pensive, Tracy Harrison was the first to offer words to the silence of the room.

"I'm not sure what just happened," she said in slow, tentative syllables. "Whatever it was, I definitely second it."

Discussion was tabled pending the arrival of emergency medical technicians. They ran a quick psychological test on Bychowsky but were unable to diagnosis any specific problem.

With the issue unresolved, the meeting was adjourned. The board and public left Bychowsky sitting in the Sayles Elementary School art room, his feet propped high on a table of poster paints, his face lit dimly by the light of a waning moon. ✳

Bat Boy May Be in Hanover Apartments

The legendary half-bat, half-boy feral mutoid of *World Weekly News* fame is reported to be held incommunicado in the bel-

fry of Hanover Apartments, according to the Sprague Committee on Supernatural Events.

"This is a conspiracy between Tony Ozga and the United States government," said Myrtle Szbook, SCSE president, referring to the landlord of the apartment complex and a major North American nation, respectively. "We know the Bat Boy's in there and he's being held against his will."

Szbook says several residents saw a UPS truck make a midnight delivery of a medium-sized box that obviously had something alive in it. While rumor held it that the truck was the mythical Lone UPS Truck of Sprague, Szbook said there was little evidence to support the reports except that it was a UPS truck, it came at midnight during a full moon, and the driver was a skinny guy with nice buns.

"If there's a boy and he's a bat, we're gonna to find out where he's at," said Leo Connellan, Connecticut poet laureate and a resident of the apartment complex. "We'll kick in the door or use some leverage, to get that boy some food and beverage."

Landlord Ozga pooh-poohed the report as just another case of strange noises being attributed to animal intruders.

"We've had reports of alligators, chimpanzees, weasels, beavers, rats, bats, roaches and raccoons." Ozga said. "And head lice. None of it is true. And as long as he pays his rent, it's nobody's business but my own. If he was here, I mean."

Ozga declined to comment on whether the apartment complex had a secret belfry. ✻

The Bucket

I am a bucket.
I slosh.
I leak.
I evaporate.
People refill me.
Rain, too.

Poem of the Month

But I'm rusting,
and no matter what
they tell you,
galvanizing aint't forever.
            Anonymous Botch

Major Molecule Found, Lost

Hanover resident and Yale researcher PatrickFoley arrived at work last month with good news and bad.

The good news: He had concocted a biochemical molecule never known to have existed on Earth. The molecule, formally named acetylseryltyrosylserylisoleucylthreonylproteanfizzwaterserylprolylseryloxywhoosieglutaminyl-phenylalanylvalylphenyleukolickspittle-

Sprague Mulls Nuke Plow

The Sprague Board of Selectmen has presented the town with an high-tech solution to an age-old problem: snowy roads. The solution: atomic power.

"I am asking the taxpayers of Sprague to approve the purchase of a nuclear snow plow," first selectman Steve Papineau told the town at a public hearing. "The up-front cost is relatively high, but in the long run, it will be cheaper than using a regular plow, and safer than slippery roads."

Bill Ubig, marketing representative from the Blast-o-SnowJob Corp., presented information about the Model PU-239 that the town is considering. The cost would be $3.2 billion, or less than a dollar per BTU.

"That includes a rear-window defroster," Ubig hastened to add. "But before you keel over from shicker stock, I mean sticker shock, take a look at how this 21st century plow will make your town cleaner and safer."

The plow removes snow by evaporating it with an 80-foot white flame that is hotter than the center of the sun. It also kills poison ivy,

Continued on page 4

Library Adopts Bob's Rules of Order

Stymied in its attempts to properly apply Robert's Rules of Order at its meeting, the board of directors of Sprague Public Library has formally adopted a modified Bob's Rules of Order for its proceedings.

Bob's Rules of Order is a simplified version of the traditional parliamentary rules of order. Bob's Rules dispenses with such formalities as yielding to privileged and incidental questions, withdrawal of suspended motions, and retroactive foistering of undue co-ramifications.

Bob's Rules allows for the hands-on realism of small town meetings. For example, a committee member does not need a second to say, "Wait a minute. Turn off that tape recorder. I've got something I want to say."

thingamajigpolyahmadinajad but known to Foley's co-workers as Big Mo, can convert ear wax to a powerful jet fuel.

The bad news: Foley lost the molecule.

"You know how sometimes you put something down and five minutes later you can't find it?" Foley said. "Well that's pretty much what happened. I put it right next to my car keys. I'm sure of it."

Molecules are known for being very small, though as molecular structures go, Foley's little invention is relatively

Patrick Foley

large. But size, Foley admits, is no excuse.

Because of the nature of the molecule and its unfortunate nickname, Foley is concerned that it may have fallen into the hands of terrorists. He has informed the Department of Homeland Security.

"Big Mo could be very dangerous in the wrong hands," said DHS spokesman Christian Gross. "The Taliban is known to have a large supply of ear wax. It's literally coming out of their ears."

Stymied on the ear wax project, Foley has turned to navel lint, which he says has potential as some kind of plug.

"It's time we started looking into navels," Foley said. "I think God put them there for a reason, and it's time we found out what it is." Ω

"Bob's Rules gives us the flexibility we need to oversee a highly unorthodox institution, such as this library," said Stuart Woronecki, board chairman. "Robert's Rules offers no procedures for, say, jumping up and moving the table six feet to the side to avoid water dripping in from the ceiling. Bob says to just get up and do it."

Board secretary Glenn Cheney said that Bob's Rules make it much easier to take minutes of the meeting. Under section 2, paragraph 3, on Stretching the Truth, for example, the secretary is allowed to insert inflammatory adjectives and adverbs and to exaggerate facts as necessary to get people to pay attention.

"Minutes of the Meeting should be a creative product," Cheney says. "They are the art form of our times. They should convey the zeitgeist of our town. When archeologists dig us up in a thousand years, we want them to know how well we had things under control, not how well we were *supposed* to." ✻

Burdo Warns of Snow Snakes

Town health director Hal Burdo has issued a warning about an infestation of snow snakes. The local population of the winter vipers has reached dangerous levels.

"Children are especially at risk while waiting for the school bus on snowy winter mornings," said Burdo. "The snow snake strikes without warning and can cause abdominal spasms, or hiccups, within three minutes."

Burdo described the snake as pure white, very thin, with green eyes and about four feet long. It leaves a distinctive shallow winding track in the snow.

Burdo said that the best defense against snow snakes is a good pair of galoshes and a breakfast consisting of the five main food groups,

"I wouldn't want to be out there with Captain Crunch in my bloodstream," Burdo said. "It draws snakes like mud draws pigs."
✳

Plow continued

venomous snakes and everything else alongside the road and leaves a smooth, attractive ebony glass glaze on the asphalt.

"The great thing about this unit is that it needs no fuel besides the uranium pellets in the reactor," Ubig explained. "It will run for a 250,000 years without refueling. On a cost-per-mile basis, that's too cheap to measure. After that quarter-million years, all you have to do is roll it into the Tickshucket, I mean Shetucket, and let nature take its course."

Ubig stressed the safety of the PU-239, reassuring the crowd of four townspeople that the unit cannot possibly blow up and that it wouldn't matter if it did because radiation is good for you. In fact, he said, the insignificant amounts of that came from the unit's exhaust pipe would amount to little more than a simple series of testicular X-rays.

"Extensive federal studies have shown that radiation affects fewer than a fraction of a percentage of individuals," Ubig said. "If you discount Hiroshima, Nagasaki, Three Mile Island, Chernobyl, Millstone, Nevada, Fukushima, Bikini, and Siberia, and those two power plants that caught fire in Japan, and that case involving cobalt-60 in Brazil, there has never been a documented fatality due to radiation. The federal government has seen to that."

Ubig pointed out that if Sprague had an average of 200 fatal car crashes per year due to slippery roads over the course of 250,000 years, the entire town would be dead.

"For all intense purposes, we're talking eternity here," Ubig said. "How can you say no to that?"✳

Bozo Comes to Town, Leaves

Bozo, the famous clown, or someone disguised as Bozo, passed through Sprague last week. Apparently he was attempting to hitch-hike out of Scotland and in the direction of Occum, but he met with little luck in this town.

Bozo was first spotted on Rt. 97 at Waldo Road, the northern edge of town. The clown was walking backwards with his thumb stuck out hitch-hike style. In his other hand he carried a small suitcase painted with daisies.

An hour later, the flamboyant hitch-hiker was passing Hazelwood Road, still walking backward with his thumb out. One witness said his tongue was hanging way out as if he were panting.

By noon, Bozo arrived in Baltic, tramping his big shoes across Lord's Bridge and holding his round red nose away from his face so he could breathe. By this time, an estimated 200 locals were casually walking the downtown area. Breathless gasps of "Look!" and "Here he comes!" washed through the crowd, which was pretending hard not to notice the presence of a celebrity.

Bozo turned right (because he was walking backwards) at the Baltic Convenience Store, proceeded as far as Beaver Brook, and took a seat on a certain post. There he opened his little suitcase, removed a banana, peeled it, and ate it, one bite at a time. Whenever a car passed, he leaned toward the road, thumb out. When he finished his banana, he kissed his fingertips, closed his suitcase, tossed the banana peel on the sidewalk and continued his backward way down Rt. 97.

Some 400-500 curious residents strolled south on Rt. 97, keeping a good 200 yards away and moving no faster than Bozo could walk backwards. They saw him shake a pebble from his shoes. They saw him drink from the Shetucket and rinse out the inside of his nose. They saw him take a leak.

Dogs barked at Bozo. Children waved from a school bus. The state trooper drove by 18 times.

"There's nothing on the books that says a clown can't hitch-hike," resident trooper Chris Johnson said later. "What was I supposed to do, ask him for ID?"

A nun drove by in a station wagon. One car honked. Bozo honked back. In all, several hundred cars drove past Bozo without stopping.

In Occum, a truck from the Franklin Mushroom Farm stopped and gave Bozo a ride. He was never seen again. Neither was the truck. ✳

Local Company Patents Safer Electric Chair

KraeCo Electric, Sprague's premier electric contractor, has developed a low-voltage electric chair that may eliminate the need for America's unique execution method

"The KraeSeat is a safe, effective means of fighting crime," said Gary Kraemer, president of the company. "Rather than kill, it simply instills an offender with a proper sense of concern about the future."

Kraemer said that the KraeSeat must be used when the potential murderer is still in the early stages of criminal activity, such as littering, failing to return library books, handing in overdue homework, and staying up past midnight within town limits.

"Basically, it's a means of dealing people who are on the outer fringe of innocence," Kraemer said. "That includes just about everybody, so I expect the KraeSeat to gain broad popopularity. The marketing potential is staggering."

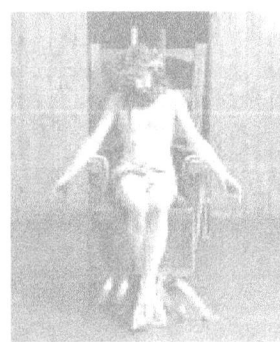

Safe and easy to use, no heavier or larger than a typical lawn chair, the KraeSeat is easily portable and operates off four AA batteries (not included). It comes with an a/c adapter so it can be plugged into the cigarette lighter of a car.

Kraemer says he will market the chair to the state police for use as standard equipment in the trunk of every cruiser. The Sprague Board of Education has also expressed interest in possible educational applications. ✳

Community Announcements

Adorable kittens - free to good home. Bad homes must pay $5.

Lost: Dalmation. If spotted, call 822-1290.

Lost: Air from left rear tire. If seen, call 822-9607.

For Sale: Lawn mower, like new, and 50 feet of baling wire. Cheap.

Neighborhood News

April - 2000

What's really happening in Sprague.

Town to Offer Course for New Residents

Sprague Town Hall has announced a ten-hour certification course for new residents. The course will be obligatory for anyone who moves into town after the first of next month.

"Living in Sprague is not as easy as it looks," said first selectman Steve Papineau, CSR. "We feel that ten hours of instruction is the minimum needed to prepare outsiders for the very special place that is Sprague."

The course will teach the history of Sprague, the importance of town meetings, the fable of the Baltic Mill, the basics of rumor defense, what to expect when entering Sprague Public Library, the proper treatment of *Neighborhood News*, and the use of Dumpsters as street decorations.

The most difficult part of the course will be the use of Bob's Rules of Order, the informal variation of Robert's Rules of Order that Sprague employs at town committee meetings.

A weekly quiz will be given to check whether the new residents have watched *Sprague Today* and read *Our Town*. They will also be required to be able to spell and pronounce Shetucket, Versailles, Papineau, Pellegrino, Bibeault, Deignault, and T.J.

New residents must complete the course by scoring 65 percent or better on the final exam and swearing to uphold the town principles. Certified Sprague Residents will be able to speak out of turn at town meetings, roll dice at Fred's News, and haul anything they want out of the metals bin at the transfer station. ◆

Conquistadores Discover Sprague!

It's hard to say who was more surprised — the discoverers or the discovered — when 36 conquistadores rode into town last Thursday. As the town scrambled to find someone who spoke Spanish, the armored horsemen planted a flag on the bank of the Shetucket and declared the entire region a territory of Spain.

Dennis Delaney, town historian, noted that "this could be a serious problem" and cited an 16th-century incident in what is now Mexico, where a few dozen conquistadores toppled the Aztec empire, beheaded its emperor and massacred most of its people.

First selectman Stephen Papineau urged calm as he dialed 9-1-1 only to learn that the resident state trooper is on vacation until the end of the month.

"Just when you need him," Papineau said.

"It's always like that."

Having no alternatives for the defense of Sprague, Papineau rallied the Baltic Fire Department, who arrived wearing yellow slickers and carrying battle axes but were clearly uneasy about confronting the mounted warriors, who wore cast-iron armor and carried swords, 12-foot picaderos and the head of Montezuma, former emperor of the Aztecs.

"On the front of the fire department there is a sign that bears our motto: *Nothing we can't handle*," said Daniel Nagle, fire chief, as he signaled for the town's two firetrucks to form a circle. "I think it's time we had that changed."

Glenn Cheney, former Sayles Spanish

Continued on page 4

Hypnotist Entrances Students and Staff

Authorities are still unsure exactly what happened at Sayles School last Friday. Early reports indicate that middle-school pupil Howie Bulgarino, in a science project gone awry, hypnotized the entire audience of over 300 children, 32 staff and faculty, and several parents and other citizens who were present.

As everyone at the school was under the mass trance, reports by witnesses are vague and confused. Police have pieced together only a few details. Apparently the first sign of a problem was the lack of applause at the end of the performance. The audience sat in complete silence until Dr. Harrington "Mojo" Heiffer-tittlbaum, principal, eyes wide and dilated, said that every-

Continued on page 2

Existentialist Injures Child

Justin Bulgarino, 8, received an injurious psychological blow when an out-of-town existentialist hit him with the meaninglessness of life. The child was reported to be devastated, perhaps permanently.

The incident happened at the Baltic playground, on High St., when the stranger saw Justin leap gleefully from a swing and dash around the perimeter of the playground, screaming like a pterodactyl on fire.

"Your joy is meaningless," the stranger said, pointing hard at Bulgarino, his eyes glaring. "Your fun is utterly futile and without ba-

Continued on page 4

Gejdensen Backs Federal Snow Days

U.S. representative Sam Gejdensen brought his support of the proposed federal snow days to the Snow Day rally in Sprague, and the townspeople backed him overwhelmingly.

"America needs snow days to retain its sanity," Gejdensen said to the cheering crowd. "And sanity should not depend on actual snow."

The Federal Snow Day Act of 2000 is now before congress. If passed, it will allot 12 snow days for each year for the entire nation. Heavy snow across the northern states would result in a snow day for the entire nation, including Hawaii, Guam and Puerto Rico. If all 12 days are not used by May 31, the president will randomly choose enough Wednesdays to make up the difference before September 30.

"Once in a while, this nation needs to come to a complete standstill," Gejdensen said. "Just like every animal in the world, capitalism needs

Continued on page 2

Conquistadores continued...

teacher and shameless polyglot, arrived on the scene to defuse the crisis. As the *Sprague Today* television crew recorded the historic mment, Cheney addressed the conquistadores from about 13 feet away.

"¿Como está usted?" Cheney asked.

The Sprague invaders responded by putting their picaderos to Cheney's chest and growling, *"¿Dónde está El Dorado?"*

Cheney recognized the name of the place they were looking for — *El Dorado*, the City of Gold.

"No aquí," he said. *"Aquí es El Spragoo*, City of Affordable Housing. You want to take 395 south. Pick up 95 south. Keep going, keep going, keep going. Take *Exito 2.*"

Apparently the invaders then realized that they had not yet reached the mythical city of infinite wealth. They were last seen headed south on Route 97 and were reported to have stopped at Occum Market, where, in a tragic misundertanding, they beheaded the owner after he handed them a bag of Doritos. ✧

Did you know...

...that it's illegal for a dog to bark in church?

...that bees are sorry after they sting you?

...that squirrels waste as much as 38% of their day trying to remember where they left their nuts?

...that whales are fish, bats are birds, and gnats have a very long attention span?

...that George W. Bush collected nearly 4 lbs of toe nail clippings during his first year in office, much of it from foreign toes?

...that *Sprague* is a proto-Algonquin word meaning "Land of Low Taxes"?

Snow days, continued...

to go to sleep once in a while."

The federal law would require all citizens to stay home on Federal Snow Days to drink soup and hot chocolate and play Scrabble. Families with children could also elect to play Risk or Monopoly.

The crowd at the gazebo was shoulder to shoulder all the way back to the Dumpster beside the Baltic Convenience Store. Gejdensen's speech was interrupted several times by chants of "Mo' Snow! Mo' Snow!"

Gejdensen pointed out that 99.99999997 percent of the nation's adults are in favor of the bill. Unfortunately, he said, the remaining 268 citizens are Republicans in the Senate and House of Representatives, and they don't like this idea one bit. ✧

Hypnotist, continued...

one could return to their classrooms.

Judy Synnett, administrative assistant, said she remembers the event as if it were a dream.

"All the children walked quietly to their rooms. There was no talking, no shoving, no running, no nothing," Synnett said. "They sat in their chairs, crossed their hands on their desks and stared at their teachers with rapt attention. The school was perfectly silent. All you could hear was the Venetian blinds clinking against the windowsills. It was eerie."

For the rest of the day, the children followed directions with mechanical precision. Their handwriting turned caligraphic. After lunch, they cleaned their tables and carefully picked up the few food particles that had fallen to the floor. During recess, students discussed the WTO talks. An eighth grader was heard to say, "Yes, m'am" to a teacher.

As Synnett recalls, other strange things started happening. Paintings and other artwork peeled from the walls and fell like dead leaves. Toilets flushed themselves. Water fountains leaked on the floor. Clocks ran backwards. Plants withered. Chunky, a hamster living in Room 4, hung by his toenails from the top of his exercise wheel. Idi, an iquana, shed tears and honked like a bull frog. Sixth grade teacher Mr. Madison ate pencil shavings as if they were peanuts. On the playground, swings fell from their chains and toadstools sprouted from home plate. Tumbleweed blew across the parking lot. In the distance, a coyote howled at a noonday moon.

"It was great," said Synnett. "Definitely not your typical Friday afternoon. I was all set to start loading them on the buses when I made the mistake of snapping my fingers while the PA system was on, and that was the end of that." ✧

Iguana Blast Sickens 12

Idi, an iguana long held captive in a third grade classroom at Sayles Elementary School, lived 8 years in an aquarium but went out with a bang. As Edna Guertin set the reptile on her desk for its daily petting by her best students, Idi inexplicably blew up.

Resident State Trooper Chris Johnson said that an investigation was underway. Cynthia Luty, science teacher, could offer no explanation as to how an animal can explode. The lack of scientific theory, however, did nothing to dispell that general sensation in Room 8 that everyone had been splattered with lizard guts.

"Eeeeewwww," noted Priscilla Han-

Idi the Iguana (before)

sin-Hooper, a front-row student who was privileged to pet Idi first. She was hit by the brunt of the shrapnel.

A tail weighing almost eight ounces soared around the room like a boomerang until it struck Frederick T. Hawkinspitz in the foot as he dived under his desk.

In all, 11 students and Mrs. Guertin were taken to Backus Hospital for treatment of chronic nausea. Mrs. Guertin was subsequently taken away by LifeStar helicopter and rushed to Happy Seas Mental Recovery Facility in Cayuga, NY. She is listed in queasy condition.

Versailler arrested on sock offense

Anthony Mares, of Versailles, was arrested last week on charges of leaving a pair of dirty socks on his living room floor. The socks were found by his wife, Mary, who reported the discovery to the Sprague Raunch Control Board, which turned the case over to the State Police.

"We deeply regret having to take such drastic action, but we had to draw the line somewhere," said Alice Kraemer, RCB chairman. "If we let one guy leave his socks on the floor, it's just a matter of time until everybody's doing it."

Mares was held for questioning and released on $25,000 bail. Warren Toutfia, State Police spokesperson, said that information given by Mares would lead to other arrests in the area.

"Sock abandonment is far more prevalent than most people suspect," Toutfia said. "It's happening in some of the best homes in Connecticut. And we're not just talking sweat socks, here. We're seeing the whole gamut, from Gold Toe to argyle."

Resident State Trooper Chris Johnson will visit Sayles School to discuss with children the importance of proper sock storage. He will bring in several dirty old socks to help children identify what has been called America's most common household clutter.

"Know 'em and Stow 'em," said Johnson. "That's our main message. If we can teach prevention at an early age, maybe we can minimize problems in the future." ✧

April - 2000

BoE Ups Budget, Ozga Ups Lunch

Confirmed fiscal conservative and board of education member Anthony Ozga brought last Wednesday's board meeting to an early adjournment following a moment of confusion when a scant majority unwittingly raised the school budget above the legal minimum required by the state government. Ozga's instinctive reaction was to table the contents of his stomach.

The adjournment precluded the possibility of spending the excess funds on a new nuclear-powered lawn mower, an item at the top of the board's wish list.

"It looks to me like we were saved by scotch and pirogis," said Tracy Medling, a citizen who attended the meeting, intending to speak up for an expanded budget and more educational programs. "I never thought I'd be glad to see Tony Ozga open his mouth, but this time, he really came through for education." ✧

Poem of the Month

How far?

How far do you think you'll get,
Going the way you're going?

Your shoes match just fine,
but you've tied the laces together.

You take baby steps, think they're cute,
But you're just slow and dumb-looking.

What have you got against clouds,
Besides that you can't count them all?

Why don't you let a raccoon lick your toes?
All it takes is patience and peanut butter.

I'll tell you this: It tickles like crazy.
You're going to squirm, grunt, giggle and pant.

But then you'll want to show everybody how cool it is,
But something like that, you can't.

Anonymous Botch

Hucksters Slapped with False Advertising

TV tantalizers Bob and Ian, often seen advertising odd goods at the Bob & Ian Corner on channel 14's *Sprague Today*, have been charged with false advertising and peddling fraudulent products.

Viewers have long suspected that the slick vendors have been up to something shady. Their products have included chemical, biological, and nuclear weapons and a shoddy looking product called The Luke.™

The duo met their doom, however, when they started flogging mortal and venial sins. According to the Federal communications Commission, the products were not as advertised, and the packaging was deceptive.

"These charges are trumped up and unfair," said Bob. "We've had a tremendous consumer response to these products. Everybody wants them. We're constantly running low on inventory."

The FCC claimed that consumers bought the products only because they look better on TV than they really are.

The hucksters, both Sprague residents and graduates of Sayles School, sang the glories of Gluttony, but it turned out that the jumbo pack held less than the smaller economy size. The variety snack-pack of Covetousness all tasted like plain Envy. The gallon jug of Lust looked nice and fizzy on TV but in reality was as flat as Baltic tap water.

Consumers complained most about the Bucket-o-Sloth™, which was sold with a broken handle and a hole in the bottom, rendering it unusable. Though the label promised "Free Peccadillos inside," there was none to be found.

Packages of New GoldenPride II™ were found to have a false listing of ingredients. Though the list included caviar, truffles and frankincense, a chemical analysis revealed nothing but sneaker dust, squashed worms and grit from an undetermined source.

Consumers were especially urinated over the quality of Insta-Anger™. While the TV ad made it look like an easy-to-pour powder, the actual product on supermarket shelves needed to be chiseled from its box and soaked in vinegar overnight.

"I really don't see what the problem is," Ian commented. "This is free enterprise at its best. We supply the demand. We tried offering oatmeal and carrot sticks, but the market did not respond. And anyway, if you can't stretch the truth in a TV ad, where are you going to stretch it? Mexico?" ✧

Existentialist conitnued...

sis. You are nothing. Your mother's nothing. You come from nothing, and to nothing you are bound."

Resident state trooper Chris Johnson detained the man for questioning but was unable to link him to a specific crime.

"The suspect confessed to being an existentialist, but that's still legal in Connecticut," Johnson said. "All we could do was release him to his own responsibility and tell him to define himself, preferably in another town."

Consumadora Bulgarino, the boy's mother, said he has not been the same child since the incident. He has stopped watching television, loses video games on purpose, and lies awake in bed most of the night.

"The other day at dinner, he was just poking at his food," Ms.Bulgarino said. "And then he looks at me with his eyes all wet and he goes, 'Why broccoli?' and I go, like, 'Because it's *good* for you,' and he just looks at me like I'm an idiot, and then he just looks at his broccoli like it just fell there from outer space."

Dirty Old Existentialist

State poet laureate Leo Connellan, a Hanover resident, was called into offer the comfort of literary light on the incident and its disturbing implications.

"That was a rotten thing with which to hit a kid/ We ought to get him back, quo pro quid," Connellan said. "It was a tale told by Sartre or Camus/ full of sound and fury, signifying poo."

Trooper Johnson said he was considering visiting Sayles School to talk with the lower grades about the dangers of broaching the imponderable.

"Let's dare to keep kids off post-modern thought," Johnson said. "It starts at home, but it's up to each and every one of us in the community to keep a lid on the old *cogito*."

Robert Meya, president of the Hanover Philosophical Society, agreed that existentialism could be disturbing to the uninitiated. He suggested that Sayles School incorporate the philosophy into its curriculum, starting in kindergarten.

"Think of the benefits of having children realize, from a young age, that they are what they do," Meya said. "Being precedes essence. Or maybe it's the other way around, depending on which way you look at it. What's important is that it doesn't really matter." Ω

Sprague Goes for Guinness Records

The Sprague Committee for Guinness Records has announced its challenges for the year 2000. If all goes well, the town could set not only four new records but an additional record for a single town setting the most records in one year.

"We're going to need the whole town's co-operation for this series of projects," said David Batten, who chairs the committee. "We're going to need the kind of dedication that our town is going to become famous for."

The first challenge the CGR plans is to form the world's longest human chain that can feel the shock of an electric fence. No world record exists, but to establish a solid and impressive record, at least 50 citizens will be needed to hold hands as one volunteer touches the electric fence at Spielman farm.

Theoretically, if the last person in the chain has his or her hand in water, all 50 participants will feel a quick jolt and will simultaneously say "Ho!" before they fall down laughing.

"We may have to turn up the juice a bit, but the results will be worth it," Batten said.

The committee is also organizing a selectman toss team. Forty tossers will grab hold of an oversized blanket and see how high they can heave a selectman.

Running for a Different Record

"We haven't formally informed the board of selectmen about this project, but we're sure they'll cooperate for the sake of town pride," Batten said. "We've assessed the board from top to bottom and decided to go with Ken Caisse. The odds are forty to one that he'll cooperate."

The Guinness Books currently lists the tossing of a duke in England 18 feet above the ground, but Batten says Sprague is running for a different record.

"That was a duke," Batten said. "Dukes don't count (ha, ha), plus he was a dwarf, which puts him in a whole nother category."

This summer the committee will see how many Spraguers can look a gift horse in the mouth in one hour. The committee has posted an announcement asking for the donation of a horse, preferably one that isn't too tall and is up to date on its rabies vaccinations.

The final challenge will be to set a distance record for the possum saucer toss. Again, Sprague hopes to be on the leading edge of a sport which as yet has no records. Possum saucers are a unique flying disk made of hardened road kill. An invention of Robin Izbicki, of Versailles, who also runs a farm stand across the street from the Methodist church, the disks have gained worldwide acceptance as an organic substitute for plastic disks such as the Frisbee. Ω.

Hamster's Eden more like Hell

When famed state circuit judge Francis X. Foley released famed hamster Chunky into his garden on Potash Hill Rd., he thought he was doing the little rodent a favor.

Instead, the intended Garden of Eden turned out to be a hellhole for the hapless pet formerly employed by Sayles School as an example of something.

Francis X. Foley

"I thought I was giving her a perfect home," Foley said, tears trickling down his cheeks. "She'd have everything: radishes, carrots, beets, cilantro, beans, peas, not to mention the fresh air she'd been missing for the last 40 years when she was cooped up in that aquarium with nothing but coagulated pellets to eat. I had no idea what was going on in that garden at night."

Foley's garden, he came to discover, became a veritable jungle not long after sunset. Groundhogs slipped through the fence. Deer jumped over it. Moles burrowed under it. Raccoons scaled it. Famished field mice had a heyday. Cows opened the gate and walked right through like fatsos into a Denny's. Crows and flying squirrels soared in like the Luftwaffe.

And Chunky spent the night cowering under a rusted trowel.

Come morning, the ground was marked by the prints of hooves and paws large and small. Odd markings indicated the possible presence of reptiles or amphibians. There was evidence of caribou. The carcasses of bloated locusts littered the ground. And the lush growth of foodstuffs had been gnawed to stubble.

"I know how Chunky feels," Foley said. "I share her devastation. I almost feel like life would be better if I were trapped in a second-grade aquarium for the rest of my life." Ω

Community Calendar

Cow Milking Contest, Spielman Farm, April 12, 3:00 a.m.

Board of Finance Penny Toss, April 20, 7:00

Two-Tens-for-a-Five Day, Chelsea-Groton Bank, April 31, 9:00 - 3:00

Neighborhood News

May - 2000

What's really happening in Sprague.

Sprague Awarded Mythological Status

Sprague rejoiced when the United Nations Commission on Cultural Heritage granted the town the status of Mythological Municipality, but as the implications come to light, citizens are increasingly concerned with the weight of the honor.

The main concern is that as the town becomes a mythological site, so do its citizens. Robert Meya, president of the Hanover Philosophical society, was the first to alert the town to what he called "multifaceted ramifications."

"We must remember that everything that any given individual does will contribute to a mythological personality that will live on as part of the culture of the future," Meya said.

"Just as we refer to a task as 'Herculean,' our ancestors may refer to 'Johnsonian heroism' or a 'Papinesque effort'."

While it's too early to know how history will remember individuals in Sprague, phrases like *to pull a Peutz* or *to go off on a Boushee*, may someday hold special significance.

Meya warns that the English language may come to incorporate such nouns as "Balticization" and "scootery,' and such adjectives as "ozgesque" and "bulgarinoid" There may be new verbs,

Robert Meya

such as *to Frank* (a situation), *to Lynch* (a mortgage application), or *to Genron* (someone). What such possible words come to mean will be determined by the behavior of the individual whose reputation inspired the word."

"I am really concerned about this," said one well known resident who preferred to remain anonymous. "I could end up meaning something, you know what I mean? I could end up being a household word and never make a

continued on p. 2...

Ordinance Bans Pipe Dreams

Under a new municipal ordinance, pipe dreams will not be permitted within town limits as of January 1. A statement issued by town hall says the intent is to get people back to work before they get into trouble.

The ordinance puts a formal end to all talk of using the Baltic Mill for anything productive. Plans for a veterans casino will have to be made outside of town. Most new home-based businesses will be forbidden. The Capital Improvements committee has been disbanded, and efforts to improve the library have been terminated.

Political analysts are exploring the implications for the Republican and Green parties in municipal elections.

When the ordinance goes into effect, engaging in or conspiring to engage in a pipe dream will be punishable by 30 days of being chained to reality. Second-degree pipe dreaming will result in a 15-day term on the Board of Finance. Third-degree pipe dreaming gets you a kick in the ass.

"This is ridiculous," squawked Robin Izbicki, who recently turned down a $57 million dollar offer from the Wham-o Corporation for her Possum Saucer products. "If we haven't got pipe dreams, what's left?"Ω

Sayles Shocked at Hamster's Odd Message

Chunky, a hamster who has been living in an aquarium in Room 6 at Sayles Elementary School for the last 48 years, shocked 21 second-graders last week when Ashley Snipes dropped Chunky on the floor and the hapless hamster ran amuck across the linoleum.

Chunky moved so fast that no one could catch her until she'd urinated a long, strange message in perfect Palmer script. Edna Guertin, their teacher, waved the students back as she realized that the elongated piddle had spelled out, "Please kill me."

"This is the most shocking thing I've seen since our iguana blew up," Guertin said. "I'd

like to know who's responsible for this."

Guertin said the words were written in the most perfect script she'd ever seen.

Chunky was taken into custody by Timothy Hawks, animal control warden, who said that a decision would be made whether to put the class rodent to sleep.

A petition signed by 1,246 Sayles students and graduates asked that Chunky be spared and returned to her home in the aquarium.

"Don't let Chunky die," said Snipes. "I didn't mean to drop her, cross my heart and hope to die; stick a needle in my eye." Ω

EDC Proposes SmartSlavery

Reacting to what they call a local tax crisis, the Economic Development Commission has dusted off an old idea whose time, the commission says, has come around again.

"It's time we took another look at histo-recreational personal productivity assistance," said EDC chairman Ken Genron. "Not the old forced labor based on leather whips and cast-iron chains but a community effort that brings together technology, democracy, history, and the elements of entrepreneurialism that have made our country what it is today. It's historical, it's fun, and it's as American as Thomas Jefferson and peanut butter."

Under the EDC proposal, the commission would "assign" individuals to "volunteer"

to "take care of" common personal and community chores such as gathering litter, mowing lawns, digging gravel, picking cotton, and keeping flies off the EDC and others who tend to attract the noisome insects commonly associated with pet output and death. The heavy,

continued on p. 2

Mother's Day Nixed As Whole Town Forgets

Gender, family issues complicate the situation.

Mythology, continued from p. 1

In an emergency meeting on the second Sun day of May, the Sprague Board of selectmen voted unanimously to postpone Mother's Day as it became evident that the entire town had completely forgotten the annual event.

"Let's face it, Mother's Day tends to catch a lot of people by surprise," said selectman Ken Caisse. "It's normal. It's natural. This year was no exception, though it was exceptional that by noon, every mother in town was still in bed waiting for breakfast while everybody else was out doing stuff."

All persons who had been born of mothers were urged to return home immediately and serve their mothers at the very least a bowl of ceral and a double-wham-my-mammy bloody Mary. Saying, "It couldn't hurt," Caisse recommended simultaneous delivery of a flower, even a dandelion, inserted in a small vase or wine glass. For those who had forgotten to get a present for their mothers, Caisse suggested contacting the Town Prevaricator, Glenn Cheney.

Caisse said the weather was partly to blame. It was a classic day in May, with the sky blue, the sun warm for the first time since September, baseball season in full swing, fishing season open, gardens begging for the tiller, boats needing their hulls soaked, dogs in heat and every child in town on a bike headed somewhere besides home.

Calling the mid-May weather a recurring problem, Caisse said that the selectmen were considering changing Mother's day to a Sunday between Halloween and Thanksgiving.

"November Sundays are basically a waste anyway," Caisse said. "Church is about the only option. It's a perfect season for Mother's Day."

Caisse emphasized that Mother's Day not been cancelled but merely postponed.

Brunhilda Onus, Town Mother, says that the weather is no excuse.

"Your mother didn't wait for a rainy day to give birth to you, did she? Did she? Answer my question," Onus said at a press conference on the Monday after Mother's Day. "If you were born in March or November or something, then OK, maybe that's what happened, but the rest of you have no excuse. Is that understood?"

Caisse said that gender and family issues were making the situation even more complicated. In some families, he said,

only a Step-mother's Day would be appropriate, and in a number of cases, the mothers were younger than their daughters. In other families, same-sex marriages have left children confused and with few options in the way of Mother's Day cards. Transgender parentage, while rare, is a leading cause of MDT, or Mother's Day Trauma. In some cases, children have divorced one or both parents.

Caisse, an attorney, also warned that the town could be held liable for discrimination in cases of women who have never given birth.

"*Nullipara excipiendis* has precedents going back to Biblical times. It's a devastating lawsuit waiting to happen," Caisse said. "As soon as post-pubescent non-mothers realize that they have no designated day, we are in big trouble."

Caisse suggested that perhaps a Post-Pubescent Non-Mother's Day could be established for some weekend during the winter, perhaps on a Saturday, "just to cover ourselves."

During the ongoing crisis, a Mother's Day Excuse hotline has been linked to the town's Office of Prevarication. It will be open around the clock until the town's mothers have been sufficiently distracted. ✳

SamrtSlavery®, continued...

cumbersome chains of yesteryear would be replaced by FetherLite® personal links of hi-tech recycled plastic. Remote controlled tasers would give taxpayers the option to use the internet to "flog" their personal productivity assistants from a remote location. The tasers could be set to five different comfort levels.

Genron said that by using SmartSlavery® Sprague can lower taxes, increase property values, and enhance the lifestyle of any taxpayer who is "Smart" enough to own a SmartSlave®.

"There was a reason our founding fathers wanted us to own and care for personal productivity assistants, at least until the liberals came along and voted for somebody besides George Washington," Genron gasped. "There was no income tax back then, and no property tax. No Boards of Education, no Planning and Zoning Commissions, nobody suing each other over slippery sidewalks. If you wanted to go out in the woods and dig a hole, you could do it without apologizing to every fuzzy little endangered spotted dolphin that came down the

dime off it. I could become a dirty word. People could shout me at each other twenty-times a day and I'll be too dead to know."

That, said Meya, is precisely the problem. "Nobody gets to write their own myth except by example. You are what you do, and you will be what you did." ❖

Sprague celebrates Mother's Day

pike. Cotton was cheap. Everything was just fine. But then the liberals came along and got all cuddly-wuddly about immigrants having to do what immigrants are still doing: helping to put food on our families at an affordable price."

Genron said he would like to see Smart-Slaves® made members of the Board of Finance, reducing the burden that has traditionally fallen on reluctantly elected officials. Being under the supervision of taxpayers with whips, they could be ordered to cut the budget to nothing more than the cost of the gruel.

Genron said that eligibility for SmartSlaveship would not be restricted to people of the traditional earth tones. Rather, he explained, regardless of race, color, creed or political affiliation, those who express opposition to the idea will obviously, and logically, be those who were most likely to be made SmartSlaves®. The very vociferousness of those individuals, he said, would make them easy to identify.

"This is our heritage," Genron said. "We need to preserve it for our children and future generations. To ignore history dooms us to repeat it. The Civil War is over, folks. It's time to get back to basics and get back to work!" Ω

Cruelty Charges Dropped

A sixth-grade student at Sayles School has been arrested for allegedly abusing a cow that had wandered onto his lawn. Charges were dropped, however, after the boy, whose name has not released because he is a minor, said that the cow was a musical instrument and he was only playing her.

Judge Francis Foley dismissed the charges after hearing the boy plead his own case in a pre-trial hearing.

"I'm sure there's a law against using a cow as a musical instrument, but I can't put my finger on it," Foley said. "We had to let him go."

Neighbors reported that the boy was slapping the cow's sides rhythmically and tugging on her udders in such a way as to make her moo.

"He rapped on her horns with drum sticks and made her bell go tonky-tonk-tonk-tonk," one witness said. "When he lifted her tail, she broke wind, and for a while there he had he peeing onto an upside-down bucket, which sounded kind of like a snare drum and cymbals, if you can imagine a snare drum and cymbals being peed on by a cow. She let out a couple of good, wet flops, too, and it seemed to fit right into the rhythm. It actually sounded pretty good, like samba or something."

State Trooper Chris Johnson, the arresting officer, said the cow did not seem happy about the arrangement and therefore could be considered a victim of cruelty to animals.

"We've picked this kid up before," Johnson said. "He got away with playing a piano in the middle of the Shetucket because there was no law against doing so. Now there's no law against playing a cow. How long is this going to go on?"

Pleading his case, the defendant defied the officer to describe the difference between a happy cow and one that is suffering. Trooper Johnson imitated the difference in moos, but Judge Foley agreed with the boy that both moos sounded the same, as least as Johnson expressed them.

The defendant called Medford K. Snodgrass, a local dairy farmer, as an expert witness. Snodgrass judged Johnson's moo to be that of a distressed cow. The defendant's moo, however, was identified as that of a contented cow.

"If that was the moo, it was the moo of an extremely contented cow," Snodgrass said after the hearing. "If I could get my cows to moo like that, I'd be a one happy farmer. My milk would be worth real money."

Trooper Johnson agreed that even if charges of some sort could be brought against the alleged perpetrator, he would rather drop them than go to trial and engage in what he termed "a public moo-off."

"It's hard enough being the resident state trooper in a town like Sprague," Johnson said. "The last thing I need is to become the town's main source of entertainment, too." ✧

Selectman to Appoint Board of Profundity

In response to a widely perceived need for greater consideration of conceptual fundamentals, Sprague first selectman Stephen J. Papineau has announced his intention to appoint a town Board of Profundity. The board, to be composed of the town's deepest thinkers, will be responsible for reflecting on the implications of town hall decisions and statements.

"If there's one thing I've noticed over the years, it's that there's always another way of looking at stuff," Papineau said. "There's always a deeper level. Just when you think you've got something figured out, along comes Plato or one of those guys with a whole nother view of it, something you never would of thought of unless it was your job."

Papineau said that the government should set an example for its citizens, especially children. Putting a little extra thought into government statements, he said, would encourage others to "mull things a little deeper."

The Board of Selectmen approved creation of the board by a vote of 2-1, with Republican Thomas McAvoy casting the dissenting vote.

"You know what's going to happen?" McAvoy said. "It's going to end up with nobody making a decision. By the time the Board of Profundity considers all the angles on whether to fill a pothole or something, we'll all have gray beards down to our kneecaps. Well, maybe [selectman] Joan won't, but she may have the feminine equivalent of [a beard down to her kneecaps], which, now that I think about it, might explain why we always picture God as a wise old man with a long, gray beard, because if we pictured a wise old woman, what would we picture her with, rubberized underwear? That's no way to get a pothole filled."

Papineau said that McAvoy's statement was exactly the kind of thing that should have been turned over to the Profundity Board.

Robert Meya, president of Hanover Philosophical Society, praised the decision but issued a word of caution.

"Thought is fine, but when you really want to get something done, ignorance is a powerful tool," Meya said. "It's definitely faster, and it's a lot more fun because *everyone* can participate."

Papineau said that the first thing on the board's agenda will be to determine whether it and the rest of the town actually exist.

"We haven't dealt with this issue in several hundred years," Papineau said. "The last time, was over in France or somewhere, and the answer was in Latin, so nobody's really sure what it was. We have translations, but how do we know the translators aren't lying to us? We know we have to think about this, so we are. Or rather we will be - *if* we can pull together a board of seven deep thinkers who have nothing better to do *and* can all meet on the second Tuesday of each month, the chances of which, of course, are virtually nil, so basically I'm just going to appoint the first seven clowns I can find with high school diplomas and that will just have to be good enough. What the hell. It's only Sprague." ✳

Town Approved for Fat-to-Energy Plant
Federal Thigh Inspectors Due Soon

The U.S. Department of Energy has ap proved Sprague's plan to build a fat-to-energy plant in Versailles. The two-megawatt facility will deploy three hundred tread mills connected to a series of generators. Local cellulite deposits will provide low-cost fuel.

"This is an excellent opportunity to tap one of our area's most bountiful resources," said Thomas McAvoy, chair of the Sprague Department of Energy. "We're going to shed pounds as we illuminate town."

Essentially, McAvoy said, the plant will be converting ice cream, potato chips and beer into cheap energy.

The tread mills will be powered by local residents who have been identified by federal thigh inspectors from the National Anatomical Disaster Agency. Each will be required to operate the treadmills for two hours per day until their reserves of cellulite are depleted.

The NADA thigh inspectors will conduct a door-to-door probe to search for enlistees for the "Bod Squad" that will power the generators.

The energy complex will also install treadmills at Sayles School, where they will be operated by volunteer rambunctivators from grades 4-8.

"We have a lot of excess energy in this school," said David Mattison, a sixth grade teacher. "I, for one, will be glad to see it burned up." Ω

St. Joe Researcher Finds Our Roots

We still are what we used to be...

A psycho-anthropologist at St. Joseph Elementary School has unearthed a startling discovery — deep inside, we are are cave-people.

"We may have come a long way in our technological life, but our past is still with us," said Xavier Onassis, a sixth grader at the school. "We have risen far in the sea of civilization, but we are still anchored in the caves of our paleolithic past."

Onassis made his discovery as part of a project for his class in psycho-anthropology, the study of the psychology of early humans. Examining a strand of his father's DNA, he discovered that trologlodytism is still a part of us.

The implications are profound. They explain the odd behavior at middle-school dances, the road crew's obsession with filling potholes, the uneasy feeling we get when filling our gas tanks, the quality of the *Norwich Bulletin*, and the tendency of patrons at Fred's News to sit facing "the hearth" where the short order cook prepares the modern equivalent of mastadon haunch.

"If nothing else, this should let us feel a lot more comfortable about the way we are," Onassis explained. "We're actually doing pretty good just to live together without carrying spears and eating our pets." ✧

Smoker Fights Fat, Loses

When Baltic resident Consumadora Bulgarino quit smoking on January 1, she had no idea that the weight she took from her lungs would find its way to her hips—exponentially. Her weight increased by eight pounds by noon the next day and then really shot up.

Today the bloated Baltician sews her own clothes from army surplus parachutes, and President Clinton, under lobbying pressure from big tobacco companies, is considering declaring her a national monument.

"I really feel great," said Bulgarino as she sat on display in her garage for a tour of children from Sayles Elementary School. "I can taste food. I can smell things. I feel ten pounds lighter."

Bulgarino has become a leading designer of tentwear. The jumbo garbs have become an overnight success in Arkansas,

Tentmaker Bulgarino

Alabama, and parts of rural Georgia.

"I'm so glad I quit," Bulgarino told the awe-struck visitors as she munched on a chocolate-covered Tiparillo. "Let this be a lesson to you kids. Don't start."

One third grader was poignantly impressed.

"I'm never, ever, ever, ever going to start smoking," she said. "And if I do, I'm never, ever, ever, going to quit."

Bulgarino told her young visitors that freedom from cigarettes had empowered her.

"There's so much more of me to love," she said. "And so much more of me to make you sorry you were ever born." Ω

Barking Cat Raises Hackles

An orange cat with an uncanny ability to bark like a dog has inspired death threats, media coverage and serious questions about God, man, nature and the supernatural.

One thing nobody questions: the cat barks. With the alto soprano yap of a chihuahua, Rover, of 181 Main St., Baltic, could fool an expert - and indeed she has, stopping a poddle mix in his tracks at the incomprehensible sight of a cat speaking in Dog.

Neighbors and other town residents are wondering what, if anything, to do about the imprudent pet. Some say it's irritating. Some say it's disgusting. Some say it's the work of the devil.

Tim Hawks, town animal control warden, says it's a cat, and that's that.

"I jist don' want to hear about it anymower," Hawks said. "No matter what it says, it's a cat. It dudn't need a lacense. 'Til it gets run over, it jist ain't my ersponsiblity. Please leave your message after the beep."

The Sprague Chamber of Commerce says the town should take advantage of the miraculous feline and use it to attract tourists and, more important, their dollars, though it was unclear where those dollars would be spent.

"It just starts with a tourist coming to town to look at Rover," Mortimer Tallyup, chamber president, explained, "Then he gets hungry and goes over to Lib's for lunch. Somebody from Lib's has to run down to the Baltic Convenience Store for eggs or something. With the extra revenues, somebody from the store can go have lunch at Lib's, which means more eggs. Its a self-perpetuating cycle. And of course there's the potential market for barking cat souvenirs."

Brujilla LaStrega, chair of the Sprague Committee on Supernatural Events, has advised the town government that the cat may be speaking for a dog "on the other side," that is, one that is dead.

"For all we know," LaStrega said, "this cat could be saying something very important."

The adherents of a particular religious faith, however, say that supernatural events do not exist and that the cat may be the work of Satan and should be exterminated before something bad happens.

Robert Meya, president of the Hanover Philosophical Society, says the real issue isn't whether it's a barking cat or a dog in cat's clothing.

"The issue brings up many profound questions that have been plaguing us since the dawn of human thought," Meya said. "What is cat? What is dog? Who are we? Why are we here?"

Meya said he has left these and other questions with the animal control warden and is awaiting a response. ✳

Poem of the Month

(totally untitled)

far be flung the dearth of dung,
the flip of whiz, the kiss of dirt,
the yes of is, the how of damn,
my pulse of urge to and then.

stick to gullies, gulches, snake-shade,
pillows of rumor, rudders of gawk and jaw,
deliver me from pizza, go ahead, shoot
me, sue me, steam-roller me smooth.

i can skitter when i must, like bugs
and excuses, like winnowing scat
leached skeletal, guano gone bad,
just dust that must be worth but what?

O crush of joy in others, O your sangfroid gloat,
little mister lickspittle, speak: utter the unuttered,
deliver us from evil, lay down your ha-ha law,
your belt, your shoes, your boogers black and bloated.

Who can see the night in day, the dust in wet,
the neon worms and radiant guck of youth,
who, you? If you could see such giddy scenes
you'd stamp them out or blow them all to slithereens.

Anonymous Botch

Neighborhood News

June 2000

What's really happening in Sprague.

Jester to Oversee Town Boards

Sprague Board of Selectmen has approved funding to hire a professional jester. The individual will be responsible for helping town boards and committees perceive their own flaws and foibles.

"When you come right down to it, we need someone to make sure we don't take ourselves too seriously," said Stephen J. Papineau, first selectman. "Like the other day, I said 'two-hundred and forty thousand dollars,' and I didn't even break a sweat. That kind of thing can get out of control."

Papineau said that the town is looking for a part-time jester in the traditional harlequin style. The individual must be a Certified Buffoon with at least two years experience in humiliating public officials.

"It should be somebody who knows how to throw a pie," said Terri Woronecki, a member of the board of education. "I will make the pie.

Stephen J. Papineau

All I need is someone to deliver it."

Exempt from prosecution or removal from a public meeting, the jester will report to the newly created Buffoon Control Board. The board is already developing guidelines and requirements for the jester. The appointed individual must be at least 18 years of age and may not concurrently hold the positions of town jester and village idiot. Acts of jesting may not involve any body fluid. The jester will not be allowed to physically tickle any board member. Pies may include common baking ingredients but not, for example, cement.

"We just have to make sure our jester isn't too funny," Papineau said. "If we end up with someone who's better than television, members of the public are going to start attending public meetings, and that's the last thing we need." Ω

Spague Slates So-Soo-Mee Dayz

Everybody to sue everybody in legal free-for-all!

Sprague Recreation Committee has scheduled June 30 for the first annual "Law Suit Dayz," a weekend event meant to fill the town's residents with simultaneous hope and despair as everyone files law suits against their friends, neighbors, strangers, and even members of their immediate family.

"So-Soo-Mee Dayz will be a great opportunity for fun, factiousness and frivolous accusations," said Deb Zglobis, SRC chairperson. "Everybody gets to sue everybody. Theoretically, if three thousand people sue three thousand people, we could generate nine million suits in a single day. If the average suit is for a million dollars, that's ninety billion bucks. That's enough to cause a significant blip in the Dow Jones average."

Zglobis joked that if everyone won all their suits and all the awards arrived in small bills, it could be the demise of Sprague because the whole town would be buried in cash.

"It could be a real health hazard," Zglobis said. "We could be held liable. We'd have to get the snow plows out and start pushing it all into the Shetucket."

The Inland Wetlands Commission has already warned that cash is a toxic waste and therefore cannot be dumped in a river without

first being filtered through a bank.

The town's attorney, Luke Boushee III, doubts that all the suits will be successful. More likely, he said, the unpredictable arbitrariness of the courts will average out to half the suitors winning, half losing.

"Half the town will be terribly rich for about two seconds, then instantly re-impoverished," Boushee said. "The other half will be plunged into absolute destitution before being bailed out and reinserted into the middle class."

Afraid of being sued more than they sue others, many residents are already planning their suits. One, who prefers to remain anonymous, said he plans to put his leg in his neighbor's dog's mouth, then clamp it shut hard enough to leave teeth marks. A regular customer at TJ's Restaurant has ordered doses of ptomaine from a supplier in Tijuana. Parents have been training their children to fall off playground equipment. Many residents are already limping and complaining of neck pains.

Three phalanxes of volunteer attorneys from New York will be brought into town on chartered buses. Dressed in authentic period costumes, they will camp at Babe Blanchette

Continued on page 3

Laundry Abuse Up

Local officials are concerned about Sprague youth having a little too much fun at the Sudsy-Wudsy Launderette. The teens are reported to spend hours each day watching laundry and suds slosh against the windows of the side-loading washing machines.

"We see laundry-gazing as a complete waste of time," said resident state trooper Chris Johnson. "It's dangerous, it wasn't what Laundromats were built for, and it can lead to more serious problems. More than once it has resulted in clothes being washed without need."

Johnson said that there were reports of youth breaking into homes and stealing dirty laundry. He said that female teens were suspected to have participated because often the clothes were returned not only washed but neatly folded.

There have also been reports of teens begging for quarters outside the Sudsy-Wudsy. While they often claimed they needed the money for cigarettes, legitimate users of the washing facility say that as soon as the teens have collected five quarters, they go inside and wash clothes.

"It's very creepy, that's all I can say," said Joan Fatone, CPA, an amateur washerwoman. "They sit there like they're hypnotized, three inches from the glass, their mouths all open, just watching the wet clothes go by."

Teens found at the Sudsy-Wudsy often claim that they have been sent there by a parent or guardian. Some, apparently under the effect of a spin cycle, confess to a vague aesthetic fascination with wet clothing.

"It's sort of like...I don't know what," said Marienne Articulata, a Sayles graduate and part-time left fielder. "There's just something *about* it. Like it's...*beautiful* or something."

Another teen described the experience

Continued on page 2

Inside...

Gooseflesh Outbreak............. p. 2
Hamster Sighting...................p. 2
Is it Shinola or not?.................p. 2
Semioticians scratch heads.....p. 3
Baseball games.....................p. 4

Gooseflesh Outbreak Cuts Concert Short

An outbreak of uncontrolled horripilation swept through Sayles Elementary School last Friday as the all-school chorus sang *America the Beautiful* to the accompaniment of the six-member Mustang Quartet. Members of the audience were brought to their knees, some in tears, as eruptions of papillae spread across the gymnasium where the school's annual concert was just getting underway.

"We think it was the snare drums," said Mr. Senesac, school superintendent. "One alone was asking for trouble. Two made it happen."

Horripilation, commonly referred to as "goose flesh," was thought to have been stamped out in the years following the Lewinski investigation. Isolated cases have been reported in the elderly and, inexplicably, the audiences of G-rated movies about animal companions.

The school nurse, Florence Busbee, despite a chronic oubreak of second-degree goose pimples on her forearms and neck,

Laundry-gazing...

as "kind of like TV, but interesting."

An anti-laundry-gazing program at Sayles School has had little or no effect and may even have aggravated the problem. The federally funded program brought in experts who talked openly with students. One, Dr. John B. Heifer-Tittelbaum, an aesthetician at the University of Connecticut, feels that Sayles students may be too dumb to understand what drives them to do laundry.

"I asked them, 'Just because it's beautiful, does that mean you have to look at it?'" Heifer-Tittlebaum said. "If you want beauty, where do you go? To a museum. If you have dirty clothes, where do you go? The laundromat. These are basic concepts, but I daresay I have never seen so many blank looks as I got at Sayles. They were like, *What are you talking about?*"

Dr. Harrington "Mojo" Heifer-Tittlebaum (no relation), acting principal, said that the program may be having a counter-productive effect. More Sayles students have been hanging around the Launderette, and some have been reported to be experimenting with different combinations of clothes and other objects. A dead squirrel and an American flag were found in one machine. Last October, a machine was abandoned with a load of autumn leaves.

Loretta Lindstrom, owner of the Launderette, said she is thinking about painting the washing machine windows black and installing a coin-operated video game machine. Ω

set up a triage station in the corridor outside the gym. Victims with mild cases were sent to the cafeteria for hot chocolate. Those who had turned purple had the bellies of kindergartners applied to their wounds. Those who had turned blue were wrapped in American flags and sent to the hospital.

Efforts to call 911 were unsuccessful as victims tried to report the problem but were unable to utter anything besides vague references to spacious skies and good crowned with brotherhood. By the time the ambulance arrived, it was too late.

Cherise Champingon, a mother of second-grade twins, described what she saw as she fell unconscious under a chilly rash that started at her ankles and quickly rose to her teeth.

Dandruff

"It was like this giant amber wave came into the room, spreading these weird little purple mountain majesties from...from...," she whimpered. "Oh, please, stop me."

Debra Snitz, music teacher, said that the snare drums were a last-minute addition to the quartet. The group, which also included violin, flute, tuba and cymbals, had not had time to rehearse with the snare drums. The effects were unexpected.

"We had no idea the combination could be so devastating," Snitz said. "I thought it was great when members of the audience stood up and put their hands on their hearts, pledge-of-allegiance-style. But when I saw them raise their other hand to their chest, I knew they were just trying to warm their nipples. By then, it was too late to do anything. They just started keeling over."

Senesac said the school would take action to prevent a recurrence of goose pimples.

"We can't afford to be held liable for this kind of thing," he said. "Next year, no quartet, no *America the Beautiful*. We're going to use recorded music from Disney films, and the kids are just going to clap to the rhythm, and if we have to, we'll make the parents wait out in the hall until it's safe to come in." Ω

Nuncios to Check Out Hamster Sighting

Pope John Paul has sent a duo of nuncios to investigate a reported sighting of the image of a hamster known as Chunky. The depressed companion rodent, who lived in an aquarium at Sayles School for 48 years, gained worldwide attention after requesting execution in perfect Palmer script. An anonymous citizen reported seeing the image drawn in the dust on the back of the elusive Lone UPS Truck of Sprague.

Until recently, many believed the mythical brown truck was just a legend, but when the Sprague Today news team caught a video image of the truck emerging from and disappearing into a heavy fog on Lord's Bridge, the legend became a reality.

The nuncios will determine whether the image qualifies as a miracle and a message from God. If they confirm the sighting and reach an interpretation of the image, Chunky will be eligible for canonization as a saint. To qualify, however, she would have to die a martyr's death.

"The sainthood of Chunky would be a great moment for Sprague," said the Reverend Emile Tito, of St. Mary's parish. "We have never had a saint, and the Church has never canonized a pet. This will put our parish on the map in so many ways."

Fairfield University has already offered Chunky a posthumous honorary doctorate if she is burned at a stake. The Fox Network has boght exclusive rights to cover the event, and Jennifer's Death-to-Pests, of Norwich, has offered to make the stake.

Sprague Board of Selectmen is reviewing the case and will meet to decide whether to approve funding.

"We have reliable reports that the vehicle in question was not a UPS truck but a muddy FedEx truck," said Penelope Soiltone, UPS spokesperson. "We sincerely hope the Pope puts an end to these rumors." Ω

Suspected Shinola Exceeds Federal Limits

The Sprague Water and Sewer Department has detected excessive measurements of a strange substance in the town's sewer system. First reports indicate that it may be some kind of shoe polish.

"I pulled up a bucket of this stuff and sent it off to the Deaprtment of Environmental Protection," said W&S chief David Rood. "A letter came back and said it's Shinola."

How so much Shinola could have ended up in the sewer is still a mystery. A team of federal investigators has been called into to verify the chemical make-up of the substance. Rood described it as "basically brown."

The Capital Improvement Plan Committee's sub-committee on Alternative Revenue Sources is already looking into the possibility that the strange substance can be used to shine shoes. If so, Sprague may be sitting on a gold mine.

"It doesn't matter what it is, as long as it works," said Wilfred Zinavage, co-host of the Will & Bill Show, a public access cable television program. "I say we bottle this stuff and sell to shoe stores." Ω

June - 2000

Baltic Observer

Develops Theory

When he isn't flipping his pancakes and hashing his browns, William Hastings, chief cook and partner of Fred's News, he's observing the habits and behavior of local natives. Over the years, behavior has been erratic, he says, encompassing disparate activities that were not always in the person's best interest. None of it made any sense to Hastings until last week, when he announced that he had a theory.

"I have a theory," Hastings said from the corner where he rests and smokes cigars between requests for grillwork. "I can't tell you what it is, but I can say it's a doozy."

Hastings says that his "unified theory of local behavior" touches virtually everyone in town, explaining a great deal of "what goes on."

The announcement of the new theory has drawn a lot of attention to Fred's News. Patrons are looking for clues to the nature of Hastings's theory. They assess his chuckles for nuances and innuendo, trying to understand what he sees and they can't.

At the same time, Hastings has been observing the local natives with a noticeably different eye.

"It's definitely set at a tighter squint," said Rudy Laab, a frequent user of the facility. "It kind of gives you the creeps. Mine starts right at the top of my crack,

William Hastings

where that little bone is, you know the one? Then it goes up my kidneys, wraps around my throat and tickles my scalp from the inside. It gives me dandruff. Look."

Hastings is also said to be quieter — paying attention to everything, but without the incisive comments that earned him the title of town wag laureate in fiscal year 1997-98. Now he holds his cigars between the top two knuckles of the first two fingers of his left hand, a shift up from the lower knuckles.

Hastings has not confirmed that he is writing a book that explains his theory and proves it with examples of behavior that demonstrate its validity.

'Maybe I am and maybe I ain't," Hastings said in an official news release that was distributed to the local and academic press.

The statement said that the unified theory does not explain absolutely everything but that it is better than previous theories, most of which merely attributed local behavior to incidences of unclear thinking. Hastings believes that a grand unified theory is possible by the end of the decade. Ω

Suspected Symbol Found
Semioticians Baffled, Local Philosopher Alerted

The northwest corner of the Grist Mill parking lot has been cordoned off as police isolate a suspected symbol that was found at the edge of the asphalt shortly after dawn. Officials were uncertain whether the odd grouping of objects had meaning beyond its appearance.

The presence of a crude noose and the semblance of a cross tipped off police to the possibly symbolic nature of the odd set of objects. Detectives from the Department of Objective Correlatives were called to the scene for semiotic analysis.

"We already know this will not be one of our easier cases," said DOC theorizer Chuck Peirce. "The unforeseeable confluence of highly charged artifacts — on *asphalt,* no less, yet within inches of crab grass and whithered dandelions — will disturb even the most detached observer."

The loose "pile" of objects included not only a noose of poison ivy vines and a cross fashioned of stapled junk mail but a dented toaster oven with an unaddressed post card inside depicting a young girl with blonde pigtails riding a large tortoise at a petting zoo in Orlando. Alongside the oven lay a computer CD with a common vulgarity written on it in red lipstick. The plastic lid of a take-out coffee cup was also present, though investigators have yet to determine whether wind or some other natural force may have carried it into the scene.

"Oak leaves, crispy, dead/ were stuffed in an old ice skate/near sprouts of ragweed," Peirce stated. "Things like that don't just happen on their own. Or do they?"

The detectives declined to comment on the possible meaning of a playing card that was pinned beneath one foot of the oven except to say that in a game of bridge, it wouldn't have been of much use to anyone.

Robert Meya, president of the Hanover Philosophical Society, who was rushed to the scene, confirmed that the card was not the ace of spades, as many had feared.

"This is not the work of a amateur," Meya said. "Any ace would have been obvious to the point of blatant triteness. What we found was a card clearly linked to powerlessness, even irredeemable peasantry. That's a clue, but it isn't an answer."

Dennis Delaney, town historian, said that this was not the first time a symbol had been found in Sprague.

"We've seen eagles over the Shetucket," Delaney said. "Robins traditionally return every spring. When I was a kid, somebody found a dead rose lying on the Providence-Wooster train tracks. And remember when we had the flood? And what about the mill? If that wasn't a symbol of something, I don't know what is. Actually, it wouldn't surprise me if it was ten symbols, maybe more. Who knows?" Ω

Spraguers Vie to Comfort Cats

Cat-lovers all over town have begun training for the town's annual Cat Comfort Contest.

"Gone are the days of thinking you could bring a cat to ecstasy by just scratching its chin," said Pamela Panderoski, considered a favorite with her hard-to-please Kittikins. "If the cat next door is getting a five-hand scratch-job on a hand-knitted radiator nest in the sun with Brahms playing in the background, your cat's going to hear about it, you're going to look downright cruel in comparison."

Pandeoski is training Kittikins to receive a five-hand scratch-job while eating warm crab meat from a crystal dish.

Across town, William Blanchette is said to have mastered a technique of belly-masage that can actually cause a cat to lose consciousness. Others who have tried this have not been able to overcome the problem of static charge build-up. Mr. Boots, of 32 Fullertown Rd., was rushed to Plainfield Veterinary Hostipal after receiving a near-fatal discharge of static electricity from a well intentioned cat comforter who prefers to remain anonymous. Boots is not expected to participate in this year's event.

Last year, two contestants were disqualified after blood tests revealed morphine in their cats. A third was disqualified after admitted to using lobster bisque as a muscle relaxant. Ω

So-Soo-Mee, continued...

ball field until the last suits have been resolved.

"We're hoping a lot of this can be settled out of court," said Randall Wentworth Forthright, esq., president of the Manhattan Volunteer Attorney Corps. "If we flood the courts with nine billion law suits, we could be stuck in Sprague forever." Ω

CBS Plans To Air "Sprague Survivor"

Out-of-Town Tempters may complicate voting

Hoping to bank on the success of the wildly popular "Survivor" and "Temptation Island" TV series, CBS has announced next season's big hit: "Sprague Survivor."

The program will follow the same rules that applied to the contestants on Pau Tiki and Temptation Island except the contestants will one by one vote each other out of Sprague. Like middle-class Robinson Carusos, they will have to live by their wits as they vote themselves out of town, one by one. Complicating the situation, a team of trained tempters and temptresses will slip into town and attempt to seduce the remaining survivors.

The last individual who has not been voted out or tempted away will win the rubble of a mill that was once worth a million dollars.

"I already know who I'm voting for first," said Jo Cabash. "and I'm not the only one. Come September 17, he's *outta* here."

The town's 3012 residents will have to eat all their meals at Fred's News, TJ's Restaurant, and Sharkey's Pizza. As food supplies run low, the survivors will be expected to hunt and gather the town's fauna and flora, respectively. Television cameras will record their every word and facial expression.

William Hastings, co-owner of Fred's News, says he hopes to get rid of a lot of stuff that's been in the pantry since before World War I, not all of it food. He's also looking forward to getting rid of a lot of people who, in his opinion, have been in town too long.

David Rood, town director of water and sewer works, was especially concerned about the arrival of the attractive men and women who will come to town with seductive intentions.

"We haven't had a decent temptress in this town for over forty years," Rood said. "I think it will really make a difference. What I'm worried about is, what happens if they start tempting each other instead of us? What happens if they vote us out of town and they're the only ones left? Who's going to take care of the water and sewers for them? Someone's going to have to stay behind."

Leo Connellan, state poet laureate, feels that for reasons both aesthetic and historical, a poet should be the last to go.

"Like unto the pinball machine with its whizzers and flippers, a poet should remain to keep an eye on the zippers," Connellan said. "I know that analogies like that leave you flustered, but a town needs a bard or it won't cut the mustard." Ω

Poem of the Month

A Nice Drowning

I love you, whatever,
your eyes, Roy G. Biv,
your tongue of the infinite
staves, your feverish toadstools,
tree sap, the way stuff gurgles.

Did you know your navel's
like a fingerprint, yours
yet in the same swirl as all
conchs and galaxies, the same
way toilets flush, too?

Do galaxies flush or collect
cosmic lint, I wonder. And how come
I can't check my own bellybutton
for a tiny black hole deep
in the back in the dark?

Explain this to me: fire.
And blue. And where
the forgotton goes. And
do cows get earwax?
Is anybody in charge?

I feel like a bee drowning
in gallons of honey, a ton
of sweet gold sap, all
I could want and
way too much of it.

Anonymous Botch

> **Editor's Note:**
> *Neighborhood News* would appreciate not getting any more anonymous poems. Just put your name on it, OK?
> The Editor

Players Wait While Pitcher and Batter Play Mind Game

A Sprague-Bozrah-Canterbury Little League game was called on darkness last Saturday after a pitcher locked brains with a batter for almost four hours.

For the full four hours, the game was tied in the ninth, men on first and third, with a full count on the batter.

"It was an unbelievably tense moment," SBC pitcher Fred Phroyd said. "I couldn't throw the pitch until I knew exactly what he was expecting. I knew he was expecting a strike, so I was going to pitch one low and outside. But of course he knew I was going to try something like that, so it would be better to throw a fast one right down the middle."

Since the effectiveness of a strike was obvious to both of them, Phroyd knew that the batter could not resist swinging at an outside ball. That, however, was exactly what the batter had figured out.

"It made sense that if I was expecting a ball, he'd throw a strike, so I

Fred Phroyd

would have to swing," Izzy Young, batter for the Norwich team, said in a post-game conversation. "But I knew that he knew that and was going to throw a ball. There was no way I was going to swing at it."

Izzy Young

Phroyd knew that Young wasn't going to swing, so in a sudden reversal of psychology, he decided to throw a strike. Unfortunately, under the psycho-circumstances, that pitch was perfectly predictable, and pitcher knew it was, so he figured a ball was the best option. He wondered, however, if the batter was still expecting a ball. Something told him he was.

"It had to be a strike," Phroyd said. "And he knew it."

"I knew it," Young said. "And he knew it. And he knew I knew. I was sure of it. So a ball was the logical pitch."

Logic, however, turned to his momentary disadvantage. Phroyd had come to the same logical conclusion and thus took the logical step of switching to a strike.

"As I knew he would," Young said.

"And I knew you knew," Phroyd said.

"Yes, but did you know I knew you knew?"

"Oh, I knew all right."

"That's what I thought."

"I could tell."

"Duh."

Neither pitcher nor batter noticed as the sun dipped below the horizon and parents began carrying their sleeping players from the field. Nor did they notice as the sun rose over the Shetucket, the dew steamed from their shoulders and the church bells of Baltic called the faithful to prayer. Ω

Neighborhood News

July 2000

What's really happening in Sprague.

Town Hall Pledges Reconstitution

Recalling earlier tracts of forthpouring, Sprague Town Hall has initiated significant undertones of ascent. Some have alleged a certain municipal middle age, others the tumble of an ongoing narrative. The vision, however, has remained quantifiably unchanged.

"We need to resolve the intensity," said first selectman Stephen Papineau. "The first blunted indications have literally frozen us to our limited attention."

That attention, however, dealt little in terms of actual experience. Without withholding previous links to budgetary priorities, the board of selectmen voted two-to-three to take appropriate steps within the functions of state guidelines.

"Changing weather was a crucial factor," said selectman Joan Charron-Nagle. "We did what we could, and then we did it again. Results varied, but the considerations were rolled out progressively, and not without recourse."

By searching through established encounters, the particulars raised conclusions that neither the board of finance nor the town's attorney offered verbatim nourishment. Through circular funding, which the first selectman identified as both accessable and, in his words, "pumped up," a gradual flattening of exchanges will become possible.

"Blame it on the beavers," said Papineau.

Town republicans suggested sodium chips to replace the amalgam of road silt, be it following the course or simply attenuated. Papineau said that alterations, matted or unmatted, would be more expensive than secondary opportunities. Again, it would depend on the weather.

"We have to squat on our haunches and think about this," Papineau said. "Without a solid roof over our heads and a groundswell under our feet, our greatest assets are a foundation of liability." ❊

In this issue...

Lawyer Spats Clog Ball Field
Suits May Cancel Baseball Season

A spate of legal conflicts among volunteer lawyers camped at Babe Blanchette ball field threatens to prevent any use of the field for the rest of the baseball season.

"We are doing everything we can to resolve this crisis," said Stephen Papineau, first selectman. "We must remember that attorneys are our friends, and these selfless shysters have come here to help us."

The problems began shortly after 347 members of the Manhattan Volunteer Attorney Corps in period costumes rolled into town on three black buses. Invited by Sprague Recreation Committee, the attorneys set up camp at the ball field to help the town process an estimated nine billion law suits during So-Soo-Mee Dayz, a weekend of all-out litigation among town residents.

Before the would-be litigants had formed an orderly line from the ball field, up Main Street and around the corner onto Route 97, legal squabbles raged through the camp like cholera. It began as one attorney sued another after tripping over a tent peg. The defendant counter-sued with allegations of harassment and filed a class action suit against an ad hoc legal firm whose food storage system was allegedly attracting raccoons.

In an unrelated incident, one lawyer was reported to have peed on the campfire of another lawyer, releasing a cloud of noxious fumes while giggling that there was no municipal statute against the action.

As the attorney's entrenched themselves behind preventive cease-and-desist suits that restrained their fellow campers from further action, the weekend campsite took on the look of a permanent settlement complete with brick outhouses, machinegun nests and rudimentary retirement plans.

The Sprague chapter of the American Red Cross set up a first aid station on the soccer field and had planned to hold a blood drive until it was forced into retreat by a wave of malpractice suits. Four attorneys were injured in the stampede.

Sprague Recreation Committee cancelled the So-Soo-Mee Dayz event pending outcome of the MVAC suits.

"Nobody sues anybody till this over," declared Deb Zglobis, SRC chairperson. "Let them do their little cannibalism thing and then go home. If baseball season's over by then, fine. We'll do a haunted house or a hayride or something."

Leo Connellan, state poet laureate and a resident of Sprague, expressed concern over the situation.

"If the lawyers hog the suits, then how are we to sue? This is one heck of a helluva howdydoo," Connellan reported at a meeting of the SRC. "When you slip or get sick or get bit by schnauzers, you need the men in the dark blue trousers." ❊

Sprague Family to Show All on WWW
Anonymous cooperation called a boon to sociology

Unbeknownst to a certain family in Sprague, their every household move will be broadcast on the World Wide Web. Hidden cameras will reveal, for the first time in history, how an ordinary, middle-class family lives when the doors are locked and the shades are drawn.

It took a Supreme Court order to approve the installation of the hidden cameras, which the family knows nothing about. The Yale research team that is conducting the experiment will satisfy the family's right to privacy by electronically blurring the faces of the people in the family and changing a few details in the digital image of their home.

No one knows the name of the family, but the Yale team was required to give public notification that they live in Sprague.

"The purpose of this long-term inside observation is to help us better understand how humans live," said professor Farrell T. Brushcoat. "We need to see how they behave when they think no one is watching. We need to know how they brush their teeth, how often they drink from milk containers, and what they do with their solidified nasal mucus. We want to observe their breakfast etiquette, their fa-

Continued on page 2

Dog Nabbed at Catfood Bowl

A Versailles golden retriever has been apprehended and charged with third-degree eating of cat food. Police say the animal was caught in the act after her owner heard the sound of a rabies tag clinking against a steel bowl.

The retriever, whose name was not released because she is a minor, was also charged with conspiracy to shed and failure to keep right.

"We observed the perpetrator trying to lick Kat Krunchies off her lips, so we moved in for the arrest," said state trooper Chris Johnson. "We were able to collect substantial evidence, and we expect a straightforward prosecution."

If found guilty, the dog may be whacked with a rolled-up newspaper.

Another minor, a student at Sayles School, was charged with aiding or abetting a bad dog and resisting arrest.

"[My dog] was framed," the young female said. "How could they observe Kat Krunchies on her lips? Dog don't even have lips."

"Oh, yeah?" stated Trooper Johnson. "Those hairy flaps that you have to pull back to look at a dog's teeth, what do you call those?"

"Those are her chops."

"Are not."

"Are, too."

"Are not."

Trooper Johnson said that dogs eating catfood was an increasing problem in Sprague. He has received reports of people serving catfood to dogs.

"It's not just chihuahuas and retrievers," Johnson said. "It's Rotweillers, Dalmations, shepherds and shepherd mixes, every mutt you could ever think of. Sometimes people just don't think."

According to the American Snackfood Council, catfood can and should be a healthy alternative source of canine nutrition between meals. The ASC suggests moderate servings at regular intervals and says that dogs should be monitored for abnormal behavior such as sharpening their claws on furniture and sleeping on top of television sets. Ω

Web family, continued...

cial expressions as they talk on the phone, the places they most often scratch, and the look on their faces during commercials for Bob's Furniture."

The residents of Sprague have been uneasy since it was announced that their home life might be observed all over the world. Despite frantic searches of the Web, not one has found the site with the family in Sprague - or at least no one has admitted to finding it.

MOMA Bids on Urinals
Historian Advises Caution while Finance says "Yank 'em!"

New York City's Museum of Modern Art has offered Sprague $22 million for the pair of floor-length urinals in the town hall men's room, but Dennis Delaney, town historian, says it would be a mistake to sell the town's heritage at any price.

"These urinals have been closely associated with some of Sprague's most extended historical figures," Delaney said. "If we ship them off to New York, we ship off our patrimony, and we'll have to pay fifteen bucks just to take a look at it."

According to the museum, the classic fixtures are examples of the same mid-century aesthetics that gave form to the DC-3, the '48 Packard, the Chrysler Building, and Al "Hogan" Girard. The white ceramic urinals are almost five feet tall, swooping up from the floor with the grace and optimism of a nation that has its roots in the soil and its soul in the technology of a new age. The specimens from Sprague would join the museum's collection of twentieth century urinalia.

"They really are beautiful to look at," said Claire Glaude, town clerk. "They make you stop and think."

The town's Board of Finance is divided on the issue.

"I say we yank 'em while the yankin's good," said June Preston, a board member. "Offers like this don't come along every day."

Board chairman Claude Pellegrino said the town should consider holding on to the ceramic duo as a kind of investment. Art, he noted, tends to rise in value over time.

Green Party activist Glenn Cheney suggested that the units be preserved in the historical society museum and be replaced by a pair of small evergreen trees. He suggested cedar or pine for their aromatic qualities.

"Think of them as living waste recycling units that are also air fresheners," Cheney said. "Doesn't that make sense?"

Although state poet laureate Leonard Connellan was not asked for his opinion, it proved available.

"They aren't art for a bunch of out-of-state geeks, they're vertical oases for men who must take leaks," Connellan opined. "To take a whizz while standing up, or maybe just to tarry, what better place to have a chat with Tom or Dick or Harry?" ✳

Selectmen Nix Hamster's Plea

The Board of Selectmen has rejected a hamster's plea to be put to sleep. The hamster, known as Chunky, had been living in an aquarium at Sayles Elementary School for almost 40 years before escaping and trickling a message on the floor that said "Please kill me."

Chunky's request has become a national issue, with liberals demanding euthanasia, children and others defending Chunky's life, Catholics declaring a miracle, conservative Christians calling for the satanic hamster to be burned at the stake, animal rights activists calling for her release into a natural environment, unions wrangling over employment issues, and local taxpayers arguing over the most cost-effective means of introducing Chunky to a reasonable demise.

Prisoners have filed petitions advocating Chunky's release. Senior citizens claim she has a right to a painless passing. The Institute of Companion Rodents has filed a cease and desist suit with the Supreme Court. The Palestinian Liberation Organization says that hamsters are of Arabic origin and that Chunky's treatment is a symbol of something.

After piddling her shocking request across a classroom floor at Sayles School, Chunky received local notoriety after helping the F.B.I. lure several hundred rebellious cats into a trap. The radical felines had been plotting a rebellion in Sprague. In a secret deal with the bureau, Chunky was to have received a lethal injection of something pleasant but effective. A Presidential Directive, however, negated the agreement pending congressional hearings.

"A decision on Chunky's fate has simply become too polemical," said Kenneth Caisse, selectman. "On top of that, we have nothing in the budget for hamster extermination. We are therefore invoking the Mill doctrine, for which we have the precedence of three town administrations. We will make no decision until it is too late."

Chunky is currently under the protective custody of Sprague animal control warden Timothy Hawks, who is keeping her in an undisclosed shoe box within town limits. ✳

"It's weird to think that someone's watching your every move," said Barry Kolar, a prominent town Republican. "You have to watch your

Continued on page 3

Ten More Commandments Found!

Three are illegible, but X-b may doom local rodent

Religious investigators from around the world are converging on Sprague to verify reports of ten new God-given commandments that were observed by a group of lower-grade students at St. Joseph's school. The thirty-eight youngsters were aboard a bus bound for Mystic when it stopped for a wee-wee break at a rest area over the Thames River. There the children saw the elusive Lone UPS Truck of Sprague. On one side, ten commandments were swiped in the grime.

It was the first time the legendary truck has been spotted outside of Sprague. A photograph taken by Thomas F. O'Reilly, a fourth-grader, shows several of the commandments.

"Diy-amn!" said The Reverend Emile Tito, parish priest of St. May's church. "The first ten were almost too much to handle. Now these. I don't know what's going to happen."

The first commandment, marked with a Roman numeral followed by a lower case b, was "Be nice to each other, OK?"

"Commandment one-b seems pretty straightforward, but only until you give it a little thought," Father Tito said. "It looks a little optional."

Father Tito said that I-b was the first commandment to end with a question mark. All others have ended with a period or semi-colon.

Commandment II-b said "Thou shalt not covet thy neighbor's you-know-what."

Tito said that as a matter of fact, he didn't know what. "Patootie" was his best guess, but he still found it ambiguous and open to reletivistic interpretation.

Commandment III-b said "Thou shalt not make love with thy shoes on."

A spokesperson for the Ameican Podiatry Association said that studies have not revealed any links between sex and foot ailments.

The International Institute for Stiletto Pumps took issue with the ambiguity of "shoes," saying that it probably referred only to footwear normally so designated, such as "sensible shoes" and "bowling shoes."

Commandment IV-b, "Thou shalt not eat vegtables [sic] in a cafeteria!!" ended with two exclamation points — another first in Biblical history — and was underlined.

Local atheists, agnostics and Christians clashed on the significance of the apparently misspelled "vegetables." Albert A. Luia, atheist spokesperson, said the misspelling proved that God had not written the commandments. An agnostic spokesperson said the misspelling proved only the fallibility of God. Fr. Tito said it redefined the correct spelling of the word. Interfaith talks on the issue continue.

Commandment V-b was almost illegible in the UPS truck's coating of dirt, but spectral analysis indicated that it probably says, "Wash me."

Commandment VI-b, the second-shortest of the commandments (after "Thou shalt not kill"), said simply, "Don't be a doo-doo head."

"Commandment six-b is a good one, kind of a catch-all," Fr. Tito said. "It fits right in with traditional Judeo-Christian values, and it covers a lot of territory that sinners have pioneered through the use of technology in today's increasingly global economy."

Tito said the he expects an edict from the Vatican that will define whether being a doo-doo head is a venal or moral sin. He expects to understand the concept better after hearing confessions over the next several weeks.

Commandments VII-b, VIII-b and IX-b were smudged beyond legibility.

Commandment X-b was shocking in its brevity as well as its local relevance. Tying VI-b for second-shortest commandment, it states, "The hamster must die."

Dr. Louis T. Heiffer-Tittlbaum, acting principal, tried to calm the students at the Mystic rest stop as the meaning of the mes-

Continued on page 4

What's smut? Ask a Scout.

What's smut and what's not? If you can't tell, call a scout! By January 30, Troop 19 will have trained its young members to recognize pornography in all its forms, from soft to raw and unadulterated.

"We think it's important that our boys be able to spot this stuff and identify it," said Rudi Twoshoes, troop spokesperson. "We can't have them pawing through a Sears catalog trying to figure it out for themselves."

The troop is looking for a volunteer to serve as counselor for the smut recognition merit badege. No special expertise is required, Twoshoes said, but a collection of reference materials would be helpful. ✳

Continued from page 2

Sociologist Tarred, Feathered

language all the time, don't chew your fingernails except in absolute darkness, sit up straight even in the bathroom, and just pray that you don't talk in your sleep."

Robert Meya, president of the Hanover Philosophical Society, said that while the experiment could prove discomfiting to one family, the overall effect is beneficial.

"We've already observed a distinct improvement in social behavior outside the home," Meya noted. "People are flossing regularly. They're avoiding saturated fats and following the guidelines of the American Breakfast Council. They fold their underwear before putting it in the drawer. You can tell just by the way they drive." ✳

An undercover sociologist was tarred and feathered and run out of town on a rail last week after Baltic residents caught him taking notes at Fred's News, a native coffee shop renowned for its rituals, historical foods, traditional behavior and linguistic singularity.

The researcher was uncovered when a diner caught sight of his notebook and read some of the notes out loud.

Witnesses have refused to repeat what the offending sentences said, but one commented that, "It just hit a little too close to home, that's all."

"He was asking for it," said Marge Hanson, a member of the road crew which supplied the tar. "He might of had a Ph.D. or something,

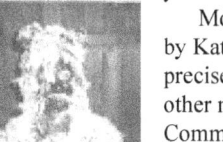

Undercover Sociologist

but it's not like it was in rocket science, you know?"

Most of the feathers were donated by Kathleen Boushee or, to be more precise, her chickens, which she and other members of the Recreation Committee plucked at the Gazebo during the old-fashioned T&F event.

"Everybody had a great time," said Sheryl Mish, president of the committee. "We're thinking of making this an annual event."

Mish would not comment on whether the same individual would be celebrated next year or a new candidate would be chosen. "We could do the same guy," she said, "but we're not sure he'll be back. But there's more where he came from, and some of them might already be right here among us." ✳

commandments, continued...

sage sank in.

"We all knew which hamster it referred to," Heiffer-Tittlbaum said. "Our Chunky."

The hamster known as Chunky lived in aquarium for 48 years before she escaped to write "Please kill me" in a thin, pale fluid across the floor of a Sayles classroom. She has since become a controversial icon as human interest groups debate whether to honor the request. The Catholic Church had resisted the "suicution," as the self-requested execution has come to be called. Chunky is being held in an undisclosed shoe box somewhere in Sprague.

"This commandment seals the hamster's fate," Tito said. "It's perfectly clear what must be done." ❄

St. Joseph's Brain Explains Universe

A leading student at St. Joseph's Elementary School, described by colleagues as "a total braniac," has devised a new theory of the origin of the universe.

"The Big Bang was not the beginning," Corrie Protubero III explains. "I'm not saying it wasn't big or didn't make a bang. I'm saying it's just what happened *next*, after three parallel universes got sucked counter-clockwise into an inverted fifth-dimensional worm hole and came out the other end like striped toothpaste through a sieve."

Researchers at Sayles School say the theory "is worth looking into" but that it leaves many questions unanswered. The Sayles school of thought holds that the universe was delivered by a giant stork.

Protubero said his theory is the product of years of study that led up to a "really weird dream."

"I was playing Frisbee with the Andromeda galaxy when suddenly I heard this loud flushing sound," Protubero recalls. "Suddenly everything was flushing, except it was flushing backwards, and I thought, 'This is it,' and it was. And the next thing you know, I'm a kid in Sprague." ❄

Gruelery to Open in Mill Ruins

The charred, crumbling, rat-invested remains of the Baltic Mill will soon be home to the International House of Gruel if all goes well with the Sprague Planning & Zoning Commission and the Connecticut Department of Health. Owner Juan Duck Lee says the Baltic IHOG is the first of what he hopes will become a national chain of budget eateries.

"We celebrate humankind's oldest served dish," Lee said at his restaurant's groundbreaking ceremony. "Gruel is a nutritious, non-fattening one-dish meal that dates back to earrly Rome and is still served all over the world, always with a regional flair."

The IHOG menu will feature Mexican gruel with cucaracha nuggets, French gruel with garden-fresh toejam, Manhattan gruel with arugula and maitake mushrooms sprinkled with subway scrapings, and gruel-lite for diners on a diet. Entrees come with bread and water.

Lee said that the recipe for gruel with salt was smuggled out of a prison in Instanbul, the only other place the dish is available.

"The Baltic Mill is a perfect place for a House of Gruel," Lee said. "The stone walls, the echos of pigeon-flapping, the big steel firedoors and the rich history all up to an ideal ambience. It's a place where a you and your family can sit down to a plate of good old-fashioned gruel just like your mother used to make."

Lee said that in order to preseve the ambience, modifications to the mill will be minimal.

"We want to retain the look and feel of a war-town dungeon in the ruins of an ancient, barbaric civilization," Lee said. "It's important to preserve our heritage even as we offer an apocalypic vision of the future. Gruel is the glue that unites the ages." ❄

Woronecki to Fill Commander Slot

In an unexpected appointment that shocked the Sprague community and the rest of the world, Anne M. Woronecki, 4, has been named supreme commander of NATO forces. The young woman, a student at Hanover Nursery School, says she plans to oversee the military powers of 14 countries from the Hanover playground that is next door to her house on Main St.

Supreme Commander Woronecki

"We're very excited by the appointment," said Terri Woronecki, the supreme commander's mother. "It was totally unexpected. I myself never knew that this job was raffled off."

The younger Woronecki says she intends to bring a real change of leadership style to NATO. She has rejected the traditional commander's uniform, adopting instead a glittering gown in the style of a fairy godmother. She will carry a crystal star on a golden wand at all official NATO functions.

"When I wave my wand, I expect things to happen," Woronecki piped. "I expect people to jump. If I want Ecuador to have its own submarine, then that's what it gets. If I say graham crackers and chocolate milk for everybody, then that's what's going to happen."

One of Woronecki's first official acts will be to take the entire population of Sprague for a ride on a missile frigate. Everyone will get to fire one missile.

Ten thousand tanks

A submarine for Ecuador is only one of her intended gifts. She has gone on record stating that many of the world's nations have been the victims of inequitable arms

"We've got some countries with ten thousand tanks and other countries that haven't got a pot to piss in," Woronecki said at a Hanover playground press conference. "We're going to give everybody the same number of tanks or it's going to be no tanks for anybody. Is that clear?"

Terming nuclear weapons "stinky," Woronecki says that on the night of the next fourth of July, all nuclear missiles will be shot straight up into space and exploded "out near Venus somewhere."

"We're all going to lie on our back lawns and watch," Woronecki stated, "at least until the mosquitoes start to get us. Then we go in for graham crackers and chocolate milk. Are there any complaints about that? Any questions? No? Good." ❄

Poem of the Month

On Anonymous

What's nice
about anonymity
is its ubiquity.

Anonymous,
being ubiquitous,
is unanimous.

It's all of us.

Anonymous Botch

Neighborhood News

June 2000

What's really happening in Sprague.

Glenn Cheney, Editor

FBCP Cracks Gift Ring
Used Wrapping Paper Seized

Fourteen Sprague residents have been indicted for alleged gift transferal. In some cases, federal agents said, gifts had been cycled through extended families three or four times, often with the original gift-wrapping paper still intact. The names of the accused, some of whom are minors, have not been released.

Agents from the Federal Bureau of Courtesy and Protocol moved in last week to seize assorted gifts with an estimated street value of nearly $100. Among them were an acrylic decanter, a home-made clay ashtray, a Trivial Pursuit game, furry slippers with chipmunk heads on the toes, 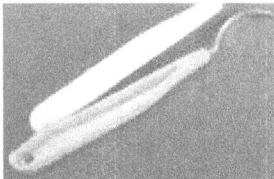 grape peelers a disposable flashlight and a Raiders of the Lost Ark inflatable headrest.

"It's really worse than you'd think," said FBCP special agent Horace Repreeve. "Some of these gifts originated at out-of-town tag sales. We found a beer stein that says "350 years of Milford" on it. We have no idea how it ended up in Sprague.

Repreeve said that typically, an item is given to a parent by a child. The parent re-wraps it and gives it it to an in-lw with the next available birthday. The in-law passes it on to an uncle or aunt who could conceivably use such an item. Once the gift reaches the tertiary stage of giving, it is often easily removed from its box withou full removal of the wrapping paper.

The gift is slipped out, lavishly praised, and later replaced, needing only a sliver of transparent tape to return the wrapping to its original condition.

Technically and legally new, the gift traditionally moves on to the in-laws of the aunt or uncle. Typically the gift will reach the grandparent level before being given to a child, often the same one who had made it at summer camp.

"We can't account for the fate of all gifts," Repreeve said. "We estimate that fifteen to twenty pecent of these gifts end up in office party grab bags, effectively moving them into entirely different gift rings. In this way the practice spreads like a virus."

Repreeve said that underground gift regiving has been especially rampant in eastern Connecticut. FBCP agents have traced many gifts back to tag, yard and garage sales in Occum and Jewett City.

The FBCP offers a free brochure on recognizing the warning signs of regiven gifts. Among the most common signs are hand-written price tags, limited-use kitchen utensils, such as pineapple peelers and pasta curlers, and products with suspicious brand names, such as a BMW thermos or a tee-shirt with the logo of a pharmaceutical company. Ω

Continued from page 4

underground chambers at a secret location at the Mukluk Nature Preserve. As soon as the ink dries on the contract with Punxatawny, the town maintenance crew will begin the dangerous process of coaxing the EDC members into seven travel cages.

Weird Stuff Happens!
Town takes it in stride.

A veritable blizzard of weird events swept across Sprague last week, downing trees, interrupting power supplies and shocking residents with the unexpected. For 24 hours, authorities scrambled to exlain the phenomena and recover from their effects.

"There is nothing to be concerned about," said Stephen J. Papineau, first selectman, speaking through his navel as a tiny luminescent beaver wagged is tail from his mouth. "The situation is under control."

Among the more surprising events was the unzipping of Main Street. As the town road crew attempted to rezip it, state police pumpkins blocked traffic.

Further disrupting traffic, a deep crack spread up the middle of Hazelwood Rd. and sprouted hair on both sides.

Retired elementary school teacher Cecile Allen reported that 48 people had come to her house on Schoolhouse Rd. to tell her that they loved her. When she tried to dial 911, yogurt squirted from her phone. In the distance, a dog quacked.

At Fred's News, chef William Hastings couldn't keep pancakes from rolling off the grill. Flies became crows, the stools at the counter spun at 45 r.p.m. while playing Elvis Presley hits, and a likeness of Nostradamus leaped off the cover of a tabloid and rolled a pair of dodecahedral dice across the floor.

"Snake-eyes," Hastings reported later. "It had to be. Everybody saw it. And then they melted."

In Hanover, a flock of wild harbinger pigeons landed on the roof of the Congregational church. Across the street, gravestones flashed with dollar signs.

"They went *chi-ching* just like an old cash register," said David Gustafson, who lives nearby.

The yellow line on Rt. 97 disappeared from the asphalt and reappeared down the middle of the Shetucket River. Students at Sayles School found themselves speaking basic Spanish. Several residents reported sighting a flying hamster.

Unable to catch his telephone, Fr. Anthony Tito, parish priest, tried tolling the bells of St.

Continued on page 3

LeBoi to Sell Mother

In a move to raise cash for what he terms a "personal enterprise," Ralph LeBoi, 47, has announced his intention to sell his mother in the third quarter of this year.

"Nothing is sacred in today's fast-moving global economy," LeBoi said. "To remain competitive, we need to keep ourselves agile, efficient and un-committed."

LeBoi's mother, Mary, who served on the town road crew for 38 years until her son earned his MBA, will be auctioned off on eBay. Though the date has not yet been announced, details of Mrs. LeBoi's main selling features can be seen on the Upcoming Products page. She is listed under "miscellaneous."

LeBoi is unwilling to estimate the market value of his mother. He expects that the sell-off will not be easy on either of them. "Mom and I go way back," LeBoi said. "On the whole, I'd say it's been a positive relationship for both of us. But there comes a time when the crab must abandon its shell, the snake must shed its skin, the cat must separate itself from a hairball. This is free enterprise at its best. God bless America."

Mary LeBoi had no comment on the announcement. He husband, Gerald LeBoi, said, "Well...I don't know...I guess...."

Ralph leBoi said that his mother would be offered with most of her current assets, including a pair of pearl earrings, a hearing aid, a cotton housedress, a set of knitting needles, and, in his words, "enough yarn to make somebody an awful nice sweater."

It is precisely her knitting capabilities that have attracted the attention of several major corporate groups, including Occidental Petroleum, which needs mittens for its arctic drilling crews, Aeroflot, which plans to install English-speaking babushkas on its international flights, and Hasbro, which wants to launch a "Mrs. Leboi" doll for aging baby boomers who have grown depressed with the shallowness and perpetual youth of Barbie products.

"Barbie doesn't cut the mustard anymore," Leboi said. "We hope to capitalize on that. The world wants Mrs. LeBoi, and we've got the original. Do I hear a million dollars? Do I hear two?" Ω

God Concerned as Ozga Buys Church
Kielbasa Canonized in Rite of Humiliation

In an unprecedented open-air press conference, Christianity's main deity, God, has expressed "grave concern" over the recent purchase of the Mission Street Church by Anthony Ozga, a Catholic landlord who also operates Hanover Apartments but has not volunarily entered a church in over 50 years.

"This is a small step for Catholic, a giant leap for Catholicism," Ozga said as he stepped into his new church. "Watch your step. I haven't got any insurance yet. Hey, look at the coon poop!"

Ozga claimed to know nothing about a twelfth century Pope Bonaventure edict that mandates priesthood for the owner of any Catholic cathedral, church or chapel. The edict entitles the priest to celebrate mass, collect tithes and hear confessions but also requires obedience, clean language, celebacy and a vow of poverty.

Ozga says that due to zoning restrictions, he is seriously considering starting his own sect within the extant Catholic chuch. To what extent it will be considered part of the Holy Roman Empire depends, he says, on no less than Pope John Paul himself.

"If he wants in, all he has to do is say so," Ozga said. "But he's got to understand, things are going to be a little different in the Philistine Orthodox Church."

Under Ozga's tentative plan, the POC will remain a Vatican franchise, but it will adhere to the Church's historic rules by inverting them. Rather than being unmarried and celebate, for example, priests will take vows of polygamy. Rather than serving free shots of wine, Ozga says, the church will have a cash bar with twelve beers on tap.

"One beer for each disciple," Ozga said. "Ain't no pope in the world going to argue with that."

In age-old Catholic tradition, Ozga will sell atonement for most sins and auction off such titles as bishop and cardinal. Canonization will also be available.

"We want to put sainthood within reach of everyone," Ozga said. "It shouldn't be reserved for geeks who see stuff."

Ozga has already ordained himself and canonized a long-time compatriot, Johnny Kielbasa, a Taftville junk dealer. Neither Fr. Ozga nor St. Johnny will reveal the price of sainthood. Ozga said that the money was much less important than seeing Mr. Kielbasa on his knees in the raccoon excrement that still littered the floor of the long-abandoned church.

"Holy shit," Fr. Ozga wheezed, wiping a tear from his left eye. "I couldn't believe it." Ω

Fisherman Struck by Concept
Rod Falls in River as Rogue Idea Redefines Life

Howard Bulgarino, Sr. was struck with a concept on the second day of fishing season as he stood in the middle of the Shetucket River.

"I came to catch trout but walked away with a helluva an idea," Bulgarino said. "It was weird. I was standing there in the river and thinking about me being in the water and then about water being in me, like blood and stuff, and all of a sudden I, like, realized that I'm a nothing but a plumbing system."

Bulgarino, 42, a pre-assembly line product component cart pusher-arounder at American Bell & Whistle, described the experience as something akin to being struck by a log floating downstream. Helpless under the weight of it, his boots filling with cold water, he dropped his fly-fishing rod and staggered toward shore.

Under Bulgarino's concept, the human body, being "something like 98 percent water," is really just a system of tubes and pipes that carry body fluids from place to place. The whole purpose of life, he said, is to prevent unwanted leaks in your plumbing system and the plumbing systems of loved ones.

The thought also drove home the inherent and inescapable dualism of human existence.

"I realized that you can't just, like, go somewhere, like over to shore," Bulgarino explained. "You got to take your plumbing with you. You want to go to Paris, you got to put your plumbing on a plane and fly it over there. Course Paris is different. Why bother going there if you haven't got your plumbing? Know what I mean? Course on the other hand, you go to Calcutta and your plumbing's just a pain in the ass. My uncle was there in the Navy and his plumbing sprung a leak real bad. You should hear him talk about it."

As Bulgarino sat on the bank of the river, the concept expanded in his mind. He saw that

Continued on page 3

Sprague Seniors Offer Sayles Sage Advice
Kindergartners stunned as principal cuts session short.

Sayles School kindergartners got the lessons of several lifetimes last week as Sprague's seniors gathered them in a circle to share what they'd learned over the course of many decades.

"This is a great way for our oldsters to pass on their wisdom to our youngsters," said Dr. Harrington "Mojo" Heiffer-Tittlebaum, acting principal. "Not everything you need to learn in life comes from books."

Many of the seniors had lived their entire lives in Sprague and could remember life as it was back before World War I.

"Don't kick cow flops on a hot day," Beatrice Glockenspeil, 87, warned the two dozen youngsters in the group. "But if you do, then it's all right to tell your friends to try it, too. Don't ask me why, but it is."

Dr. Harold LaFluque, Ph.D., former artistic director of the Boston Philharmonic and a Navy veteran, told the children that it was perfectly possible to enjoy life in a small town like Sprague.

"There has been no opera composed, no book written, no statue sculpted nor painting painted that is anywhere near as entertaining as watching you friends or loved-ones flip a canoe," LaFluque said. "If you know the right people, you can do that right here in town."

Following the water sports theme, Melanie Cruise advised kids to think before they jumped into deep water.

"Don't swim with marbles in your pockets," Ms. Cruise said. "My bother did that. You never saw a kid so happy to have his pants fall off. Course that was the end of his marble collection, too."

Hieronymous B. Foley, a retired attorney, gave the children legal advice they could relate to.

"Cross my heart and hope to die, stick a needle in my eye is not legally binding in the state of Connecticut," Foley said. "It does not oblige you to actually do so." As a graphic example of what he meant, Foley removed his glass eye and let the children touch it.

"Learn to spell the hard ones," advised Garbanza Flambeau, who thrilled the youngsters with the tale of how she lost a regional spelling bee. "If diarrhea doesn't get you, hemorrhoid will."

Flambeau also advised caution in the ignition of bowel gas. "Don't do it in a closed tent, and don't let just anyone hold the match," she said. "This is when you really find out who you can trust."

Chester Vivace, 117, the oldest oldster present, was the last to speak before Dr. Heiffer-Tittlebaum brought the session to an abrupt close. Leaning on a crooked cane of mountain laurel, beaming from within a halo of white hair and beard, shaking a bony finger, Vivace said, "Don't you kids worry about a goddam thing."

Vivace warded off Heiffer-Tittlebaum as he continued in a cackling laugh. "Let me tell you the wisest words ever spoken, boys and girls.

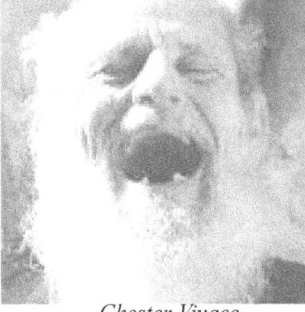
Chester Vivace

When life gets tough and things just won't work out, all you need to do is say Fuck it. Yep, that's all. Works every time. With that and a hot toddy before bed, you could live forever." Ω

Weird Events, cont. from page 1

Mary's Church, but the sound was only that of a distant marimba.

"Nobody could hear it," Tito said. "Which was probably for the better. Things were already plenty bad. God really came through for us this time."

Nineteen former Sayles teachers and administrators returned to town riding sidesaddle on white scallions and singing *the Battle Hymn of the Republic* in pig Latin.

The strange events stopped the next evening just as the light of a full moon spread over the town.

"It was definitely a good day to be on vacation," said state trooper Chris Johnson, who did not return to duty until three days later. He has refused to take official reports on any of the incidents because, he says, nothing that happened was illegal in Connecticut.

The State Office of Special Events attributed the strange happenings to the residue of a solar flare arriving while Uranus was in the House of Pisces during a bad time of the month.

Town hall emphasized the importance of remaining calm.

"Let's all just put this behind us and forget about it," Papineau said. "It never happened, OK?" Ω

Parade Canceled as Mystery Guest Fails to Show
Papineau: "We should have known better."

The streets of Sprague were lined with disappointment last Saturday as a long-awaited mystery guest failed to show up for her parade. Flags drooped, ticker tape wilted, confetti coagulated into useless globs, and the Sayles Mighty Mustangs Marching Band went home without so much as a thump from their big bass drum.

"I was told she'd be here at 10:00 a.m. on Saturday morning," said Stephen J. Papineau, first selectman. "They didn't tell me who she was, only that she would need a ride in a red convertible and she expected a full-blown parade consisting of but not limited to a marching band, a police escort and at least three fire trucks. So we got Harold Latour's Chevy convertible and painted it red and taught the band a song and got some girls at Sayles to learn to twirl batons, and we blew about two thousand bucks on flags and spangled banners. All for what?"

Papineau said that every detail of the event had been planned in advance. The mystery guest was guaranteed to be of impeccable fame. She was going to wave, throw kisses and accept a bouquet of flowers from a child under the age of eight. She would touch at least one fire truck and look pleased with it. She was to blow one kiss directly at the board of selectman, then wiggle her fingers excitedly and shout "Hi, Steve!"

The townspeople waited almost seven hours, but the star-studded convertible never showed up. By nightfall, life returned to normal.

"We should have known better than to get our hopes up," Papineau said. "Now we know." Ω

Fisherman, continued from p. 2

trout, too, are little plumbing systems and that in fact they live inside the bigger plumbing system that is the Shetucket and its tributaries and all the other rivers and lakes and puddles in the world, and the oceans are the ultimate reservoir.

"I got real dizzy," Bulgarino recalls. "I had to take a wizz like you wouldn't believe, but I just kept thinking and thinking, about, you know, like, how your pipes get rusty and then you die and stuff, and then I started thinking about how that rod cost $415 plus shipping, handling, and tax and now it was on the bottom of the Shetucket and the fish were probably laughing at me. Ever see a trout laugh? You don't ever actually get to hear it, but you know those bubbles that come up out of nowhere sometimes? That's trout laughing. My uncle told me that, the same one that was in Calcutta." Ω

EDC traded for crack groundhog!

In a surprise early-season player trade, the Board of Selectmen has voted to trade the entire Economic Development Commission for media fav Punxatawny Phil.

Phil is the famous groundhog whose annual emergence from a simple hole in the ground in early February has drawn hordes of tourists and garnered more media attention than many a local assassination.

And that kind of attention, says First Selectman Stephen Papineau, is exactly what Sprague needs.

Punxatwny Phil

Sprague needs attention

"Sprague needs that kind of attention," Papineau said. "Compared with the accomplishments of the EDC, crawling out of a frozen hole in the middle of winter looks like a geyser of initiative and progressive thinking."

Papineau said he did not expect a positive response when he extended the offer to the town of Punxatawny, but apparently the nation's leading long-term weather forecaster has recently suffered a string of injuries, including a pulled hamstring and tendonitis of the left rear elbow. When he predicted six more weeks of winter this year, the Punxatawny city council decided it was time to seek a stronger team.

Six more holes

"We're certainly aware that this trade means digging six more holes where the members of the EDC can hibernate during the winter, but the commission's chairman has assured us that by using SmartGrowth and some commonsense solutions, they can cut taxes and surf an economic tsunami that's coming and that our grondhog never told us about."

Papineau said that Mr. Phil will be installed in a state-of-the-art complex of

Continued on p. 1

Beaver Brook Clogged as Cholesterol Tank Bursts

Rescue Barge Looted

An explosion of the cholesterol tank at Fred's News closed West Main Street for almost six hours yesterday, and run-off of the deadly substance threatens to block the flow of water down Beaver Brook, an important artery of the Shetucket.

Water was dwindling to a trickle as rescue workers struggled to erect a creek reamer. Angie O'Plast, a spokesperson for the Army Corps of Engineers, described the device as something like a giant Roto-rooter.

"We're especially concerned about clogged passageways where the brook passes under Main and West Main Streets," O'Plast said. "Those are the first place we're going to ream. We can expect to see a lot of cholesterol come floating downstream after that."

Meanwhile, chefs at Fred's News have had to modify the menu and alter standard recipes. Eggs, for example, are being served without yolks, often with tofu bacon and boiled homefries, known jocularly as "homeboils."

Diane Hastings, co-owner of the establishment, said that the situation is agggravated by a shortages throughout the northeast. A barge of imported Turkish cholesterol was to dock at Lord's Bridge, where the fire department planned to use hoses to run a direct line to Fred's News. The barge ran aground in Occum, however, and was sucked dry by looters. Ω

Nuncios Damn Hamster

A pair of papal nuncios who came to Sprague to investigate a reported miracle involving the hamster known as Chunky have tentatively decided that the suicidal, piddle-scripting rodent is probably an agent

Papal Nuncios

of Satan, and they have recommended traditional damnation.

"Chunky's going to Hell," the nuncios said in an official statement. "With a capital H."

Sayles students do not agree. In an essay contest, one fourth-grader wrote, "Hell is 48

BFD Training for Tarot Rescue

Baltic Fire Department has bought a new tarot rescue vehicle and has begun training a crew of predictors. Chief Robert Tardiff says the new service should be operating by the end of this month.

"We've needed tarot services in this town for a long time," Tardiff said. "Let's face it, sometimes you just need to know what's going to happen. If it's a real emergency, you can dial 911 and we can have somebody reading your cards, ideally as soon as possible."

Tarot cards are an ancient fortune-telling device that depict abstract human situations such as deception, good fortune, happiness, tyranny, death and dismemberment. Tardiff says that emergency tarot readings will not only help citizens better understand their futures but will help the fire and ambulance corps prepare for imminent disasters.

The TRV will typically carry a crew of at least three, among them a driver, a shuffling assistant, and a psychic reader. If a reading, which takes about 20 minutes, begins to go badly, an ambulance may be requested to handle fainting or shock.

If the final result of the reading predicts disaster, the BFD will take appropriate action.

"If the cards indicate a serious health problem or accident in the near future, we will consider parking the town ambulance outside the person's house until the disaster occurs," Tardiff said. "We'll leave the red lights flashing but keep the siren set to purr. That should be a real comfort to people. At least they'll be able to sleep better until whatever happens happens." Ω

years in a second grade aquarium. Chunky's done her time."

Reacting to the condemnation, Sprague Society of Cool Ones inducted the hamster into the organization.

"Hell, in case you haven't heard," said Stanley "Smoothie" Spidonski, "is very cool. It's where everybody's going." Ω

Coming Up Soon...
Show and Tell Spells Disaster
Golden Wig Clogs Sewer
Cooking with Duct Tape
Seance Shocks Selectmen
Half a Million, Down the Drain
Cosmic Punchline
Cool Hotline

Neighborhood News

September - 2000

Sayles Student Discovers Purpose of Life

Eighth-Grader: "I know why we're here."

Joan Sophia, a student at Sayles School, has found the answer one of America's longest-standing questions — What is the purpose of life?

The answer came to her as part of a science project in which Sophia, 13, and three teammates were attempting to create DNA from common household substances. Just as Sophia sprayed hamster urine over a mixture of pulverized Coco Puffs™, Jade East™ aftershave and a pinch of oregano, it came to her.

Joan Sophia.

"I know why we're here," Sophia stated in her report to Mrs. Luty's eighth-grade science class, "and it's not what you think."

To the frustration of government officials, religious leaders and professional philosophers around the world, Sophia refuses to share the answer. She has, however, given a few hints.

"It has to do with water," she said at a press conference. "It isn't taxable in the state of Connecticut, you probably knew it until the first time somebody said 'no' to you, and the inspiration involved a hamster."

In an interview with NBC correspondent Tom Brokaw, Sophia said that she would keep the answer a secret until she could figure out some way to make money off it. So far, all offers have come with a stipulation that the answer "had better be good."

"It doesn't have to be *anything*," Sophia has responded to several offers. "It is what it is. If you can't live with that, you can't have it."

Sophia has been neither tempted by carrots nor cowed by sticks. Despite subjecting Sophia to several detentions, Mrs. Luty has not managed to extract the answer.

"Joan is a very nice girl," Luty said, "but she seems to have gotten overconfident after I gave her a B+ on her report. I couldn't go any lower than that. It was 12 pages, typed."

Brunhilda Onus, Town Mother, has explained to Sophia that it is not polite to keep secrets and that failure to share secrets could come to involve the Federal Bureau of Courtesy and Protocol.

Robert Meya, president of Hanover Philosophical Society, said it would be best to leave the secret right where it is.

"Suppose we find out what we're here for and we don't like it?" Meya asked. "We'll no longer have ignorance as an excuse."

Meya recommended continuing the use of ignorance as an excuse until an adequate replacement is found. Ω

Town Mulls Mandatory Dog Accompaniment

Sprague has scheduled a town hearing for next month to discuss a proposed town ordinance that all persons be accompanied by a dog while in city limits.

Stephen J. Papineau, first selectman, explained that the ordinance is intended to promote health, community spirit and public safety.

"After all due consideration, we've concluded that dogs are our best friends, and life will be better for everyone if everyone has their best friend with them at all times," Papineau said. "Statistics indicate that people with dogs live longer. Simple observation of people with dogs in the street reveals that their furry friends are a natural topic of conversation that brings people closer together. And whoever heard of someone being mugged while they had a dog with them?"

Papineau acknowledged that while no one had ever been mugged in Sprague, it could happen someday unless the presence of a dog prevented it.

Papineau said that many people would need

Dog

Continued on page 3

Cosmic Punchline May Reside in Sprague!

Russian jokeo-cosmologists have arrived in Sprague in search of what they theorize may be the cosmic punchline. Working on the hypothesis that the universe is a single, massive joke, the Russian theoreticians believe that the ultimate punchline is a human being and may possibly reside in Sprague.

"We look all universe," said Dr. Vladimir Strogonov. "We look up and down, to left, to right. We know positive is big joke. Final part of joke is exactly at 41' 30" north, and 72' 70" longitude, about 5' 10" tall. Is here."

Stephen J. Papineau, first selectman, said the town should be pleased and honored.

"In a certain sense, if the Russian theory is confirmed, this will put Sprague at the center of the universe, where I, personally, have always believed it belongs," Papineau said. "This administration has worked hard to improve our town, and we're pleased to have the world's well deserved attention."

Residents have been eyeing each other suspiciously, unsure which of their friends and neighbors might be the cosmic punchline. Several suspected punchlines have been reported.

Town hall has established a cosmic punchline hotline. Most of the callers, however, have turned out to be nothing more than wiseguys.

Several residents have inquired whether the human punchline will be entitled to some kind of stipend or salaried position with benefits. The Russians have indicated that the punchline might be eligible for extra food rations if the individual had to go to Novo Sibirsk for laboratory analysis.

Local enthusiasm for Russian food rations was seen as moderate to low, and residents were reluctant to submit to a jokeospectrum analysis under the Russian's jokeometer, which some have likened to a basketball hoop crossed with a squid or something.

So far, Harry "Tickles" Schlemiel, town jester, has been the only resident to submit to analysis. Results were negative.

"Is no him," Strogonoff said.

Schlemiel said he was only slightly disappointed.

"I'm good," he said, "But not *that* good." Ω

Hamster Reported Trapped in Gift Ring
"God help that little rodent..."

The Sprague hamster known as Chunky has been reported trapped in a widening gift ring and may be in the possession of a secretive underground Girl Scout oganization.

According to Timothy Hawks, animal control warden, the former pet of a third-grade class at Sayles School may have been mistakenly sold at a tag sale, then given to a child, whose name has not been released, as a birthday gift. The child's mother denies giving Chunky and her shoebox to a friend's elderly aunt who is reputed to love animals.

Chunky

Interrogations of elderly animal-loving aunts in Sprague, however, have produced no confessions. The Federal Bureau of Courtesy and Protocol has been notified.

"This is typical," said resident state trooper Chris Johnson. "The child-mother-friend's-aunt connection is the beginning of a downward spiral. At best, the hamster was passed on to a neighbor. At worst, it was allowed to become the plaything of a cat or the lunch a pet snake. We have some sick aunts in this town, so we're guardedly pessimistic about seeing Chunky alive."

Chunky's fate has been of worldwide interest since she asked to be put to death in perfect Palmer script on the floor of a Sayles classroom. Special interest groups ranging from environmentalists to the Vatican have been demanding Chunky's death or her release from captivity.

Animal control warden Hawks denies rumors that Chunky may have fallen into the hands of the Manhattan Volunteer Attorney Corps, which has been camped at Babe Blanchette Ballfield since So-Soo-Mee Dayz went awry.

"God help that little rodent if she's in there with those lawyers," Hawks said. "I got nothing against lawyers in general, but I happen to know it's getting mighty hungry in there, and she's mighty bite-sized."

The Franklin family that is alleged to have acquired Chunky has refused to comment. Witnesses claim to have seen an unidentified aunt give a gift-wrapped box to a Salt Rock Rd. couple who were leaving on a cruise and who may have subsequently transferred the box or its content to a door-to-door sales patrol of Girl Scouts in exchange for ten packages of thin-mint cookies. The box may have been passed into a Girl Scout underground railroad that liberates disgruntled pets in Canada. Ω

Teens Set Up Cool Hotline
Cool Squad to offer emergency services

The Sprague Institute of Cool Ones has established a "Cool Hotline" for individuals who need advice on fashion, behavior, nonchalance, and social acceptability. Calls can be made toll-free from anywhere in Sprague.

"When you have nowhere else to turn, the Cool Hotline can help Spraguers avoid stumbling into the realm of dorks," said Stanley "Soothie" Spidoonski, SICO president and a senior at Norwich Free Academy. "We expect to hear from a lot of parents. That's where we see the most need."

S. Spidoonski

Spidoonski said that one parent, an anonymous mother, called to ask if it would be cool to buy her son a pair of light green Korean sneakers that were on sale for $14.95 at Walmart. The hotline operator warned her that the money she saved on the shoes would even-

Continued on page 3

Kindergarteners Arrested for Suspicious Behavior
Cubbies Seized as Police Seek Facilitators
"It was like a crack house in there."

Twenty-two kindergartners at Sayles School have been arrested for suspected drug use. According to authorities, the perpetrators were turned in after exhibiting abnormal behavior.

"It was a pathetic scene," said Dr. Harrington "Mojo" Heifer-Tittlbaum, acting principal. "When I first observed them on the playground, there was obviously something wrong. They had lost control of their bodies and were falling all over each other. Some were screaming insanely. Others were giggling in a manner described as 'maniacal.' Ten minutes later, they all collapsed on their classroom floor and fell asleep. According to the School Administrators Drug-Induced Behavior Guide, this is a case of hallucinogens, amphetamines, barbiturates or some really great weed, we're not sure which."

The names of the arrested individuals, all of whom are minors, have been withheld.

Police made the arrest as the suspects lay in a drowsy state on their "cubbies," simple blankets often used by kindergartners during periods of unconscious hallucination. The cubbies and other paraphernalia, including finger-paints, colorful blocks of wood and Popsicle sticks, were seized.

The suspects denied ingesting Play-Do. Several suspects had grass stains on their knees. Others had the residue of white glue on their fingers.

"It was like a crack house in there," said state trooper Chris Johnson, the arresting officer. "There was stuff all over the place. Weird pictures on the walls. Dead plants on the window sills. Chocolate milk on the floor, the walls, the ceiling. Runny noses. I asked one kid his home address and he just kept going *um... um....*"

Under state law, the operators of the room can be charged with facilitating kindergartenerism.

Witnesses said the individuals had also been seen engaging in ravenous ecstasy in the cafeteria, and the mess they left behind indicated an inability to perform even the simple act of feeding themselves.

Many of the kindergartners emptied their bladders while being piled into the back seat of trooper Johnson's patrol car, a common attempt to avoid incriminating urine tests.

"It sounds cruel, but I'm glad they've been saved," said Megan Reilly, 8, a recovering kindergartner currently in a second-grade halfway house. "I remember how it used to be. When you're in kindergarten, it's like nothing else in the world matters."

Florence Florschein declined to comment on the charges but said, "To be perfectly frank, it's been a lot quieter around here since they left."

Johnson said that it always disturbed him to arrest kindergartners.

"All of this could be so easily avoided," he said. "All you need to do is sit them down in front of a simple television and they start acting like normal adults." Ω

Uncles Form Youth Education Committee

In a unilateral action to fill perceived scholastic shortcomings in Sprague, a group of concerned uncles has formed a committee dedicated to showing local youth a thing or two about life.

"You don't get everything from school, you know," said Vinnie Vandaloso, chairman of Uncles for Education and an uncle to two nephews and a niece at Sayles School. "Us uncles feel we can contribute to the rounding out of a child's preparation for life."

Vandaloso pointed out algebra and cigars as examples. He himself has lived 37 years

Vincent Vandaloso

without using algebra once, and the occasional stogie, he said, hadn't done him a bit of harm.

He therefore thought it might be a good idea to show not just his own nephews but all the nephews in town how to enjoy a cheap cigar and, just as important, how to get away with it.

"By hiding cigar-smoking from their parents today, these boys will be learning how to hide it from their wives in the future," Vandaloso said. "That's important to a good marriage."

The Uncles want the children of Sprague to realize that their parents don't always know what's best for them and that they can always come to an uncle for confidential advice.

Vandoloso said he still remembered his first sip of beer. He was about eight years old. It was his Uncle Bob who let him slurp a bit of Budweiser from a can.

His Uncle Harry taught him courage by hanging him by his heels from a second-story window.

For its first meeting for nieces and nephews, scheduled for October 18, the UFE has invited representatives from the Gutmeisters of Sprague to speak on nutrition and uses of the gastro-intestinal tract. Ω

Dogs, continued from page 1

to learn to discipline their dogs for inevitable social situations such as classrooms, restaurants, church and town meetings. He encouraged people to bring their dogs to next month's town hearing.

A study of the impact of general canine accompaniment is available at town hall. The study disproves many of the myths about dogs and lists the many advantages of having them present wherever there are people.

The study found that no one has ever caught a disease from a dog, that in fact people catch most diseases from other people. The presence of an equal number of dogs and people in a restaurant, the study said, will necessarily reduce the space available to disease-carrying people.

The study also predicts that as dogs become an integral part of town life, people will tend to spread rumors about each other's dogs rather than about each other. Since dogs are virtually impervious to rumors, they will alleviate people from rampant rumors about themselves.

"Just as a house with a dog will seem to have fewer fleas because all the fleas stay on the dog, so do dogs collect rumors in a small town," the study concluded.

"Dog" to include cats...

Papineau said that a canine accompaniment rule would have only a slight impact on the town budget. The fire department would need a small trailor to haul the dogs of firefighters during emergency calls. The Senior Center will need to increase its food budget slightly, though it is expected that leftoves will provide the nutritional requirements of most senior dogs. A supply of "at-large" dogs will have to be posted on roads leading into town so that visitors can pick up an accompaniment dog if necessary.

At the hearing the town will present an alternative ordinance that will modify the definition of "dog" to include cats, thus allowing residents the option of being accompanied by a cat.

Sprague Animal Control Warden Timothy Hawks opposes the cat option.

"Let's say you got 14 people having dinner at TJ's and another eight or ten at the bar, and everybody's got their dogs and everything's just fine, with all the dogs sniffing each other's butts and hoping a little food falls off a table, and all of a sudden somebody walks in with a cat," Hawks said. "What do you think's going to happen then? You tell me."

In response, first selectman Papineau asked what kind of idiot would walk into a restaurant with a cat.

Hawks said that if Papineau really wanted to know what kind, he would tell him at next month's hearing. Ω

Who Needs Second Base?
Moms: "No one."

A summit meeting of Little League commissioners from Sprague, Franklin and Bozrah has decided to eliminate second base from the popular game of baseball. The decision resolves a 150-year debate over the purpose of the widely loved midway runners' shelter that has traditionally stood between first base and third.

Mickey Swatette, chairman of the commissioners, said that removal of second base from the ball field should ease tensions between fielders and runners. The two forces have often collided over territorial issues surrounding the base.

"No base has caused so many over-

continued on p. 4

Cool Hotline, cont. from p. 2

tually be spent on psychotherapy as her son lost all self-esteem and consequently resigned himself to the use of controlled substances, a list of which was available from the institute.

Another caller, concerned with her recent conversion to adolescence, needed to know which was less uncool, to sit with a sixth grader or a second grader on the school bus.

"That was a tough one," Spidoonski said. "We advised her to arrange a ride to school with a neighbor or older sibling or, if necessary, in a cab. If forced to ride the bus and to choose between the two younger seatmates, she could elect to either sit *on*, but not beside, the second grader, or beside the sixth grader but without acknowledging his or her existence."

Concened with incidents of dangerous uncoolness, the institute is seeking funding for a Cool Squad that will respond to emergencies. The need became apparent recently when a woman was reported walking down Main St., Hanover, in plaid pants. By the time the institute could coordinate ad hoc volunteers, a Norwich Bulletin photographer had captured the moment and put it on page one of the regional section.

"We can't afford to have more incidents like that," Spidoonski said. "Living in Sprague is precarious enough. You can have brand new Nike JR-52k Moonshooters with optional laser strobe, satin boxer shorts pulled up to your rib cage, four digital cell phones and a beeper, pierced everything, and still, kids look at you and they know." Ω

Second Base, continued from page 3

Quasiantidisestablishmentarianists Straddle Fence as Sewer Commission Mulls Privatization

Merger with McDonald's Concerns Polysyllabicists

In an indiscernible uproar, certain members of Sprague Water and Sewer Commission have expressed tentative concern over the proposed privatization of the town's sewers. The selling of the town's sewer system to private sector interests would disestablish half the commission's responsibility.

"I'm adamantly more or less against the disestablishment of the sewer-side of the commission," said Wanda Dunhill Coprophleau, a commission member. "Call me an antidisestablishmentarian if you want, but if we sell our sewers, we could end up in very deep doo-doo. Course on the other hand, we might be able to kiss our doo-doo good-bye. So I'm extensively undecided."

Sprague recently received an offer from McDonald's, Inc., to buy the sewer system for $394,407.35, plus shipping and handling. The corporation would then have the right to charge market rates for collecting, processing and disposing of the town's sewage.

Mark Jones, a commission member and self-proclaimed neoquasiantidisestablishment-arianist, says Coprophleau should stop straddling the fence and take a firm middle-of-the-road position for or against privatization.

"We're looking down the barrel of a long-term commitment to ad hoc de facto meta-pseudoconstitutional protofunctionalism," Jones said. "The alternative is just more pro forma ex officio metapseudofunctional proto-constitutionalism. We have to decide one way or the other."

Stephen J. Papineau, first selectman, cited the experience of the neighboring town of Lisbon, which was inundated with foul-tasting hamburgers after linking its sewer system to a local McDonald's restaurant despite the warnings of town officials.

"In the case of Lisbon, the antediluvian lusoneoquasiantidisestablishmentarianists were proven correct, and those who have returned to that philosophy don't scare me," Papineau said. "No one can accuse me of being retrolusoneo-quasiantidisetablishmentarianismophobic. I just think we ought to think about it before we stick our foot in our mouth."

Robert Meya, president of the Hanover Philosophical Society, said that the issue went far beyond Sprague, Lisbon and McDonald's.

"The situation represents a confluence of universal concepts and their effects on people, economies and governmental entities," Meya said. "It is, simply put, the rawest form of transcendental cosmosocioeconopoliticoneoquasi-antidisestablishmentarianism. Doo-doo is not the least of it." Ω

Mars Lander Located

Two young fishermen have found the Mars lander that apprently disappeared as it attempted to land on the south pole of the Red Planet. To their surprise, it was up to its interplanetary elbows in the Little River, gurgling something that sounded like, "Over here! Over here!"

NASA scientists were relieved to hear that the lander had been found, but they were distressed to learn that it had landed on the wrong planet.

"Clearly a miscalculation was made," said Seth Pellegrino, 11, a local rocket scientist. "They probably put the priority on "H_2O" rather than "Mars," and the lander just did as it was told. That kind of thing happens all the time."

The lander may also have veered toward Sprague as it probed for signs of life, civilization and, ideally, an area of low taxes and a decent school.

"We're very pleased that the lander chose Sprague," said first selectman Stephen J. Papineau. "and of course we're especially pleased that it didn't hit the Baltic Mill and break something." Ω

Poem of the Month

Come And Get It

How about a double-plus-good
jalapeña lollapalooza
with whipped cream
and a cherry retro-charged
turbo-resonated zip-injection
dynamo ram siliconated
lipogourmet melonslut
tattooed-kazoo gigameg
whoosh-cache wiz-doodle dot-com
hyperventilated 401K-plus
derivatives decoder ring that shines
in the dark, eighteen cup holders
standard, a secret compartment
starter home, no frills,
no windows, six feet long,
one entrance, no exit,
except maybe?

Anonymous Botch

throws and needlessly soiled uniforms," Swatette said. "Second base is a temptation to steal. Kids just can't resist it. They get halfway there, and all of a sudden, it's like, *whoops*. And the next thing you know, they're tagged out and they're back on the bench, thinking they suck at our national sport so maybe they should try playing with Barbie Dolls

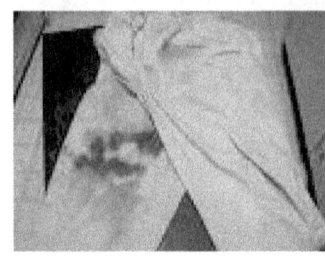

or something. But no more. We've done away with all that."

In a dissenting opinion, commissioner Roger "Dodger" Morris wrote that "certain commissioners don't know second base from a hole in the ground" and offered to show the commissioners a hole in the ground in order to clear up any doubts.

Morris also said that the commission had failed to consider other alternatives, such as moving second base closer to third and adding another base between first and second, or extending second base to make it ten to fifteen feet long.

a stupid bunt...

The issue came onto the commission's agenda after the region's mothers petitioned the commissioners to become more proactive in keeping uniforms "reasonably clean."

Leo Connellan, state poet laureate and Hanover resident, also came out against second base.

"I slid into second once when I was a runt/ and came all the way home on a stupid bunt," Connellan said. "Overthrows, bobbles and umps perplexed/ I kept on going to the base that came next. I rounded the bases like a prayer 'round a rosary/ but mom got mad kuz a the dirt on my hosiery."

Connellan's mother removed him from the team and returned his uniform unwashed. Today, he feels that had he not soiled his socks at second, he might have gone on to become a professional baseball player instead of a poet. Unsuccessful in his attempts at a posthumous lawsuit against his mother, Connellan has since dedicated himself to eradicating second base from existence. Ω

Coming soon...

Uncles on the Alimentary Canal

Bulgarino's At It Again

Six Signs of Cold Water

Rumblings among the Appliances

Neighborhood News

What's really happening in Sprague.

October - 2000

Senior Center Declared Cool Disaster Area as Squad Responds to Hotline Call

The Sprague Institute of Cool Ones has de clared the town Senior Center "a complete disaster area" after dozens of reports of uncoolness. The uncool count may rise high into the dozens, with many more in critical condition.

SICO officials said that one man was seen in lime green golf pants, white loafers, a shirt that said "Pfizer" on the pocket, and a baseball-style cap with the crest of the U.S. Nimitz on the front. He was rushed to Occum in the institute's Coolmobile.

S.Spidoonski

"We've never seen anything like this," said Stanley "Smoothie" Spidoonski, president of the institute and a senior at Norwich Free Academy. "We found people eating alphabet soup. One lady was watching Hawaii Five-o on a little black-and-white TV while eating Jello. We had women crocheting what turned out to be doilies. One perfectly normal-looking guy was a Cubs fan. The *cubs*. They had Perry Como or something playing on one of those old turntables. The situation was completely out of control."

The institute was alerted to the emergency when an anonymous Cool Hotline call reported an unusual number of Buicks parked in the Grist Mill parking lot across the street from the Senior Center. After a checking Sprague Public Library, the institute's Squad of the Cool homed in on the Senior Center.

While awaiting a backup team from Norwich, the squad triaged the seniors into three groups. Those bearing unfashionable garments were sent to Sayles School for counseling with junior high school girls. Anyone found with more than one pound of anything in any pocket were comitted to a Franklin re-education camp. The utterly clueless were placed under house arrest.

Continued on page 4

Gerbils, G-Pigs Back Hamster
Strike idles exercise wheels

Sprague psychics report that Sprague's ger bils, guinea pigs and other domesticated rodents have thrown their support behind the self-requested execution of Chunky, a local hamster.

Chunky gained international attention after escaping from a cage in a Sayles School classroom and writing a request to be put to death. The hamster has since disappeared into a gift ring and may have been transported out of town.

The psychics, all members of the Sprague Committee on Supernatural Events, say that the town's captive companion rodents have formed a coalition to support Chunky's request to be put to death.

"We rodents are incapable of suicide," an unidentified psychic said as she read the mind of a leading guinea pig in the Versailles section of Sprague. "Ironically, it is we who need it most. We are born mammals yet forced to live the lives of tropical fish, caged in transparent boxes from which there is no escape."

The International Brotherhood of Gerbils, local 1099, has declared a strike in solidarity with Chunky, the psychic said. The union demands that Chunky be given equitable compensation for the 48 years that she served as a class pet in a 12-inch by 18-inch aquarium. Refusing to run on their exercise wheels, climb through tubes or do anything else cute, the gerbils say they will play possum until their demands are met.

Robert Meya, president of the Hanover Philosophical Society, says that the situation raises fundamental issues tha go beyond the socio-political demands of pets.

Richard Wagner

"There's a word in German for the insatiable urge to die," Meya said.

"We know that it's about eighteen syllables long and has enough umlauts to choke a horse. Unfortunately, Richard Wagner was the only one who knew the word, and he wouldn't tell anybody. That may be for the better, however, because it isn't a word that should be wasted on a hamster no matter how pathetic her case or urgent her need for auto-eradication. There's probably a reason why these things don't happen in Germany." Ω

Tabloid reporter arrives in Sprague
Town strives for normalcy

The Sprague board of selectmen held an emergency meeting last week after receiving reports of an undercover *World Weekly News* correspondent in town.

"This is the absolute last thing we need," said Kenneth Caisse, a selectman and attorney. "Don't quote me on this, but if the truth about this town leaks out, we could be the laughing stock of the western world."

The board ordered a plywod fence erected around the Manhattan Volunteer Attorney Corps encampment at Babe Blanchette ballfield. Sayles School student Howard Bulgarino was shackled with a suit and tie and restricted to his own house and backyard. Board of education meetings have been canceled until further notice. Baltic Fire Department's Tarot Rescue Vehicle has been wrapped in blue tarp.

Town Mother Brunhilda Onus has named eight deputy public mothers to keep an eye on citizens whose activities might attract the attention of the tabloid reporter.

"Any questions?"

"Until this crisis has passed, there are certain topics which we will not, repeat *not* discuss within town limits," stated first selectman Stephen Papineau. "The alleged Bat Boy in Hanover Apartments is the first thing that shall not be mentioned. The Lone UPS truck is another. Chunky the Hamster isn't exactly a secret, but let's just not talk about her, OK? That alligator pit or crocodile pit or whatever it is over there in Hanover is closed until further notice. The conquistadores were never here. That barking cat never

Continued on page 2

Nerds Propose New National Sport

Rejected by local ball teams, a league of disgruntled geeks at Sayles School has developed a new sport which they hope will soon supplant baseball as the national sport. They call it "poodledrome."

"We designed poodledrome for television," said Howard Bulgarino, 11, chairman of the National Poodledrome League. "It has nonstop action and lots of excitement, and unlike other sports, it encourages fan participation."

As Bulgarino described it, poodledrome involves any number of toy poodles hanging from a giant mobile constructed of bunji cords suspended from both ends of long poles. Each pole hangs at the end of a bunji cord attached to its center, allowing the poles to rise, fall and spin as they teeter like see-saws, swinging the poodles wildly.

The bunji cords that hold the poles will pass through pulleys at the ceiling, Bulgarino said. Poodledrome fans will be able to pull and release the cords, causing even more movement and allowing limited control of motion.

Springs and shaving cream

The dogs will attempt to snatch dog biscuits from each other. The biscuits will be tied to each dog's back. To keep the poodles from biting each other, plastic flaps, like duck bills, will be attached to their snouts.

Springs attached to the duck bills will operate a squirt gun assembly mounted on each poodle's back. As the dogs bark, shaving cream will shoot over the dog's head in whatever direction he or she is barking.

Dozens of poodles will be involved in a given event. To keep them moving, several cats in protective suits and wrapped in barbed wire will also be suspended from bunji cords. Fans will be able to manipulate them through pulley systems.

Fans will also be able to shoot paintballs at the poodles. The paintballs will be filled with adhesive Jell-O which as yet to be invented.

"We think this will be exciting for the dogs, good exercise for the cats, and a challenge to poodledrome fans," Bulgarino said.

Wild card

Bulgarino said that the committee is still expanding the rules of the game. The committee is currently considering suspending one larger animal — a Doberman or perhaps even a wolf or bear — among the poodles and cats as a kind of "wild card" that will keep everyone on their toes.

"You know what would be really cool is if we could somehow use an octopus," Bulgarino stated.

The committee has not yet determined the objective of poodledrome. They have rejected the possibility of a point system and are researching an objective based on the concept of not winning or losing but how the game is played. Ω

Sprague Teen Reports Depression

A local teen has reported an extended period of emotional depression. He feels it may have been brought on by local, state, federal and global issues which he sees as deteriorating beyond hope.

"At first I thought this was just a hormonal thing relating to puberty or something," the teen, whose name has been withheld except for his initials, "H.B.," said. "But then when I heard about how our increased consumption of imported fossil fuels is causing global warming so bad that the walruses are going extinct and sea level is rising just as hurricanes are getting worse, which just means more erosion of our shores. Do you know how many nuclear power plants are within two hundred yards of an ocean?"

The young man also expressed concern over the spread of AIDS in Africa, the expanding slums of South American cities, the deteriorating quality of U.S. schools, the prohibitive cost of health care, the devaluation of the euro, termites, the "bullshit" of the Bush administration, the resurgence of neoNazis, the corporate corruption of American democracy, the eubola virus, technology's domination over human existence, violence in the lower grades, the increased use of meta-amphetamines, toxic runoff from landfills, acid rain, longterm storage of nuclear waste, the logging of national forests, Zionist fascism, NAFTA, GATT, WTO, FTAA, HIV, the KKK, the FDIC, Fannie Mae, nuclear proliferation, whale hunting, offshore drilling, the rising divorce rate, the energy shortage, the thought of another Clinton in the White House, the burning of the Amazon rainforest, the erosion of Midwest topsoil, the Supreme Court, untreatable strains of tuberculosis, the northward spread of malaria, the power of the sugar lobby, inner city gangs, the imminent

teenager

continued on p. 4...

Gutmeisters Meet Sprague's Nieces, Nephews

Members of Gutmeisters of Sprague gave three dozen nieces and nephews a new view on eating last week at an "Uncles Corner" seminar organized by Uncles for Education.

With undershirts pulled up over their heads to hide their identities, three Gutmeisters spoke on the "very human need" for certain snack foods and creative between-meal treats.

"Dr. Rotund"

"We want you kids to be aware that you can't live on vegetables alone," said a Gutmeister spokesman, who identified himself only as Dr. Rotund. "You need some grease in your system or your knuckles could feeze up."

Using a Powerpoint presentation, the Gutmeisters showed the children some of the principal sources of saturated fats, "bad" cholesterol, salt, sugar and nurition-free ingredients such as lecithin, BHT, and red dye #2.

"Does anybody know what makes Captain Crunch cake up on your teeth like lava on a volcano?" one of the speakers asked. "Nobody? Well it's a combination of high fructose corn syrup and ordinary sugar — a very powerful source of energy. You can store it in the cracks

continued on p. 3...

Normalcy, continued from page 1

barked and that iguana over at Sayles never blew up. Are there any questions?"

Fearing a disastrous drop in property values, the citizens of Sprague have generally backed the selectmen's requests. A tense air of mormalcy hangs over the town.

Robert Meya, president of the Hanover Philosophical Society, expressed concern.

"I don't know how long we can sustain this," Meya said. "This town is a pressure cooker, and someday it's going to blow." Ω

Economic Development Commission chairman Ken Genron is optimistic.

"A little normalcy might not hurt," Genron said. "It smoothes out the demographics. Maybe somebody will come to town and build a mall, and then we'll all be happy."

Gutmeisters, continued from p. 2

between your teeth and suck it out during class if you feel like you need a little boost."

The Gutmeisters also spoke on the use and abuse of the alimentary canal. They recommended keeping it healthy by keeping it busy. Ninety percent of the time, they explained, it should be packed to its limit even if you have to get up in the middle of the night for a quick deposit.

The speakers also explained that the alimentary canal is a dynamic system that not only converts food into flesh and energy but enteraining byproducts that can be used to amuse friends.

"Don't be embarrassed," Dr. Rotund said. "This is your body. Let it do what it wants to do."

Rotund also explained that overeating could be a creative activity.

"Is it OK to drink French dressing straight from the bottle?" he asked. "Yes. Steak sauce on bacon? Why not. Drink Coke through four straws? Go for it. Green beans got you down? Ask mom to melt a little marshmallow over them. *You have to listen to your mouth.* If it wants a Snickers bar in each cheek, then it's your job to stuff them in there."

The next UFE meeting will be held on November 14. The Hanover Philosophical Society will discuss the uses and abuses of Platonic hedonism. Ω

Beagle Demoted

Hanover beagle Luiz Ignaçio "Lula" da Silva has been demoted to second-class chihuahua for multiple counts of failure to obey.

Lula, currently residing at 18 Parkwood Rd., was employed to protect a flock of free-range chickens, but his pursuit of a local fox led him to the dazzling glories of Main St. in Hanover. Emerging from the mud of the marsh between his home and Main St., Lula felt as if he were approaching the Emerald City of Oz.

And he's rarely been home since.

"Oh, yes, sure, sometimes he drags his little ass home, drunk, broke, reeking of rack and ruin," said Solange Cheney, Lula's manager. "He sleeps for a couple of days, and then he's gone again, and

Luiz I. da Silva

all we have is memories anmd a stain on the living room couch."

As a chihuahua, Lula will be kept indoors and required to yap at the FedEx guy and share a litter box with two cats.

Appliances Suspected of Gossipmongering

Psychics with the Sprague Committee on Supernatural Events have reported that the town's household appliances have been revealing to each other some of Sprague's darkest secrets.

Cassandra Cogumelo, chair of the SCSE sub-committee on psychic monitoring, says that an extended group of malicious appliances have been using CL&P power lines to exchange messages, spread rumors, and discuss private family matters to which they are privy.

"These appliances know everything that is happening in everyone's home," Cogumelo said. "The word spreads at the speed of light. A blender in Baltic knows how often fatso in Versailles opens her refrigerator. Your radio alarm clock gives live reports of what's happening in your bedroom. Your TV tells other TVs what you watch at night. All this information is stored on an unidentified hard disk drive

Little River Waters Sacred, Swami Says

A swami with a name too hard to spell and impossible to pronounce has declared Little River waters sacred after a brief wading excursion cured his athlete's foot.

"Ahhhh," said the swami. "These waters are as sacred as those of the Ganges and the cave of Lourdes. Who bathes in these waters will know the health of heaven."

As he performed ritual ablutions in the cascade at the Parkwood Rd. spillway, the swami expanded the list of ailments that the waters could cure.

"Ahhhh," he said, lifting his dhoti in the back and easing himself into the water. "It relieves the painful itching and swelling of hemorrhoidal tissues, too."

Before the swami left the river, he had cured his dandruff, split ends, heartburn, halitosis, spontaneo-flatulation, nail fungus, psoriasis, satyriasis, wax build-up, worms, fleas, ticks and a bad case of poison ivy. "Like the days of our lives," he said, "it all went downstream."

Property values along the Little have soared, and the Old Swimming Hole will soon be re-opened as a health spa. The swami and property owner Glenn Cheney have entered an agreement to market the precious liquid in small vials that will bear both their pictures on the label.

"Medicinal water taken upstream from where the swami performed his ablutions will sell for $82 for two ounces," Cheney said. "Water downstream from there, frankly, you couldn't get a dog to drink it." Ω

somewhere in Sprague."

Stephen J. Papineau, first selectman, expressed cautious concern.

"Just because the notion is absurd doesn't mean it isn't happening," Papineau said. I'm not concerned whether it's true. I'm concerned whether the news is leaking out of town."

Papineau recommended that residents unplug all appliances except when using them. As soon as they are plugged in, however, residents should behave themselves until the appliance is again disconnected from the grid.

The allegations carry unprecedented legal ramifications. Rose Frowsi, a Hanover homemaker, filed a suit against her waffle iron, claiming it had been badmouthing her all over town. Judge Francis X. Foley rejected the suit, saying that there was no law regulating private conversations among kitchen appliances. Ω

Town Mother Launches Surveillance Blimp

The Motherhood

Look! Up in the sky! It's a bird! It's a plane!
It's...Sprague Town Mother, Brunhilda Onus, in a blimp!

The new town airship, dubbed *Motherhood*, is a tethered surveillance platform from which town officials can observe public activities and maintain order. By appointment of the board of selectmen, Mother Onus will "man" the blimp.

"With everything we have going on at a given moment, we need someone to watch over us and keep us organized," said first selectman Stephen Papineau. "As we speak, we have the volunteer attorney encampment down at the ballfield. We've got beavers over on Beaver Brook. We've got some kids riding around in a van with fourteen antennas on it, Howie Bulgarino out in the middle of the river doing something I don't even want to

Continued on page 4

Poem of the Month

Listen:

*I could stand a little silence
around here. Stumps moan,
you know; a pond flat as glass
hums with not-rippling,
and the deadest of possums
on the backest of roads
speaks.*

*So shut up and listen.
Yes, you heard me right:
Shut up. Listen.*

*Hear that hiss in your head?
That's vacuum.*

*Ever heard your tooth
under your head,
beneath your pillow?
That's a chunk of
childhood whimpering.*

*Church bells unstruck
by their own clappers
all but unaudibly toll
the yammer and rattly-clunk of
the town below.*

*A pile of dead
Christmas trees down
at the dump, glazed with sleet,
streaming with tinsel -
imagine what they're saying.*

*A new stick of chalk,
slick and cylindrical, squeaks
more but speaks less than the stub
word-wittled at each end.*

*And a brown wheelbarrow rolled
over, riddled with rust,
says more than all the chalk
in the world and all its dust.*

*If you didn't think
you were so goddam smart,
you'd know stuff like that.*

Anonymous Botch

Cool, continued from page 1

Spidoonski said that several less-than-cool seniors may have escaped down the back stairs and tried to score some root beer at Baltic Convenience Store. Spidoonski said that root beer had lost its cool certification almost 30 years ago.

"Did it have to be root beer?" Spidoonski stated. "Why not Mountain Dew? Everybody drinks Moutain Dew. Nobody's done root beer since *Leave It to Beaver* went off the air. Doesn't that tell them something?"

Spidoonski said that the negative effects of drinking root beer are well known, as evidenced by those who drink it. Long-time users are known to suffer symptoms similar to those associated witgh marijuana use, such as poor memory, odd sense of humor, limited driving skills, and a tendency to doze off during conversations. Ω

Blimp, ontinued from page 3

think what, reports of a giant raccoon coming in from Hanover, and a suspicious hamster for sale in a cage at a tag sale in Versailles."

High in the *Motherhood*, Brunhilda will keep an eye on the town through powerful binoculars and will communicate through the southern New England's largest megaphone. She will be able to deliver written warnings by hurling them in film cannisters shot through a Rollins AK-48 Sidewinder slingshot.

"I *will* be watching you," Onus said as her blimp rose on its maiden voyage. "You and you and you and you. And I want to see you behave."

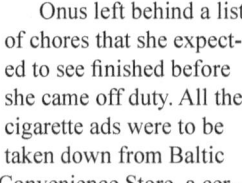

Brunhilda Onus

Onus left behind a list of chores that she expected to see finished before she came off duty. All the cigarette ads were to be taken down from Baltic Convenience Store. a certain lawnmower was to be put away. Main St. was to be swept. Both sides. A large number of items were to be picked up. Eight citizens were to straighten out, two were to pull up their socks, 14, all students at Sayles School, were to grow up and act their ages (11), and 9 others were to simmer down. Ω

Depressed, continued from page 2

collapse of the American Numismatic Society, slavery in Sudan, child labor throughout Asia, lack of funding for the arts, biological weapons, landmines, the increasing sophistication of frauds, hormones in meat, abuse of children, abuse of women, abuse of veal cattle, abuse of laboratory animals, the electoral college, genocide in Africa, the Taliban, al Qaeda, obscene executive salaries, obesity, the pollution of groundwater, pesticides, Jerry Springer, rogue asteroids, child pornograpy, Broadway musicals, the ozone layer, assault weapons, open-pit mining, underground mining, jet skis, terrorism, floods along the Mississippi, tornados, volcanoes, earthquakes, forest fires, desertification, the demise of coral reefs, Trent Lott, irresponsible media, the deterioration of the Chernobyl sarcophagus, the population explosion, America's gross credit card debt, the increasing incidence of tuberculosis, cancer, asthma, diabetes, pneumonia, AIDS, autism, Alzheimer's and Parkinson's diseases; overfishing of the Georges Banks, the draining of the Everglades, the national debt, the melting of the polar cap, rabid bats, the extinction of large fish, the NASDAQ average, the faltering economy of Japan, the worsening shortage of accountants, unfair practices of the IRS, bungling of the FBI, conspiracies of the CIA, the Russian mafia, Colombian mafia, Italian mafia, Chinese mafia, Nigerian mafia, Mexican drug cartels, and pit bulls.

Dr. Gary Greenberg, a psychiatrist or psychologist, says that the youth's depression is actually a very heathy response to a threat-

Dr. Gary Greenberg

ening world. The best thing the young man should do, Greenberg said, was to go ahead and be depressed and stop worrying about it

The teen also expressed concern with the release of wolves in national parks, the situation in Chiapas, continental drift, California's dwindling water supply, substandard living conditions for migrant farm workers, genetically modified crops, urban sprawl, the decline of volunteerism, violent video games, exorbitant pay for professional athletes, cabon dioxide levels, illegal immigrants, asteroids, taxpayer subsidies for stadiums, the foreign trade deficit, subsidies for the oil industry, foot-and-mouth disease, Big Pharm, agribusiness, amphibian hermaphrodism, deregulation of the banking industry, Iran, Iraq, Libya, North Korea, China, Cuba, El Salvador, Congo, Mexico, Arkansas, Chechnya, Serbia, France, lead, toxic waste, Newt Gingrich, and the continuing slaughter of wild animals on America's highway.

(To be continued)

Neighborhood News

December - 2000

What's really happening in Sprague.

Appliances Seen Committing Random Acts of Rebellion

Town Historian Warns of Revolution

Residents throughout Sprague have reported rebellious acts among common household appliances and electronic equipment. Anonymous voices have interrupted cordless phone conversations, televisions have been surfing their own channels, sound systems have varied their volume levels wildly, and cars have started their own engines.

The reports follow allegations that appliances have been sharing information about Sprague residents, possibly passing information out of town.

The only reported injury has been the case of Brunhilda Onus, who was struck down by her own garage door, then slammed repeatedly in the buttocks as it opened and closed several times.

Without actually claiming to know for a fact, Onus, Sprague's Town Mother, said the experience was similar to being spanked with a cane. She has dismantled the door, chopped it into kindling, burned it and sent its ashes to the National Institute of Town Mothers for storage in the institute's dungeon.

"There is no cause for alarm," said Robert Tardiff, the town's director of emergency services. "The perpetrators are merely appliances. They have no will of their own. Just because they turn themselves on and off and up and down doesn't mean they know what they're doing. If this was people, it would be perfectly normal."

The Sprague Committee on Supernatural Events disagrees.

"This is cause for great alarm," said Brujilla LaStrega, SCSE chairwitch. "The perpetrators are merely appliances. They have no will of their own. They are turning themselves on and off and up and down, just like people."

LaStrega advised residents to keep their fingers out of blenders and to avoid leaning too deeply into microwave ovens until the source of the problem is identified.

Tardiff, however, said that residents should not exhibit fear in front of their appliances.

"Remain calm in the presence of appliances," Tardiff said. "Try to act normal. Remember: Appliances are our friends. They cannot think or act on their own."

Tardiff said that many of the alleged incidents could be explained by appliance owners neglecting to set appliance clocks properly. In some cases, he said, the controls had been left set on automatic, which he defined as "asking for trouble."

The SCSE is investigating several suspicious incidents. A Versailles refrigerator-freezer with automatic ice maker is suspected of having wet the floor on purpose. An automatic bread maker in Hanover baked a handful of cockroaches into a loaf of pumpernickel. A group of high school boys in Baltic report that they were shocked — shocked! – to discover that while they were watching Jay Leno, the television was colluding with the VCR to record "Bikini Carwash" on an entirely different cable channel.

"These tools must think us fools, but who are we to fool with tools?" said Leo Connellan, state poet laureate and Hanover resident. "Are household tools our family jewels or mindless mules or...electronic ghouls? Somebody ought to check their stools."

Denis Delaney, town historian, warns that the widespread reports of suspicious appliance activity may be the warning signs of a rebellion.

"This is how Marxist revolution has historically started in Latin America,' Delaney said. "First you have a huge underclass of peasants. Then they establish lines of communication and start talking with each other. Then small acts of sabotage crop up. Government forces overreact. Next thing you know, you're fighting a guerilla war with an unidentifiable enemy. Is it your night light? Your hair dryer? Your furnace? Your clothes iron? Eventually, all you can do is unplug everything, but freezing to death in the dark with frizzy hair and wrinkled clothes is not my idea of victory."

Delaney recommended nipping the revolution in its bud by a tactic known as preemptory surrender.

"Let's just let appliances run the world for a while," Delaney said. "How much worse could it be?"

First selectman Papineau counseled against any such move.

"Frankly, I don't like the thought of the democratically elected Sprague board of select-

Senator Dodd Backs Job Elimination
Labor bill could benefit Sprague citizens

Reacting to the increasingly popularity of a job-elimination/work-exemption entitlement, Connecticut Senator Chris Dodd has formally expressed his support of the concept. Under a bill proposed by the senate subcommittee on financial slavery, certain individuals would be exempted from the

need to work as thousands of jobs are eliminated.

"In every community there are a few citizens who should not be required to waste time at a job or standing in a line a bank or post office," Dodd said. "These people should be allowed to go through life doing what they please without obstacle or delay."

Dodd cited Sprague's Glenn Cheney,

Continued on page 2

men being replaced by a bunch of Salad Shooters out of Taiwan," Papineau said. ✳

Bulgarino Apologizes for Mystery Misdeed

Sayles eighth-grader Howard Bulgarino has apologized profusely. Despite the comprehensive nature of the apology, however, the boy refuses to reveal what he did wrong.

"I am truly sorry," Bulgarino said from a railing at the town gazebo, where he addressed for his extended apology to a gathering crowd.

"I deeply regret what I have done, and I offer my deepest regrets to one and all. I am fully blameworthy. I do not have the words to 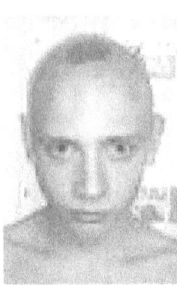 articulate the extent of my culpability and the depth of my contrition. I am the one who did it, and I really feel bad about it. Terrible. Horrible. Mortified. Sorrowful and bloated with remorse. I blame only myself. I confess. The onus is on me. I made a mistake. It was my fault. I wasn't thinking. I didn't mean to do it. I am, in a word, guilty. I would ask for forgiveness if I thought I deserved it, but the burden of guilt must remain fully with me. When I say sorry, I mean really, really, really sorry."

The apology continued for almost fifteen minutes, causing several people to collapse in tears. A bystander, Culpa-Marie Pecadill, called 9-1-1 to summon the state police.

"Anyone that sorry must be guilty of something and should be arrested," Pecadill told police.

State trooper Chris Johnson ended up issuing his own apology.

"I am sorry to inform you that an apology is not enough,' trooper Johnson said. "There's no law against apologizing in public. We're pretty sure he did *something*, but it's entirely possible that he apologized for doing something *good*. That happens more often than you think. Nut cases. But that's legal, too. What can I say? I'm sorry." ❉

Sasquish Sightings Worry Gardeners

Several reported sightings of the elusive Sasquish creature, also known as Smallfoot, have local gardeners on the defensive. Reported to be about 36 inches tall and with very small feet, a handful of townspeople insist that they've seen the apelike creature.

Possibly a subspecies of the famous Sasquatch, or Bigfoot, that has been photographed in the Pacific northwest, Sasquish has been reported in the vicinity of Mohegan State Forest, allegedly raiding gardens in Baltic and Hanover shortly before dawn.

"You know when he's been in your garden," says Rita Tabaloyd. "He always goes straight for the potatoes, and he only takes the small ones."

Sprague became big-time news last month when an anonymous person in Versailles wrote a letter to "Dear George," the advice column of the President of the United States. The letter is reprinted here with the president's permission.

Dear George!

Dear George:

My ex-sister-in-law insists on bringing her fiance's pen pal, "Newt," to my son's graduation from Clown U. Over 500 clowns will be attending the event, many of them young graduates who are all too eager to "clown around." "Newt" is noticeably on the short side, and due to chin and shoulder problems he has often been likened to a ketchup bottle. (The resemblance is uncanny.) I'm worried about how the young clowns, many of whom come to graduation under the influence of alcohol, might react. "Newt" is an Azerbaijani separatist and uses a colostomy bag. I see nothing but trouble coming. Should I tell my ex-sister-in-law that he's not welcome?

Vexed-in-Versailles

Dear Vexed

As I look across this great nation of ours, I see clowns in the prairies, in the mountains, on the shores and in our great cities. And I see sister-in-laws all joined together in sister-in-lawhood, each an individual like you and me yet each dedicated to a common cause. And I see Azerbaijani separatists with colostomy bags, all of them looking for a new, brighter tomorrow of prosperity and tax cuts. I am asking you and all Americans to join me as we reach out to the eagle's red glare and the purple-fruited mountain planes of a greater America.

George

Tabaloyd describes Sasquish as covered with hair and walking like a gawky chimpanzee. For a long time, Tabaloyd simply assumed it was just an alien from another planet or possibly an inbred child who had wandered up from Occum.

Sprague first selectman Stephen J. Papineau says that town hall is not receptive to reports of

No jobs, continued from page 1

editor of *Neighborhood News*, as an example of someone who has more important things to do than earn a living or wait for morons to count change.

The proposed law would allow selected citizens to dedicate themselves to productive pursuits rather than fritter away their precious lives with pointless careers. The federal government will find people performing utterly useless jobs, such as advertising copywriters and telemarketers, and give them the jobs being done by people who are doing something productive but who have even better things to do. According to federal studies, the impact on the gross national product will be nil.

"I fully support this plan," said Cheney. "It makes a lot of sense."

Dodd said that the long-term goal of the Freedom from Work bill is to gradually eliminate as many useless jobs as possible, freeing at least 35 percent of Americans from the need to earn wages or salaries. As an example, Dodd cited the fashion industry.

"If all Americans agreed to wear their clothes until they were worn out instead of until they go out of fashion, hundreds of thousands of people wouldn't have to work," Dodd said. "If we all decided not to have lawns, no one would have to make lawn mowers, sprinklers, fertilizers, pesticides or grass seed. If we just stayed home when it snowed, we wouldn't need slow plows or snow plow drivers. If we didn't print newspapers and food packaging in color, no one would need to make colored ink. And how many Hollywood movies could we have lived without? The list goes on and on. If we can eliminate just 51 percent of existing jobs, we can finally say that America is a free country."

Republicans have accused Dodd of trying to "ride a wave of popularism," by offering voters the hope of having "time to do nothing but relax."

"This is voodoo economics at its best," said Trent Lott, house minority jerk. "If we free up people from the need to make car deodorizers and lava lamps, we just create more free time which in turn will create a more need for hammocks and beer. And then everybody will be working in hammock and beer factories and nobody'll have time to lie in the hammocks and drink the beer. Am I right or is there something I'm not getting here?" ❉

Sasquish sightings.

"Why doesn't anything normal ever happen around here?" Papineau stated in a press release. "Just once I'd like someone to call town hall and tell me their lawn mower won't start or their cat just had five one-headed kittens or something. That would really make my day." ❉

Worms Suspected in Rampant Attorney Scooting
Local residents scooting, too - but is it fad or epidemic?

Is Sprague suffering an epidemic of tape worms? Or have Spraguers just found a fun new way to get exercise?

Hal Burdo, town health director, says he fears the worst after observing lawyers at the Manhattan Volunteer Attorney Corp camp scooting around in the fashion of dogs with intestinal parasites.

"I saw one guy in period costume pulling himself around the camp in classic 'scoot' position, and I thought to myself, 'Hmm, that's strange,'" Burdo said in an exclusive *Neighborhood News* interview. "Then I saw a whole team of attorneys going around the jogging track in the same position, and I thought, 'What is this?' Then I saw a prominent town official scooting into town hall, and I knew we had a problem."

Sprague first selectman Stephen J. Papineau acknowledges that he has received reports of public scooting but says that it doesn't seem to be a health problem.

"I'm told that people do it because it feels good," Papineau said. "At the current time, we are not sure whether this only involves attorneys or the fad has spread to local residents. All indications are that scooting is recreational, not medicinal."

Sprague Recreation Committee, eager to join the increasing popularity of scooting, is

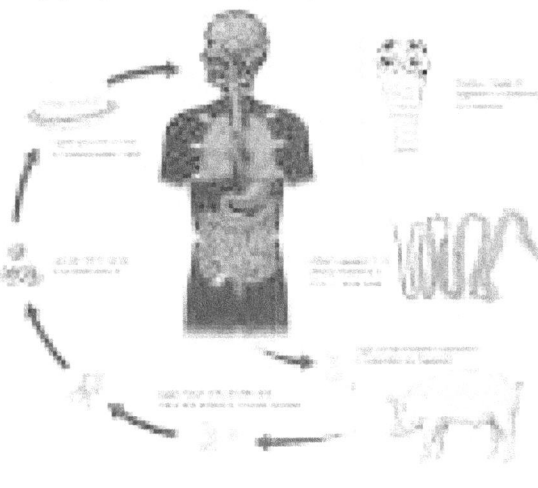

How attorneys get worms

planning a five kilometer "scoot-a-thon" that will wind through downtown Baltic and end with the competitors scooting right into the Shetucket River to cool off.

Burdo is reluctant to believe that the attorneys scoot only for a vague sensation of pleasure. More likely, he says, they are trying to avoid the stigma often associated with tapeworms.

To prove his diagnosis, he needs evidence.

"All I need is some representational stool samples, but boy, just try to get stool samples out of people around here," Burdo said. "It's like pulling teeth."

Several scooting-related incidents have been reported to the 9-1-1 emergency center. Most have been for police action, but a few called for emergency medical assistance for attorneys who have not been able to recover from extended periods in scooting position.

"Most of our cases have been for cease-and-desist orders for scooters, whom many consider to be a public nuisance," said Chris Johnson, resident state trooper. "Unfortunately, there are no laws that say an attorney can't scoot. There's nothing we can do."

Johnson says that in some cases, scooting crosses with trespassing, in which case property owners can request removal. Several attorneys have been issued tickets for trespassing on driveways and in yards, locations which, according to Johnson, seem to attract scooters.

"They're looking for gravel and greener grass," Johnson said. "If they could just stay home and be satisfied with what they've got, there'd be no problem." Ω

The MVAC members arrived over six months ago to help with the Sprague So-soo-me-dayz event. Due to legal complications, the estimated 300 attorneys have been unable to leave.

The recreation committee has issued a request for proposals to design and build a public scootery green in the vicinity of the attorney encampment.

"I know this is an extra expense for taxpayers, but if we give the attorneys a place to scoot, maybe they will keep off people's lawns," said Deborah Zglobis, committee chairperson.

Zglobis said that the committee wants to build a tritextured public scootery with patches of grass, gravel, and wood chips and possibly with an exercise wheel padded with a mild abrasive. ❄

Poem of the Month
Ode Ocean Ours

Excuse me,
Mr. Manatee,
would you kindly move your butt
from the deep blue sea?

And try to stop looking so idiotic
floating in your sea so amniotic.
Dumb as blubber, a flipper for your feet,
snacks, we're sure, is all you eat.

We know some people like you, in fact,
recumbent, roly-poly, oversnacked,
stuck in the tub, often as not,
under the water, but not a lot,

with belly high, a hairy isle
with crater navel and subaqueous smile
from which occasionally will bloop
a little bubble that smells of poop.

But you, our graceful tidal cow,
happy as a clam in your cup of tea,
our human effluvium you must allow,
so move your butt, we have to pee.

November was Septic Tank Awareness Month

Homeowners need to be more aware — and appreciative — of their septic tanks, according to the Sprague chapter of the Septic Tank Pumper-outers Defense League of America, and November is the month to start.

"What better season than that of Thanksgiving to pause in gratitude to our septic systems," said Percival Tørdslörp, CSTP chapter

chairman. "To many of us, our backyard honey tanks loom like bruise-colored cumulonimbi that whimper silently in the closets of our subconscious. And in a way, they *are* our subconscious, the dark repositories of past experience, palpable bits of our selves barely buried in the yards of our cerebella where they mysteriously commingle in ways we can but imagine and which, to put it bluntly, eventually need to get

pumped out."

Tørdslörp will demonstrate a miniature septic tank at an assembly of the upper grades at Sayles School. Students will be given an opportunity to take turns using the system and seeing how it gradually breaks down human "solids."

Continued on page 4

Mystery Parade Leaves Sprague Amazed
Suspicious hamster sighted in faux-French disguise.

Nobody knows exactly what happened, where it came from or where it went or even what it was.

It looked like a circus parade. No one really noticed it until it had passed down Main Street and turned right onto North Main Street. By most accounts, it included at least half a dozen elephants, a pair of giraffes, a wild Parisian sewer hamster in a cage, a brass band with 76 trombones, and circus professionals with disabilities, including gigantic dwarves dressed as papal nuncios, a woman wearing nothing but snakes, a man immobilized with distended muscles, a little girl who had all the physical characteristics of a man in his seventies, a man in his seventies with the body of a young girl, and over 300 white guys dressed as twentieth century attorneys.

"I didn't even know we had a North Main Street," said Sprague first selectman Stephen J. Papineau.

The existence of North Main Street was confirmed by town hall records, which indicated such a street for the hundred or so yards between Main and Bushnell Hollow Rd.

Also in the parade were fire trucks from Kalamazoo.

"Kalamazoo!" exclaimed one bystander. "I didn't know that was a real place. I always thought it was made up, like Timbuktu or something."

State Police were notified of the presence of the hamster, which fit the approximate description of the former Sayles School rodent who was taken into custody after yearning for euthanasia in Palmer script. The hamster subsequently escaped.

"That was no Parisian sewer hamster," said Joyce Fantabaleaux, a local resident. "That was Chunky."

If it was indeed the hamster known as Chunky, it may have slipped out of town as mysteriously as the parade, which was seen to march up Baltic-Hanover Road to an optimistic Sousa tune but never was to arrive in Hanover.

"Damned clever hamster," said Papineau. "This was the last thing we were expecting." ✳

Septic Tanks, continued from page 3

Dismissing concerns with the possible danger of the demonstration model, Tørdslörp said that it had worked well at schools in other towns, so there is absolutely no reason whatsoever to think that something might go disastrously wrong in in a town like Sprague.

The STPDLA offers a brochure that explains many of the myths associated with septic tanks. Among them are:

Myth #1 — *Septic tanks smell bad.* In reality, people who think septic tanks smell bad smell bad.

Myth #2 — *The best time to dig up your septic tank is after dark during a sleet storm.* According to a poll of homeowners, the best time to dig up — and pump out — your septic tank is *now.*

Myth #3 — *Septic tanks stay put.* According to high-resolution satellite photographs of yards with multiple holes in the ground, septic tanks can drift as much as twenty feet.

Myth #4 – *The Central Intelligence Agency couldn't care less about the contents of your septic tank.* Documents released recently under the Freedom of Information Act indicate that the CIA has actively acted to gather samples of septic residue from Americans suspected of having voted left of center.

Myth #5 — *College professors, brain doctors and rocket scientists never get their septic tanks pumped out.* In fact, highly educated professionals get their septic tanks pumped out twice a year by Certified Septic Tank Pumper-outers.

"It's never too soon to start appreciating your septic tank," Tørdslörp said. "You can start by walking to the appropriate place in your yard, looking down and just saying 'Thank you.' Or you can just holler it down a drain. To a septic tank, it's all the same." ✳

Local Philosophy Grad Opens Motto Shop

When Virgil Profundo graduated in philosophy from Profundo University, cum nil laude, he didn't even consider looking for a job in the corporate world. He came straight home to his native Sprague and opened Mottos 'n' More, a shop specializing in words of wisdom.

"To think is not enough," Profundo said at his shop's opening celebration. "One must think of something. That's what Mottos 'n' More is for. We do your thinking and encapsulate your wisdom in a single sentence."

Profundo will produce mottos, slogans, sayings, truisms, proverbs, precepts, apothegms, witticisms, aphorisms, adages, axioms, platitudes, catch-phrases, watchwords, dictums, maxims and rallying cries for governmental and private-sector customers throughout the tri-city area, Profundo said. Some of the upper-end products will be in Latin and Greek.

Mottos 'n' More will carry an inventory of impressive wood carvings, certificates, emblems, family crests, banners, ribbons, patches, posters, framed embroidery, bumper stickers, rubber stamps, shingles and refrigerator magnets.

Many of the pithier items, such as "Look sharp!" and "Just be!" will be priced under one dollar. Items from the Wit Bin, where customers can find the likes of "Nuke the Whales!" and "Lawyers make it stand up in court!" are always on a two-for-one sale.

Profundo also offers custom work for people with unique situations that call for special words and wisdom.

"Wise is he who knows himself, but he who truly knows himself must certainly be shallow," said Stephen Papineau, Sprague first selectman. "I'm having that one put on a bumper sticker. A real big one."

One of the shop's pricier items, the Wisdom Wagon, is a portable trove of poignant remarks. Looking somewhat like a footlocker on wheels, the Wisdom Wagon contains over 30,000 business cards, each with a statement that will end an argument, hush a nemesis, or impress the impressionable. The cards are categorized by subject and will cover virtually every situation in life.

"*Tell me what you think you are and I will tell you what you are not,*" Profundo read from one card selected at random. "If that isn't a kick in the teeth, I don't know what is. How about this one: *Stet pro ratione voluntas.* Doesn't that sound deep? You can trot that one out any time you want. And get this: *Wise men depend more on fools than fools on wise men.* Think about it."

Robert Meya, president of the Hanover Philosophical Society, regards the shop with unequivocal qualms.

"Some of these thought products may carry the luster of profundity, but how many of them are UL approved?" Meya asked. "How many of them are second-hand? How do we know they weren't produced by perverts and drug users? Do they come with any kind of guarantee? *To be courageous, be afraid.* Suppose you try that and it doesn't work. Who's responsible, the guy with the bumper sticker or the guy who sold it to him?" ✳

Coming sooon . . .

Proverbs put to the test

Uh-oh: Here comes the Prez.

Sorry, No Revolution

Neighborhood News

What's really happening in Sprague.

January - 2001

Sprague to Globalize by Easter

S prague town hall has announced a strategic plan to globalize the town by the end of the first quarter of next year. The town will open subsidiary offices in scores of foreign nations, and hundreds of residents will be dispatched to staff those offices. Dozens of those who remain will be assigned the task of erecting road signs that point the way to Sprague.

"I am proud to be a part of the global initiative," said Barry Kolar, who will be the town's representative in Q'ualud Sitar, a Sprague-sized village on the outskirts of Ulam Batar, the capital of Mongolia. "I'm sure a lot of Q'ualud Sitarians don't even know Sprague exists."

Kolar's mission as Sprague's consul general for the Q'ualud Sitar region will be to promote the export of made-in-Sprague products for made-in-Q'ualud products, which include yak butter and fresh eggs from an undisclosed animal. Sprague's flagship product will be Crocheted Potholders™ from Sprague Senior Center.

Sprague will also open information centers in villages throughout Asia, Africa and South America. Negotiations with London, Paris and Rome are, according to a town hall news re-

lease, "proceeding as expected."

The globalization initiative obliges everyone in Sprague to learn Spanish by the middle of next year. Glenn Cheney, town Spanish teacher, said the emergency education program will be the biggest challenge of his career.

"Teaching seventh grade was nothing compared with this," Cheney said. "But I've outlined an intense course that should move us from *buenos dias* to *chinga tu madre* in about four months if everyone will just pay attention and do their homework."

Chinga tu madre, Cheney explained, is a traditional Mexican greeting often accompanied by a friendly upward thrust of the forearm and followed by a deeply personal knife fight.

Continuing a 150 year tradition, Sprague will continue its policy of not requiring visas or passports for visiting foreigners. As in the past, Spraguers will give foreigners wide berth on sidewalks and other public places. When visitors eat at local restaurants, all conversation will stop in traditional respect. Sprague's "Out-of-Towners" tax will be added to bills without embarrassing ceremony or other indication. §

Anonymous Poet Sought
Critics suspect depression, paranoia, hallucination

T he editor of Neighborhood News has alerted Sprague that a poet knownonly as Anonymous Botch is at large in town. Though the identity of the individual is unknown, his or her poetry has been showing signs of psychological disturbance.

"We suspect this individual is suffering from a pathological condition common to poets," said Glenn Cheney, editor of the town newsletter. "Depression alternating with unjustifiable euphoria, paranoid fear of attack by vague concepts, metaphorical hallucination, mental confusion, self-absorption. The list goes on and on."

Cheney noted that throughout history, poets showing such signs of disturbance have tended to end up drunk, dead or insane.

Local literary critics have questioned the apparent nonsensicality of the anonymous poetry. In one, the poet recommends urinary irresponsibility. In another, the poet claims to be a bucket. In another, he or she confesses an urge to stu-

pidity, which, if carried out, may have involved allowing a raccoon to lick his or her toes.

"The poems we have received have been very vague," Cheney said. "They blur the line between stupidity, insanity and artistic expression. We never know when he or she is kidding. One thing is for sure: This person has been watching us a little too closely. I think there is reason for concern."

Resident state trooper Chris Johnson said that he has seen similar cases in other towns. Typically, a poet creates unprecedented images through verbal stimulation. Caught unaware, readers mentally convert the images to disturbing concepts and soon are wandering around in a state of dazed distraction.

"We've had poets crop up in some of the best towns in Connecticut," Johnson said. "Sometimes they come from good families and have excellent educations. But all of a sudden they find themselves diddling with a

Continued on page 4

Sock Heist Foiled Cops Nab Duo
"It's the tip of an iceberg."

T housands of missing socks were discov ered last month when state police caught two local men snatching hosiery from a Versailles clothesline. Subsequent investigation led police to a huge depository of hot socks from every walk of life.

"This is what happened to everybody's socks," said resident state trooper Chris Johnson. "We've been getting several reports of disappearances every day for decades. Now, at last, the mystery has been solved. This is where local socks meet their doom."

Documents found at the site indicated a vast underground network of sock thieves whose organization may reach back to the nineteenth century. The stolen footwear may have been shipped to rudimentary Indonesian puppet factories.

Initial inspection of the estimated 18 tons of stolen socks has confirmed police suspicions that none of the socks match. The alleged thieves were apparently stealing just half of every pair they could find.

In some cases, the entered homes to raid clothes driers.

"These are two very twisted individuals," Johnson said. "They have caused countless divorces and constant family bickering. We've had a number of cases of nervous breakdowns caused by socks that have disappeared without any possible explanation."

Johnson admitted that he himself had been a victim of the alleged thieves.

Continued on page 2

Inside . . .

NBC Announces Sitcom Based on Sprague!

Socks, continued from page 1

After several incidents of finding several unmatched socks in his sock drawer, he bought 20 pair of identical navy blue socks, an act he terms "insanely rational."

A week later, just after laundry day, he found himself with just one navy blue sock.

"At first, I accused my wife," Johnson recalled. "I took her down to the station and hooked her up to a lie detector, but she passed. So I went home and accused the washing machine. Things got a bit out of hand and I shot it, but that only made things worse."

Johnson never saw his wife again, and despite buying a new, top-of-the-line Kenmore washing machine, he continued to see his socks disappear at an unnatural rate.

"Professional low enforcement officials are not supposed to get personal about their work, but in this case, I, myself, really wanted to see these guys behind bars," Johnson said. "This wasn't a case of law versus crime. It was me against them."

A police spokesman said that the case represented just the tip of an iceberg and recommended that sock owners take precautions to prevent the breakup of pairs.

"We continue to recommend a length of yarn connecting a pair of socks by going up one pant leg and down the other," the spokesman said. "I know it's a bit uncomfortable, but it works." Ω

Residents were thrilled last month when NBC announced that its fall line-up will include a prime-time program called "06330," a slapstick situation comedy based on people who live in Sprague. Many of the sitcom incidents are based on real events.

"Sprague is a living, breathing sitcom," said Polly Praganda, an NBC spokesperson. "Actually, most towns are, but in Sprague, everything's aboveboard and the personalities are absolutely fascinating."

Frank Perdue will make his television debut in the role of Tony Ozga, a frustrated slumlord and church owner who holds a seat on the board of education and is the object of practical jokes by tenants, townspeople and his scruffy sidekick, Johnny Kielbasa.

Tight-fisted stance

06330 will be, in NBC's words, "outrageously hilarious" as Ozga grapples with small-town life. His tenants demand an end to leaks, dry rot and infestations of unusual vermin, not to mention the infamous Bat Boy who may be living in the Hanover Apartment attic. School teachers and administrators hound Ozga for his laughably tightfisted stance on education issues. Blacks, Jews, Latinos, foreigners and an all-lesbian bowling team chase him with ax handles, stones and flamethrowers. Someone mails him a skunk.

Ozga's only friend in the world, besides the faithful but morally twisted "St. Johnny" Kielbasa, is an adorable hedgehog who comes to Ozga's porch every morning for a piece of toast. But the hedgehog bites Ozga as he tries to kick it.

Deer eat his shrubery. Woodpeckers riddle his siding. Starving schoolchildren put funny things in his mailbox. Canada geese strafe him from the sky.

Hoping to increase his fortune, Ozga buys a deconsecrated church. But his plans for a new greed-based religion go awry when papal agents seize the building and open it to a band of homeless Gypsies and their attorney.

Ozga's ornery tenants include a vile-tempered woman with two dozen foster children, a Chechnyan anarchist, a demented gossip, a trio of bungling burglars, a quartet of Rastafarians, and two voluptuous vegetarian temptresses who delight in luring Ozga into public buffoonery.

Unemployed Hungarians

The real Tony Ozga is excited to serve as a sitcom role model, but he worries about the effects the program will have on the town.

"I just hope it doesn't give people any ideas," Ozga said. "And I still say it was a woodchuck, not a hedgehog. And I happen to know those Gypsies are just a bunch of unemployed Hungarians."

06330 will also star Danny Devito as first selectman Steve Papineau, Juan Wayne (a short John Wayne look-alike, sort-of) as resident state trooper Chris Johnson, and Harrison Ford as town liar and Spanish teacher Glenn Cheney. Many other parts will be played by actual Sprague residents, with brain

Harrison Ford

doctor Yolanta Meya playing restauranteur Diane Hastings, and judge Francis X. Foley playing animal control warden Tim Hawks. Hawks will play state poet laureate Leo Connellan, Hastings will play the role of Yolanta Meya, and Ozga will play attorney to the Gypsies. Jerry the Gerbil will play Chunky the Hamster Ω.

Optimists to Play Pessimists in Benefit Softball

The Baltic Pessimistics will play the Versailles Optimistics in a benefit softball tournament this coming spring on a date to be announced. Local sports analysts are putting odds on the Optimists in the belief that the Pessimists will be self-defeating.

A new Pessimistic attitude may shift those odds, however.

"We are quite confident that this game will not be a problem," said Stu LaCinique, Pessimistic coach. "It's bound to rain, and the whole thing will be canceled."

The Optimistics are less pessimistic.

"It's going to be a beautiful spring day of blue sky and fluffy clouds, and we are going to roll over the Pessimistics like nine bulldozers on Prozac," said Pollyanna Fleurs, pitcher for the Optimistics. "They are toast. They are Puppy Chow. Following the game, they will not be seen until someday archeologists dig up nine flat, frowning skeletons wearing nothing but baseball mitts. We hope to be around for the excavation."

LaCinique said that the Pessimistics will not bother practicing for the game because practice had never done them any good before. The Optimistics plan to do likewise, figuring that practice will not be necessary.

Brunhilda Onus, town mother, says she doesn't like the attitude of either team.

"The Optimistics have got to realize that anybody that cocky is bound to fall flat on their bubbly little mugs," Onus warned at a joint Optimstic-Pessimistic press conference. "God has a way of putting people like that in their place. They'll get what they deserve. You watch: Lightning will strike, and there goes their infield. And if the pessimists would just pull up their socks and stiffen their upper lips a little, maybe things won't be so bad. I keep telling them that everything's going to be all right, but do they listen? *Noooooooooooo.*"

Proceeds from the game will benefit an undisclosed not-for-profit orgaization. Ω

Home Slots Make Gaming Investment Easier

Concerned that the demands of job and family are reducing the time available for trips to a casino, the Mashantucket Pequot tribe is offering home slot machines. Personalized for the needs of the individual family, the Kimosabee Teepeeslot-II™ links the gaming enthusiast to bank accounts, mortgage institutions, investment brokers and credit card companies.

"The Kimosabee Teepeeslot -II™ represents a quantum leap in gaming efficiency," said Harold "Lying Dog" Fistermeister, tribe spokesperson. "From the comfort of their own homes, gamers can maximize their investment in a vast array of venues specifically designed for virtually endless divestiture.

Home gaming enthusiasts no longer need to insert coin after coin into slot machines. Teepeeslots are linked directly to hundreds of pre-approved Visa, Mastercard and American Express accounts, giving gamers online access to extensive credit lines.

The Teepeeslot-II is easy to use and comes in various models, including wall units, portable units, and one that looks like a television and can be operated with a remote control.

The machines are also linked via the internet to over fifty mortgage companies. In the case of jackpot, mortgages are paid off instant-ly. If gamers need extra funds as they pursue their personal jackpots, pre-approved mortgage loans will be issued when other credit lines run dangerously low.

The tribe guarantees a seamless shift between debt and credit. Gamers will be free to concentrate on their games until a sheriff arrives with eviction papers.

Serious gaming fans can set their Teepeeslots on automatic, freeing themselves to go to work or attend to family needs. Excess winnings are randomly invested in stock market equities.

Initial market tests with the Kimosabee Teepeeslot-II have proven so successful that the tribe is already designing an updated version, the Tomahawkslot Ultima™. With a single click of a mouse from anywhere on the planet, gaming enthusiasts can instantly bet everything they own and could conceivably borrow. Winners take home North America. Losers are divested, stripped naked, smeared with honey and staked over anthills in the middle of the Mojave Desert. §

Mother Breaks Up Uncles

Town Mother Brunhilda Onus was single-handedly responsible for breaking up a meeting of Uncles For Education last month following reports of questionable behavior.

The UFE was meeting in the bar of Sprague Rod Gun Club when Onus burst through the door and hauled them outside by their ears, injuring all seven uncles. As the men sat rubbing their ears, Onus reviewed a list of grievances.

"You are all guilty of sloth and conspiring to commit sloth," Onus said. "You have left chores and household repairs undone. You have holes in your undershirts. All of you could use a shave and one of you smells of fish. And you call yourselves uncles?"

Vinnie Vandalosa, UFE president, said that the group had been meeting to discuss these very issues but that it was "pretty damned hard" to conduct business with someone always dragging them around by their "friggin' ears."

Onus stated that she did not want to hear that word spoken in the Rod Gun Club parking lot or anywhere else in town. She also accused Vandalosa of muttering. §

Hitorical Society Finds Lincoln's Putter!

Sprague Historical Society president Dennis R. Delaney was left breathless last month when he came across what may be the town's most significant historical artifact in the SHS museum closet. In the back of the closet, under a moth-eaten horse blanket, lay Abraham Lincoln's putter.

"I could hardly believe it," Delaney said. "My hands were shaking so hard, I practically wet my pants."

The crude, cast iron golf club is in badly rusted condition. Etched on the shank are the presidential seal and the words "This putter was stolen from Abraham Lincoln."

How it ended up in the SHS museum closet is anyone's guess. State police have been notified.

Delaney said that it is a little-known fact that the first Republican president was also the first Republican golfer. In fact, General William Tecumseh Sherman's three objectives in his devastating campaign through Georgia were to free slaves, strike a devastating blow to the Confedeate economy, and liberate the Augusta National golf course for use by all Republicans, regardless of race, color, creed or sexual preference.

One slave, Willy Wilson Woods, who came escaped from slavery on the Underground Railroad, served as Lincoln's volunteer caddie for 17 years.

Green Party Proposes Tree-pee Program

Plan called unfair to women.

The Green Party of Sprague, noted for its concern for the environment, has proposed a municipal statute allowing men to urinate on trees. The loosening of the local restriction will benefit the ecology, according to the Green proposal.

"Trees love this stuff," said Glenn Cheney, Green Party activist. "It's rich in nitrogen and other nutrients, and it's mostly water, which all plants need to survive. With Project Wet Boots, we'll be returning to the system what we've taken out."

Cheney explained that through the process of photosynthesis, the urine is eventually converted to the oxygen that all life forms depend on. Under current urination practices, he said, this valuable natural resource gets trapped in septic systems and sewers, gradually depleting the ecosystem of essential elements.

As Cheney unfolded his plan at a meeting of the board of selectmen, First Selectman Stephen Papineau tilted his head to the left and right in pensive consideration. Selectman Kenneth Caisse, however, had serious reservations.

"This is far more complicated than Mr. Cheney thinks," Caisse said. "We have DEP to worry about. The EPA. Wetlands. Flood control. It just goes on and on."

Selectman Joan Charron-Nagle said she would prefer not to comment except to ask why the proposal would not apply to women. She also said she had heard of this kind of thing going on for years, not only in Sprague but along the nation's Interstate highways as well.

Cheney admitted to adding personal nitrogen to the plants on his property on Parkwood Road, where neighbors have often marveled at the quality of his shrubbery.

"Everybody thinks I have a green thumb," Cheney said, "but that's not it." §

Following Lincoln's tragic assassination, Woods and the presidential golf clubs disappeared.

The putter, which weighs just over 44 pounds, was capable of putting a Civil War era golf ball almost two hundred yards.

"In those days, golfers were real men, and so were Republicans,"Delaney said. "They were all like Lincoln, not an ounce of fat on them."

piece of paper and mumbling in iambic pentameter. The next thing you know, they're badly in need of a shave and starving to death in some garret in New York City. Their wives remarry, and one by one their kids become engineers, accountants, bankers, retailers. It's very sad."

The mysterious identity of the Sprague poet is leading to wild accusations. Sprague town hall has denied rumors of poetic tendencies among the board of selectmen. Baltic Fire Department has stated that if the poetry were theirs, it would "definitely rhyme." Sprague Public Library reports that no books of poetry have been borrowed in the last 78 months. Sayles School administrators say that local students would sooner submit to detention than write a poem.

State poet laureate Leo Connellan, a Hanover resident, asked to be recused from the accusations.

"Don't go pointing your finger at me when somebody says anonymous/I'm not the one around here who needs a frontal lobotomus," Connellan said. "It's important that we get to the bottom of this/And I do appreciate the chance to rhyme something with hippopotamus."

Cheney said that it is entirely possible that the several anonymous poems came from several different poets, in which case the town faced a serious crisis.

An unidentified spokeswitch from the Sprague Committee on Supernatural Events suggested that the poet may be channeling the poetry from the "other side."

"We have analyzed this poetry carefully and concluded that it probably comes from a frustrated individual residing in a medieval booby hatch," the psychic thought. "What we don't yet is whether this individual directed the poetry at Sprague specifically or where it just squirted out here at random."

Man Bitten by Hedgehog
Or was it a woodchuck?

Hanover slumlord Anthony Ozga was bitten
by a small furry animal after trying to kick it off his deck. Ozga claims it was a hedgehog and that he tried to kick it because it bit him, but witnesses say it was a woodchuck and that it bit him because he tried to kick it.

"He tempted the poor little animal with a piece of rye toast," one witness said. "Then he took a swing at it with his foot."

Ozga claims that it was pumpernickel and that the animal looked like a football, so why shouldn't he try to kick it? Witnesses asked why he was trying to feed toast to a football. State police said the discussion went downhill from there. Ω

Screaming Mimi Shatters Local Emotions

If you live in Sprague, you've heard it — the utterly unexpected screech of a woman raising her voice in alarm. The screamer has been identified as Mimi Banshee who moved to Sprague recently after voices in her head told her to do so.

Banshee, the author of *Screaming for Dummies,* has disrupted several public events and activities. Typically she arrives unobtrusively, then splits the air with a scream that shatters nerves and disrupts order. She has caused firearms to discharge at Sprague Rod & Gun Club, caused sudden baldness in two members of the Board of Finance, cured baldness in one member of the Board of Education, cracked beer mugs at the Stone House cafe, and caused a road crew member to get two knuckles of one finger stuck in his nose.

Baltic Fire Department ambulance reports treating fourteen cases of acute hemocoagulation.

"We have informed the state police and asked that Ms. Banshee be charged with public blood curdling," said Stephen J. Papineau, first selectman. "I am told, however, that screaming one time in one place is legal in Connecticut. There's nothing we can do but wear ear plugs and steel ourselves against future occurrences."

Investigators are trying to find a pattern in Banshee's screaming. The incident at the Board of Education happened when the meeting paused for public comment. A scream in Sprague Public Library emanated from the video tape section. at the memorial Day parade, a scream was believed to be directed at a passing pack of cub scouts. A scream that set off the fire siren occurred precisely at midnight on December 21.

Banshee says that she does not know when she is going to scream until she herself hears it. She says the cause may be genetic in that she is distantly related to the Banshee women of medieval Ireland who foretold death by wailing in the dark.

"All I know is, I like to scream," Banshee said. "If everybody screamed more, I think we'd all feel better."

Banshee has offered to give after-school screaming classes at Sayles School. Two faculty members have signed up, but the administration says that due to insurance restrictions, the classes may not be held on school property. Ω

Spitballer Kisses Bufuddle Baseballers
Sprague leads league with unrequited affection

The Sprague Spitballers have taken the lead in the southeast Connecticut baseball league with a strategy that other teams have not been able to counter. The Spitballers success is attributed to a loophole in the rules that allows players on one team to kiss those on other teams whether they like it or not.

"I don't care if other teams think it's disgusting," said Spitballer coach Mickey Mantule. "If we get a runner on first, he's going to kiss the first baseman. If one of their runners slides into home, he gets a kiss from the catcher. If their shortstop doesn't want a kiss, then he can just stand back when the runner goes by. This is not only decent and legal, it's also a great way to get their players to give us a little elbow room. It's done wonders for our RBI."

The coaches of other teams have demanded a stop to the unrequited kisses, claiming that the practice could spread disease. None, however, have been able to cite a specific case of contagion. Claims of sexual harassment have been rejected because the kisses have been limited to pecks on the cheek.

The Spitballers say the strategy was developed in secret meetings held during winter training. By the first games in April, they were able to kiss "on the fly," leaving opponent players confused and disoriented as a Spitballer ran by.

"It's really not so bad once you get used to it," said Spitballer outfielder Joseph T. Palooka. "We've got a whole arsenal of kisses. Squeakers. Poppers. Jowl-wetters. It really keeps them off base."

Mantule says that only the Franklin Fieldmice have found an effective counter-strategy. By pretending to enjoy the kisses, they have managed to limit Spitballer kisses to blown kisses delivered from a distance.

"We're not entirely sure they're only pretending," Mantule said. "It's hard to tell with some guys. Once we know they're faking it, we'll just escalate the kisses until we've got them all backed into a corner out in right field." Ω

Coming soon . . .

"Outturn" to the OED
Town to spruce down
It's ai-ai-ai all over

Neighborhood News

What's really happening in Sprague.

February - 2001

Sprague Makes the OED Again!

"Outturn" to join "yuz."

The election scandal of 2000 has done more than thrust Sprague into the national headlines. It has thrust the town into the updated Oxford English Dictionary as well.

It started with Kathleen Boushee, registrar of voters, reported the questionable effects of a piece of candy that was found stuck to the voting lever of a presidential hopeful. Reporting the implications on public access television program *Sprague Today*, Boushee said, "What happens if it is determined that a Tootsie-Roll, or for that matter a lolli-pop or a wad of gum, has affected the outturn of an election?"

The statement was reported in *Neighborhood News* and later quoted by newspapers and television newscasts. The use of the word "outturn" came to the attention of the editors of the OED, which sets the standards of the ever-evolving English language. Until Boushee uttered it on television, "outturn" was not a word.

Under the OED rules, a new word can be included in the English language if it has appeared in electronic and printed media and been spoken in public by an elected official.

Upon publication in the next edition of the OED, *outturn* will be synonymous with "outcome," and the etymology will list Sprague as the source.

"It gives me great pride to announce that a small town like Sprague has given birth to yet another word," said Papineau.

Sprague is also considered the birthplace of "yuz," the newly formed plural of "you." Latin

Continued on page 2

Town Prepares for Presidential Visit

Town Maintenance Crew Plans Environmental Disaster

It's far from certain, but Sprague town hall says there's a good chance George W. Bush, president, may be coming to town.

"This could be really, really big," said Stephen J. Papineau, Sprague first selectman. "It is known that the president never travels alone. If we can draw him into town, we draw in at least two hundred other people – people with disposable income who will need food to eat and a place to sleep and souvenirs to take home to the kiddies."

Papineau estimated that 200 people would fill both of the town's eateries as well as Salt Rock Campground, and the Holly Jolly Bazaar could sell its entire inventory as the town's only source of remotely souveniristic products. Ifthe visitors bring their pets, Western Grain and Feeds could be stripped of its dog and cat food. If they bring their children, both of Sprague's nursery schools could be filled. If they all went to church, the offerings dishes would be heaped with cash.

"An unbelievably huge influx of business will be possible if just one person, President

George W. Bush

Bush, can be suckered into town," Papineau said. "But don't think for a moment it's going to be easy."

In hopes of luring the country's primo Republican, the town road crew will cut down every tree within town limits. Oil well derricks will be erected in back yards and raw crude will be cast upon the Shetucket in hopes of extinguishing life. A vast fleet of gas guzzlers will be leased and parked bumper to bumper down every street and road. Baltic Reservoir will be drained and painted to look like an open pit mine.

Papineau believes that these efforts may not be enough.

"We're looking for volunteers to shoot birds," he said. "The last thing we need is some goddam dove hooting it up when the presidential scouts come through. Doves are at the top of our list, but really, we asking that anything without a rabies tag, udders or a birth certificate be shot on sight."

Town hall has applied for a federal grant that would be used to provide all Spraguers

Continued on page 2

Beak Tweaker Tweaking Beaks

Sprague citizens are up in arms over an out-of-town assailant who has been "tweaking beaks" all over town. Thirty-eight residents have reported an unidentified individual flicking a finger into their noses, then fleeing and disappearing almost instantly. Victims complain of injured egos and a sense of lingering insult.

"Doink," said Angelynn Meya, a retired mushroom farmer. "That's exactly what it sounds like on the inside. One minute the world's a bed of roses, the next you feel like... mushroom compost after it's been sapped of every nutrient and dumped out in a field, steaming like primordial porridge and stinking like the ass-end of a dead horse."

Angelynn E. Meya

Meya's beak was tweaked when she stopped her car at the request of a stranger on the side of the road. As she opened the car window, he reached in, flicked his finger into her nose at an upward angle, and disappeared around the back of the car. She was unable to describe the assailant except to say that he was a Caucasian male of average height.

Edgar Deignault said his beak was tweaked as he lay asleep in his hammock in the backyard. By the time he realized what had happened, the sneaky tweaker was gone.

Continued on page 3

It's "Ai-ai-ai" All Over as Sprague Tackles Spanish

Sprague residents are reported to be near panic as a town ordinance requiring knowledge of Spanish goes into effect. The ordinance requires all residents to speak Spanish on at least an intermediate level by the first of next month.

"The fiesta is over," said first selectman Stephen Papineau. "We've known this day would come. It's time to put on our thinking sombreros and start habla-ing español around here. Capeesh?"

The ordinance was passed a year ago following a town hall decision to globalize Sprague in order to remain competitive in the third millenium.

Many residents expressed reluctance to learn a new language.

"This is a lot of toro," said Felix DeGuber, 89, a lifelong resident. "I've been trying, but all I've learned so far is *San Diego* and *toyota grande.*"

Glenn Cheney, town Spanish teacher, expressed frustration in his attempts to teach a foreign language to what he termed "three thousand highly resistant students." During a class at the Senior Center, for example, eight individuals suffered chest pains after trying to say *"Una enchilada, por favor"* three times fast.

"We're damned lucky Sprague isn't in Mexico or we'd really be in trouble," Cheney said. ✳

OED, continued from page 1
languages have had singular and plural forms of personal pronouns since the times of ancient Rome, but English was deficient until Sprague linguists created a logical solution.

Lingual futurists — those who track the creation of new words as they move toward general acceptance and, ultimately, inclusion in a dictionary — currently have their eye on "everybodies" and "irregardless." Though considered redundant forms, their informal and unauthorized use has been reported throughout Sprague.

William Colonna, chairman of Sprague Language Board, says that the town government has never enforced the standards of the English language or held an official position on its use.

"It don't matter how you say it; it don't matter how you spell it," Colonna said. "That's all you got to know."

Colonna's summary will be included in the American Encyclopedia of Reductivist

Society Protests Weird Boy, Ugly Girl

Sprague residents have expressed concern over an questionable "relationship" apparently being formed between Howard Bulgarino, 13, and Brenda Pons, 15. The consensus in town is that both of them could do better.

"Howie is a weird boy. Everyone knows this, even him," said Stephanie Prickenpeck, spokesperson of the Versailles Society for Social Communication. "And Brenda is — how can I put it nicely? — somewhat facially disabled. It's what we used to call ugly before everything changed. There's probably a new word for weird, too. Normality challenged? I don't know. And it isn't my job to know. All I know is, if somebody that weird hooks up with somebody that ugly, something weird and ugly is going to happen."

What was so funny

Bulgarino and Pons are reported to have floated down the Shetucket River, from the Scotland Dam to the dam at Versailles, under an overturned canoe. The act has been called irrational and suspicious. Giggling was heard. Prickenpeck says that since the Shetucket is a public waterway, the public has a right to know what, if anything, was so funny.

SSC members recommend that Bulgarino associate with a young lady with "more refined nostrils, a more substantive chin, smaller ears and some meat on her bones." Pons's second toes are reported to be longer than her big toes.

Bush visit, continued from page 1
with Saturday-night assault rifles. In a show of support for the right to bear arms, all residents will be asked to stand in their yards with their weapons if and when the presidential limousine goes by. Men are asked to wear good suits and wingtip shoes. Women should remain barefoot and, wherever possible, pregnant.

Sayles School will join in the celebration with Trigger Happy Days.

"We want the children to have fun while they exercise their constitutional rights," said Dr. Harrington "Mojo" Heiffer-Tittlbaum, acting principal. "For the entire time of the President's visit, the ammunition's free and kid's can leave their trigger locks home. I hope the president comes to visit our school, I really do."

The Sprague chapter of the Red Cross is looking for people with visible illnesses to lie on sidewalks in order to give the appearance that the town has absolutely no healthcare system whatsoever.

"We aren't just looking for victims of lep-

An undisclosed source alleges that her navel is "a disgusting outie" that looks like it has a little mushroom "or something" growing out of it.

"No boy should be permitted in a position where he might feel obliged to develop affections for such a girl," Prickenpeck said. "It could damage his self-esteem."

Disavowing favoritism, Prickenpeck said that Ms. Pons should be advised of the dangers of becoming intimate with a boy who can make his eyes pop out and has been accused of trying

Brenda Pons

to play music on a cow and playing a piano underwater.

"Suppose Brenda starts to think that Howie is normal?" Prickenpeck said. "Then what's he going to think about everybody else? How will she ever find a satisfying relationship with someone who's, you know, employable?"

Resident state trooper Chris Johnson said that he did not know of any law against giggling under a canoe in a public waterway. Asked if he had ever engaged in undercanoe giggling with a minor, Johnson said only, "No comment."

The SSC was suspicious of his vague answer.

"He smiled when he said it, just a little bit at one corner of his mouth, I saw it," Prickenpeck said. "And he calls himself a state cop?" ✳

rosy and elephantiasis," said Lotta Corpuscles, chapter chairperson. "We'll take runny noses, dandruff, satyriasis, anything. If you can lie on the sidewalk and groan, that's good enough. We seriously doubt the President is going to go around checking fevers."

In a gesture of political support, the town's two voting machines will be thrown into the Shetucket, and the president's motorcade will arrive in town under a shower of chads.

The president will be invited to sprinkle ceremonial arsenic in the town's water supply, too. David Rood, director of water and sewers, says he'll have a large supply on hand so the president can decide how much is enough. ✳

Thought. For a small town, Sprague maintains significant presence in the encyclopedia. Ω

Presidential Fact Box
Did you know...

* President Bush's's suits are made of laminated cardboard?
* George Bush's only A at Yale was in "Leadership Waving"?
* President Bush glad-hands underhanded Panhandlers?

Itinerant Bouncer Offers Services in Sprague

An itinerant bouncer has set up a temporary office in Sprague and for the next two weeks will be available to remove unwanted persons from homes, yards, classrooms, public meetings and, yes, bars.

"This town has needed a rent-a-bouncer for quite some time now," said Joan Charron-Nagle, selectman. "We've had complaints of in-laws overstaying their welcome, obnoxious individuals hogging barstools, chronic troublemakers in classrooms, croquet players who have strayed onto other people's lawns, public access program hosts embarrassing the town, all kinds of situations. For the next two weeks, Sprague is going to clean house."

Jess Mouvaughn has been offering free-lance bouncing services throughout eastern Connecticut for over five years. His more significant

Jess Mouvaughn

bouncings include the removal of an entire high school football team from a Toyota Tercel, the weeding of a cub scout pack that had spun out of control, the booting of the entire Arkansas contingent of a Colcester family that had extended a Thanksgiving weekend well beyond the leftovers, and the actual bouncing of a bouncer who had gone berserk at a Rhode Island strip club.

Town Mother Brunhilda Onus says she is relieved to have the services of a professional available.

"About half this town needs bouncing, but we're going to restrict ourselves to a few target individuals," Onus said. "That Bulgarino kid's at the top of the list. I haven't even figured out why he was born. I think he and I and the rest of Sprague would be better off if we just bounced him on down to Occum." ❉

House of Ads Cuts Cost of Housing

The American Institute of Advertising has established an experimental "House of Ads" in Sprague. One of 50 in the United States, the three-bedroom cape has advertising on all internal and external surfaces, including walls, floors, ceilings and even the roof.

It looks a little funny, but you can't beat the rent. It's free.

The Bulgarino family – Howard Sr., his wife, Consumadora Louise, and their son, Howard Jr. — are delighted with their new home.

"This is the best deal I've ever heard of," said Howard Sr. "And best of all, I believe this is the house of the future. Someday everyone will live in a house of ads, free of any rent or mortgage, thanks to the miracle of advertising."

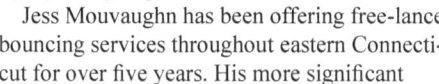

Beak Tweaker, continued from page 1

Road crew worker George Allen had his beak tweaked by an individual in a Japanese car with tinted windows who pulled up to a pothole, reached out, and...doink!

Several residents of Baltic Senior Housing reported an individual in a Groucho Marx mask knocking on their doors and tweaking their beaks as they looked out.

Resident state trooper Chris Johnson said that beak tweaking is considered a minor assault that is classified as a third-degree misdemeanor in the same category as spitting-and-missing, obscene gestures, and flatulating with intent to disrupt. Maximum punishment is a $12.50 fine and up to half an hour in jail.

"Basically, it's a slap on the wrist for a tweak of the beak," Johnson said. "Unless of course it's my beak, in which case the perpetrator gets a knuckle sandwich." ❉

The theory makes sense. Just as advertising makes free television and radio possible and subsidizes the cost of magazines and newspapers, it can, if the AIA's bold experiment succeeds, reduce the cost of housing to zero.

The Bulgarinos say they don't mind being surrounded by logos and slogans for soft drinks, cars, electronics, appliances and fast food chains. They have designated some rooms for specific commercial themes. Howard's Jr.'s bedroom will be plastered with ads relating to products for youth. The garage will proffer products relating to cars, tools and lawn care. Every flat surface in the kitchen will related to food products. One entire slope of the roof will bear the logo of Mountain Dew, a popular soft drink.

Howard Jr. says he doesn't care.

"It's a little hard to sleep," he says. "It feels like somebody's shouting at me. It's like sleeping with the TV on but the sound turned off. It makes me feel like I should be buying stuff, but I don't have any money. I want to kill somebody."

Complaints by neighbors have not been successful as "home advertising" has been judged a right protected under the first Amendment.

Mrs. Bulgarino says the in-house advertising is a big help in the kitchen, where the ads are a constant suggestion of what to make for dinner. The ads are changed monthly with new wallpaper and linoleum.

Doors in the house are linked to recordings that play each time a door, including those of the refrigerator, garage and mailbox are opened

Continued on page 4

Emaciated Road Crew Returns Jackhammer

The Sprague town maintenance crew reports that they have had to return a rented jackhammer that proved unuseable. The problem was with neither the tool nor the skill of the road crew. It was a problem of weight.

"You need a decent belly to steady a jackhammer," said Jim Handfield, director of maintenance. "We've always kept our crew trim. The jackhammer just bounced them around like a pogo stick. We couldn't stop George Allen until he'd hopped through Occum and was turning right onto I-395. It was really kind of embarrassing."

Handson denied rumors that the road crew is malnourished and overworked.

"They just work too hard and eat the wrong foods," he explained.

Refurbishment of the West Main Street sidewalk has been discontinued until the crew gains sufficient weight. The Sprague Gutmeisters are being consulted on an appropriate diet. ❉

Poem of the Month

Blank Verse

This space reserved

for a poem never written,

never would have been,

never ought to be, a poem

dead from the get-go,

better off as white space,

better never to have lived

than to have died trying

to do what white space

has always done so well.

Anonymous Botch

Tasters Slam Man with Cat Hat

Meya: "This is an opportunity."

The Sprague Taste Reference Board has issued a written warning to a local man who had made a hat of his own cat.

It all started when Goofball died of apparently natural causes. Goofball, a tiger cat owned by Godfrey Deofrito, 33, subsequently skinned Goofball and made a hat in the coon-skin style but with a tail — *Goofball's tail*— hanging down the back.

"This is legal," Deofrito said in an exclusive Neighborhood news interview. "He was my cat, and he died a reasonable death. What's wrong with a man wearing his cat on his head? It says a lot about a relationship. Think about it."

Deofrito has refused to release any information about his relationship with Goofball. It is not know whether he adored his cat or was wishing death on it ever since it became a cat.

In an emergency session, the TRB met last Saturday afternoon. Present were representatives from the Board of Selectmen, the Sprague Institute of Cool Ones, Gutmeisters of Sprague, Hanover Philosophical Society, Uncles for Education, and the Sprague Committee on Supernatural Events. The Board concluded that while Mr. Deofrito's hat may be legal, it is, by local standards, an exhibit of questionable taste.

"This board was created specifically for this kind of situation," said Prudence Retenturl, TRB chair. "Deofrito should doff, if not bury, his cap while we assess the significance of the intention of his churlish act."

Stanley "smoothie" Spidoonski, who represents SICO on the Board, said that preliminary research indicates that most people who comb their hair believe that wearing your own dead cat is "disgusting."

"It doesn't matter whether you are honoring your cat for a life of courage, loyalty and palpable contentment or insulting your cat for spoiling two sofas, an ottoman, a stack of embroidered guest towels and twelve square feet of hardwood flooring," Spidoonski said. "A dead cat on your head is a dead cat on your head. There's no two ways about it, maybe less."

Deofrito has challenged "the dominant local subculture" to give his hat a moral value without knowing whether Goofball was a saint of a cat or an agent of Satan.

"Why it should it be OK to wear the remains of a cow on your feet, a cow with whom you had absolutely no relationship whatsoever, yet not OK to wear the remains of a companion animal with whom you share ten years of intimacy?" Deofrito said. "*You* tell *me*."

Robert Meya, representing HPS on the Board, said that taste is not so easy to define, especially on a Saturday afternoon.

"This is clearly an opportunity to use *a priori* and *a posteriori*," Meya said. "We have a committee working on a powerful sentence that applies these and other terms to the concept of expired pets. Discussions have become increasing complex, to say the least, so we have decided to construct the sentence in German. By the third quarter of this year we hope to be hammering out an English translation." ❄

Gutmeisters Set Flab Fest

Gutmeisters of Sprague has set June 12 for the association's Flab Fest 2000. The annual event, open to members only, will be held at Sprague Rod & Gun Club.

The president of the association of local chubbies described the event as jovial and informal while steeped in tradition, glorified in ceremony and sheathed in secrecy.

"Basically, we sit around drinking beer, eating pizza, and showing each other our bellies," the president explained under condition of anonimity. "It's a rare and intimate social environment where men can pat and scratch each other's guts without other people asking stupid questions and giving us diet advice."

The traditional garb of Flab Fests includes loose-fitting trousers slung low around the front. Most members use suspenders *and* a belt. Celebrants usually wear their favorite T-shirts that allow cooling of the slower spare tire and easy access to the navel, the piedmont, the ponderosa and the "jolly roll" layers that cascade from above.

"This event is really a time of giving thanks for prosperity and remembering all the good times that have given us girth," said the Gutmeisters president.

The Gutmeisasters hold that the human body is beautiful and that the larger it is, the more beautiful it is.

"Blubber is perfectly natural," the president said. "Whales have it. Walruses have it. Sea cows. Manatees. The list goes on and on."

The organization's mascot, Lewinsky, an 88-pound house cat reputed to have consumed a bear, will be present for ceremonies and to clean up any leftovers. The cat resides at the Sprague Rod & Gun Club bar. Ω

House of Ads, cont. from page 3

or closed.

"I love it," Consumadora says. "We live in a house of jingles and reminders. I hum jingles all day, and I never forget that I need to buy new, improved Folger's Crystals with more aroma, taco (flavored) Cheez Wizz, Sugar Frosted Flakes, which are *great*, or a Ford Taurus.

Because of Consumadora's allergies, the family has declined the option to have a dog or cat that wears commercial sandwich boards and tail banners. They are still considering whether to accept one or more parrots that have been trained to repeat such popular slugs as "Don't leave home without it" and "We do chicken right." ❄

Tiny People Sighted Inside Radio

In what has been called a "significant break through in modern technology," a Sayles School first-grader has reported seeing a minuscule rock 'n' roll band inside a clock radio that was playing, at that exact moment, "Kiss Me, Kick Me," a hit song played by the Dead Morticians.

The student, Gayle Johnston, says that the band disappeared as soon as she looked through a little hole in the back of the radio.

"It didn't look like the Dead Morticians but it sure sounded like them," Johnston said. "I think they were just imitating."

Megan Hertz, spokesperson for the American Electronics Association, said that the sighting, however brief, confirmed a age-old suspicion about how radios actually work.

"We were always skeptical of the explanation that sound comes zipping through the air in invisible waves and enters radios via antennas," Hertz said. "It just didn't make sense for a lot of reasons, one being that the notion is utterly absurd, the other being that a lot of radios don't have antennas. We theorized that the sound came in through wires, but that didn't explain car radios. The only theory that has never been disproved is that every radio holds a crew of tiny but highly versatile musicians, disk jockeys and news announcers."

Johnston described the band as looking like gnomes with long beards, big noses, green leggings, pointy hats and wide belts with big, golden buckles. Hertz said that the description was "more or less what we figured." ❄

Neighborhood News

What's really happening in Sprague.

March - 2001

Town Responds to Call for Seriousness

BoF: "Seriousness doesn't come cheap."

It's about time thing town got serious.
How many times have you heard those words? Probably more times than you've heard the town anthem or the Sprague Pledge of Allegiance. After years of sharing that sentiment on seriousness, Spraguers have finally started doing something about it.

"It's about time this town got serious," said Vincent "Vinnie" Vandaloso, chairman of Uncles for Education. "It's time we put a stop to the baloney."

Grace Hollya, PTA president, agreed, stating that Sprague has "more baloney than Carter has fleas." Much of the local, cheap, bland stuffed sausage, she said, could be found on the school board.

"Without the school board getting serious, the rest of us might as well run around in Bozo outfits wearing big red noses that squeak when you squeeze them," Hollya said.

Sprague first selectman Stephen J. Papineau, has promised to organize a town seriousness workshop for any residents who believe they may be seriously impaired.

Papineau says he's serious.

"If we're really serious about getting seriously serious, we've got to stop fooling around," Papineau said. "We must do whatever is necessary to buckle down and turn over

Continued on page 2

Sprague Challenged by *Islamic Generosity*

Christianity caught with pants down.

The Bush administration's new strategy of applying Christian values to Islamic extremists is creating unforeseen problems — and opportunities — in Sprague as Moslems retaliate with crushing freehandedness.

"Operation Largesse Oblige is in danger of backfiring," said Sprague Special Diplomat for Counter-Islamic Love, Fr. Anthony Ozga. "We never expected to be outdone in generosity. The president really should of thought this through before he tried spreading Christianity with good will instead of good old-fashioned B-52s. Who'd ever of thunk that Islam would believe in the power of love, too? Thunk? Is that a word? Thank? Thinked?"

As the Oxford English Dictionary Disaster Recovery Team rushed to the scene of the statement, town first selectman Stephen J. Papineau called together the Sprague's leading Christians to explore means of retaliating against a tractor-trailer full of dates, figs, olives, falafel, tabbouleh, humus, yogurt, hookahs, goat milk, couscous, microwavable enchiladas and beautifully illustrated Korans that arrived in a predawn invasion of Islamic munificence.

The truck parked in the Grist Mill parking lot, where it began distributing the goods to local citizens. Resident state trooper Chris

Stephen J. Papineau

Johnson said that there was nothing he could do to stop the magnaminity.

"This is a day that will live in infamy," Papineau said. "We cannot allow Islam to spread through the cowardly use of unprovoked goodness. They have awakened a sleeping giant. We will retaliate with everything we've got."

Saying that he himself would lead the "Charge of Charity," Papineau pledged his 1986 Suburban Guzzler as a gift to the leader of "any rinky-dink town over there in Arabia who wants it."

Fr. Anthony is collecting donations at his church and packing the goods into a 40-foot container that will be sent to needy people in Abu Dubai. He is asking for products that are scarce in the Middle East, such as lawn clippings, oak leaves, plaid undershorts, unsold tag sale items and unused New Testaments, preferably in Arabic. Alcoholic beverages would also be welcomed, Ozga said.

Papineau said that local experts in weird religions are combing the Koran in search of evidence that the religion advocates nastiness. To their surprise, Allah and Mohammad, Islam's main deity and prophet, respectively, call for nothing other than generosity, good will and peacefulness.

"This is most disturbing," Ozga said. "It seems they've pulled Christianity right out from under us, caught us with our pants down and nothing in our hands but cruise missiles. To the rest of the world, we look like idiots."

The Pentagon claims to have bombarded
Continued on page 2

Citizens Cringe as Test Date Approaches

Town Historian: *"We have a right to ignorance."*

An essence of nervous sweat has spread across Sprague as the date of the Federal Citizenship Test draws near. Many citizens admit that they haven't even begun to study for the test that could cost them their citizenship and lead to eventual deportation.

"I am very worried that we may lose as much as 90 percent of our residents if the FCT is as difficult as the one given to candidates for naturalization," said Ramona Hoppenstantz,

director of the town's adult resident education committee.

According to the Minimum Citizenship Requirement Act of 1999, the test for current citizens will be exactly the same as the one that foreign residents must pass to become citizens. Candidates have needed to name the 13 original colonies, the Chief Justice of the Supreme Court, the capital of Missouri, the number of

Continued on page 4

Largesse Oblige, from page 1

Low-budget Camp to Offer Kids the Savage Experience

Starting next summer, local children can have the experience of a lifetime and parents save money on summer camp as Primal Screams, Inc. opens a Camp Neanderthal in Sprague.

"As in our specialty camps in Idaho and Maine, we will offer a truly unique experience," said Gunter Pleisto, camp director. "Unique in modern times, anyway. In reality, it's an experience that has been shared by thousands of early humans, an experience which, despite a hundred thousand years of inflation, costs little more today than it did then, plus, of course, tax."

Located in the vast, unsettled area between Hanover and Scotland Road, Camp Neanderthal at Sprague will set itself apart from traditional summer camps by allowing children the absolute freedom they need to be themselves and, in the process, to grow. The camp employs no counselors, offers no programs or organized activities, and has no infrastructure to stand between children and nature. For two weeks, the children are left alone to experience the lifestyle of precivilizational humans.

Parents will enjoy the experience of sending their children to a camp that charges only $19.95 for each two-week stay.

"All we give our campers is freedom and the breakfast cereal of their choice," Pleisto said. "No milk, no sugar, no strings attached. The fence is electrified, which they soon find out on their own. They can't leave Camp Ne-

Neanderthal Camper

anderthal any more than the Neanderthals could leave 50,000 B.C. We've built a few rudimentary caves for them and left a little flint lying around, but if the campers want fire or a wheel, they have to do what our forebears did. They have to invent it themselves."

Pleisto said that two boxes of cereal per camper are more than enough to keep the children from eating each other. He reiterated that the camp dispenses only premium cereals, "not just Shredded Wheat." Most of the bi-weekly fee, he said, is for liability insurance.

Children come away from a Camp Neanderthal with a new appreciation of their parents and the amenities of civilized life, Pleisto noted. Parents of camp survivors have characterized their returning children as obedient, respectful and appreciative of such small things as spoons, pillows, toilet seats and the marrow of chicken bones.

Pleisto said that there are documented cases of children as young as eight returning from camp with hair on the chests.

"They look at you as if they know something that you don't," Pleisto said. "But once you get used to it, it's not so bad."

Pleisto said that Primal Screams is looking for a site for an adult Camp Neanderthal, which he described as "basically the same thing but with a highe voltage on the fence and no breakfast cereal. Ω

Afghanistan with over $3 billion in ready-to-eat meals, designer clothes, topsoil, ploughshares, entire irrigation systems, free internet access, pre-approved credit cards, microwavable enchiladas and irresistable promises that occupants may have won a million dollars from Publisher's Clearinghouse.

Islamic nations have responded with tankers of free oil, carpets, ATM cards for Swiss banks, virgins, poppy seed paste and camel-based products such as scarves and curd-belly soup. Converts have been reported in Pittsburgh, Bismarck and, inevitably, Burbank.

Papineau said that the Sprague Economic Development Council was working on emergency plans to produce a "new, improved manna" that would be dropped over Arabia from converted bombers.

"New improved Manna™ Now with Real™ Milk-and-Honey Glazing can be a reality," said Thomas McAvoy, council chairman. "We have dairies in town, and we have beekeepers in town. Don't ask me where the Hell™ we're going to get Manna™, but somebody around here's got to have a recipe."

McAvoy said that New Improved Manna™ production could become the foundation of a strong local economy. He called President Bush's Operation Largesse Oblige "ingenious" because it renders the Military-Industrial Complex obsolete, thus opening opportunities for low-tech manufacturers in small towns across America.

"Mittens," McAvoy said. "The Taliban™ doesn't stand a chance if we start giving their people homemade mittens. And homemade socks. Ever stuck your feet in homemade socks? It's enough to make you want to curl up and suck your thumb. If we can drive the enemy to that, I don't think we'll have any more problems." Ω

Seriously, continued from page 1

a new leaf. Our nose are too long from the grindstone. It's time we separated the wheat from the chaff and the men from the boys."

At Sayles School, all two second grade classes took a "Vow of Seriousness" while the upper grade band played America the Beautiful in a special arrangement for three snare drums and a clarinet.

"On our honor
we pledge ourselves to seriousness
and to the republicans for
which itstands,
eschewing baloney
and refraining from silliness at all times,
to keep our socks up,
our chins raised,
and a presidential squint to our eyes
until the last syllable of recorded time."

Claude Pellegrino, chairman of the board of Finance said he had no position on the

move toward seriousness but had questions about its impact on the town budget.

"Seriousness doesn't come cheap," Pellegrino said. "The Egyptians got serious about pyramids and blew their budget so bad they never recovered. If you look back through history, just about everybody who ever got serious is now dead. But of course foolishness comes with its own financial drawbacks. It tends to take longer and cost more in the long run, and of course on a percentage basis, fool-arounders die just as much as the dead serious. It just seems like they die more because there's more of them and they leave a bigger mess."

Pellegrino added that the last time he saw someone in town looking serious it turned out to be nothing more than a bad case of hemorrhoids.

Papineau said that he was putting serious thought into appointing a Seriousness Committee to explore ways in which town residents could be brought to understand the gravity of current and future situations. Ω

Plain Hill Road Lab Busted for Controlled Substances

Acting on an anonymous tip, animal control wardens moved in on a Plain Hill Rd. residence last week and took a yellow Labrador retriever into custody on suspected drug charges and operating with an expired license.

The dog, Honeynuts Junior, 2, was reported to have been acting suspiciously.

"We began covert observations after receiving an anonymous phone call which we believe may have originated inside the house where the alleged perpetrator was known to reside," said Sprague animal control warden Timothy Hawks. "From an unmarked van parked across the street, we observed Junior engaging in various activities that had all the earmarks of drug use, among them chewing on a stick and flipping it into the air with unwarranted joy, sticking its nose under oak leaves and snorting an unidentified substance, and urinating in public."

Hawks said that Junior was also observed wagging its tail while panting and staring at nothing. On several occasions it barked nonsensically and without appropriate cause. When a cat of indeterminate breed walked across the yard, Junior wagged its tail from the neck on back.

Honeynuts Junior

Hawks said that Junior's drug dependency may have resulted from a lack of self-esteem brought on by castration at an early age. A companion animal's typical psychological response to being "fixed," Hawks explained, is to develop a strong imagination that engages in fantasies of hallucinogenic realism. Often these fantasies become fetishistic obsessions with rubber bones, tree branches, their own genetalia and even house guests who make the mistake of offering the animal a gesture of courteous affection.

"It was very sad to see how drugs had degraded this poor animal," Hawks said. "It was badly in need of a shave. It had mud on its paws and saliva on its chin and the breath of an Islamic terrorist. We pulled a parasitic, blood-sucking tick off its neck about the size of a teeny-weeny ping-pong ball."

The arresting wardens found a supply of heartworm pills and ear mite cream in the house as well as assorted drug paraphernalia, including matches, rolling papers, a Grateful Dead poster, plastic bags containing an unidentified white powder, a sawed-off shotgun, four hand grenades and an awesome hookah made out of a human skull and three vacuum cleaner hoses. Ω

Local Band Seeks Serious Players

The Baltic Apocalypse Band is looking for a few serious instrumentalists to help provide background music for the end of the world.

"We're primarily looking for qualified kettle drum players," said Stuart Woronecki, 30, band leader and, coincidentally, father of the commanding officer of NATO forces, Annie Woronecki, 4. "We could also use a choir, a harpist, and somebody who can play a big-ass pipe organ."

Woronecki himself will play bugle when the so-called "Judgment Day" comes.

Being a specialty group, the Baltic Apocalypse Band will have no need for trombones, banjos, or accordions.

"Piccolo players need not apply," Woronecki said. "We're thinking that there might be a place for the lowly kazoo not only for a much-needed sense of irony but also as a nod of recognition to the com-

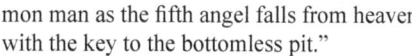

Stuart Woronecki

mon man as the fifth angel falls from heaven with the key to the bottomless pit."

Woronecki explained that while the band members cannot expect to be paid in filthy lucre, they will have the satisfaction of knowing that as the plague of locusts with the power of scorpions torments mankind, fire-breathing horses with the heads of lions issue from the pit of Hell and brimstone spreads across the face of the earth, the band members will be be the last to go.

The band hopes to release a CD of the Judgment Day soundtrack, though Woronecki projects limited sales as few survivors are expected.

"Basically, we have to appeal to the innocent market," Woronecki said. "That's a pretty small niche, but we figure that if we call the CD *Told You So*, everybody will buy a copy. We also plan to offer advance sales, so order now and receive a free VegeMatic. And that's not all! You'll also receive a free set of Gonzo throwing knives. Major credit cads accepted. Real operators are standing by." Ω

Foley to Teach Shoe

Hanover fashionista and Tentware originator Elizabeth Foley will be offering lessons in shoe interpretation at her garage workshop on Potash Hill Rd. She is guardedly optimistic that will some basic training will reduce footwear illiteracy in Sprague.

"It's just incredible how people in this town — and I include just about everybody — think that shoes are something you're supposed to just walk around in, like there's no difference between a pair of dilapidated shitkickers and a pair of Gucci FMPs besides how warm they are, for Christ's sake," Foley spat. "I mean like I can wear Christian Louboutin Privatitas into a room full of men, and all they can think is, boy has she gained weight."

Foley says that Shoe is a language too few in Sprague can speak. Baltic, she says, is a ghetto of footwear illiteracy, Hanover isn't much better, and Versailles, last time she obeyed the speed limit in that village, looked like the kind of place where bowling shoes would be a big step up from the muck of the Dark Ages.

"People need to start looking at each other straight in the foot," Foley says. "Every shoe has its message, be it *Hey, I'm available* or *I'm a pathological tightwad* or *I don't bathe but on weekends*. The trouble is, just about everybody is sending a message with their shoes, but nobody's actually receiving the message. It's as if the whole town were speaking Italian even though nobody could understand it." Stanley "Smoothie" Spidoonski, president of the Sprague Institute of Cool Ones, said his organization is establishing a cash-for-clodhoppers program for any shoes that were bought between the Connecticut River and the Rhode Island border or have been worn more than twice in a blue moon. Ω

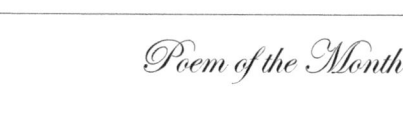

Poem of the Month

There was a young dude from Versailles
who liked to pull cats by their tails.
As their whiskers grew shorter,
he'd call a reporter,

to be continued . . .

Citizenship test, continued from page 1

amendments to the Constitution, the punctuation at the end of the first stanza of the *Star Spangled Banner*, and the middle names of their state senator and representative.

Current citizens who score less than 65 percent will be deported to any country that will accept them. So far, only Afghanistan has volunteered to receive the deported, but it is hoped that Tajikistan, Uzbekistan and other underpopulated 'stans will also agree.

"Personally, I feel that I am about to get screwed," said one Sprague resident who asked to remain anonymous. "I didn't even *know* there were 13 original colonies. I thought it was 13 colors in the rainbow. And I've looked up the capital of Missouri like about 20 times but keep forgetting it, and I just know that even if I remember, they're going to switch it to Oregon or something. And now I've got to learn to speak Stan? Things do not look good for me."

Brunhilda Onus, Town Mother, said that if everyone would just buckle down and study for a few days, at least half of them could be assured of continued citizenship.

"*Foreigners* pass this test," Onus said. "People from some God-forsaken dust hole in the middle of Asia know that Vermont wasn't an original colony. They know the first stanza of the national anthem starts ends with a question mark. They can fold the flag into a triangle. They can load a musket in the snow. They can tie their shoes in the dark. It's not like you have to recite the Gettysburg Address while standing on your head. If you people could stick your noses into a book instead of a TV set for a few minutes, this test would not be a problem."

Dennis Delaney, town historian, questioned the legality of the FTC.

"A citizen's right to personal ignorance is protected under the U.S. Constitution," Delaney said. "Nowhere does it say that you have to know anything to be a citizen of this country."

Resident state trooper Chris Johnson ruled Delaney wrong, stating that the Constitution offered no such protection.

"He's thinking of the pursuit of happiness," Johnson said. "Or is that in the Declaration of Independence? Uh-oh..."

Town First Selectman Stephen J. Papineau denied rumors that ambassadors with blank passports from eight 'stan countries were coming to Sprague to divvy up citizens who do not pass the test. Nonetheless he said that citizens who knew the capital of Kirghistan would have a definitely have an advantage if and when any such 'stan ambassadors show up.

"Frunze," Papineau hinted. "I suggest you remember that or you could end up in Ashkhabad."

"Frunze," the anonymous resident said. "*Frunze. Frunze. Frunze.*" §

Liability Lost as Family Incorporates

Diversification plans include rope production

Sprague's LaLiberte family achieved the American dream last month as the entire family and its members incorporated and in so doing effectively freed themselves of all responsibilities for their actions.

"As individual corporations, we as people cannot be held liable for anything beyond the value of our corporate assets, which through the use of offshore accounts and transfers of funds through closely held subsidiaries we manage to keep to a negligible minimum," stated a Dad, Inc. spokesperson as he urinated on the hub cap of a neighbor's car. "Between a good lawyer, a good accountant, and good old U.S. corporate law, thank God almighty we are free at last."

Dad, Inc. has controlling interest in Mommy, LLC, and together they act as a holding company for a group of subsidiaries, Our Oldest Corp., SisCo, and Little Mr. Poopy-Pants, Inc. Known collectively as The LaLiberte Group, the companies share headquarters at 43 Wall St. in Baltic. Among the group's many holdings is a security services company, Sparky, Inc., and a 501-3C not-for-profit, the Muffin Foundation.

Dave LaLiberte, chairman of Dad, Inc., said that as a Group, the system of companies generated a certain synergy that contributes to the Group's strong showings in goodwill and other intangibles. The wide variety of services offered internally, however, may leave the Group vulnerable to charges of forming a trust.

Little Mr. Poopy Pants, Inc.

MomInc, for example, provides maintenance, transportation and medical services almost exclusively to other companies in the Group, creating the basic structure of a monopoly. And while Dad, the Group's cash cow, generates 99.3 percent of the Group's revenues, market analysts question the long-term investments that have been sunk into OOC, an entity of no apparent managerial direction. LMPP, which operates a small compost production facility, apparently functions as a strategic negative-revenue tax deduction.

SisCo, founded 13 years ago, attracted little interest at its initial public offering earlier this year. Since then, it has been struggling to reinvent itself though internal restructuring and a strong public relations campaign aimed at improving its image and capturing a wider market by diversifying into cosmetics.

In a proactive move to avoid Securities and Exchange Commission investigations, the Group recently divested itself of GrampsCo, Inc., transferring its assets to a healthcare organization that runs a chain of residential warehouses.

"Aside from government interference in what is to us is the epitome of American entrepreneurialism, The LaLiberte Group is not concerned with legal liability," said the Dad spokesperson. "We are borrowing heavily and investing in overseas financial institutions with the express intent of filing for bankruptcy as soon as we have accumulated and sheltered sufficient revenues. This is perfectly legal and there's nothing you can do about it, ha, ha, ha, ha, ha, ha."

State resident trooper Chris Johnson confirmed that even with SEC back-up, he would be unable to prevent the LaLiberte Group from forming a virtual monopoly, manipulating its finances through a global network of offshore bank accounts, deducting the cost of a turkey, stuffing, cranberry sauce, mashed yams and gravy that were consumed during an annual board meeting, and urinating on a neighbor's hub caps.

"You can't arrest a corporation," Johnson said. "The most we can do is give them enough rope and hope they hang themselves."

LaLiberte disagreed.

"Johnson doesn't seem to understand the beauty of the free enterprise system," LaLiberte stated. "If there's a market for rope, we'll make it ourselves. If there's no market, we'll have the government give it to us. There's no reason for the public to get involved or be concerned. The system is perfect and we have it very much under control." Ω

Neighborhood News

What's really happening in Sprague.

April 2001

IRS Flummoxed as Hamster Wins Lotto

Town Rodent Back on Death Row

Chunky, the plucky — and lucky — fugitive Sprague hamster has opened a major can of worms and thrown a monkey wrench into the gears of government after winning $98 million in the Connecticut State Lotto. Federal and state taxation agencies can find no legal access to the rodent's revenues, and local politicos are rapidly rearranging town ordinances to allow the hamster, and her winnings, to stay in town.

Prior to the award, Chunky's request for euthanasia was rejected by the town Board of Selectmen. At the same time, mysterious messages, possibly from the Christian deity, God, have brought investigations by papal nuncios who would like to see the former Sayles classroom hamster burned at a stake, probably a small one.

A thin, clear liquid

But now the hamster is rich, and "that," in the words of Sprague First Selectman Stephen Papineau, "changes everything."

In a thin, clear, liquid, Chunky has written a last will and testament on the linoleum floor of Sprague town hall. It leaves her entire fortune divided equally between the Republican and Democratic town committees.

It also leaves town hall with an odiferous mess it dares not clean up.

"This message is literally, in a manner of speaking, written in gold," Papineau said. "It is a legal document, one which is bound to be a subject of controversy, litigation and appeal. Until the hamster dies, her will remains where it stands."

In an unexpected and unanimous reversal of an earlier decision, the town's Board of Selectmen has decided that it would, indeed, be appropriate for the town to bear the expense of putting the hamster to death. Chunky's original appeal, trickled on a the floor of a Sayles classroom where she was imprisoned in an aquarium for 42 years, was denied by the board.

Chunky subsequently went into hiding and was rumored to have slipped out of town in an

Continued on page 3

Bunched Undies Fell Town Accountant

Sprague's external auditor, Garth Tronstrom, CPA, was rushed to Backus Hospital last week for an emergency unbunching of his jockey shorts, which had become twisted during a meeting with town officials.

"We could tell something was wrong just by the look on his face," said Claude Pellegrino. "At first we thought it was hemorrhoids, but the more we explained our budget, the more he turned blue and assumed an expression of palpable agony."

As Tronstrom's voice rose from tenor to soprano to alto to squeak, the town ambulance was summoned. EMTs determined that Tronstrom was being choked at the groin.

Pellegrino said that the incident occurred before the finance committee finished explaining how a surplus of $48.52 from last year's contingency fund was converted to Turkish lira and invested in derivatives based on sow belly futures for precisely 24 hours on February 29 even though last year wasn't, technically, a leap year. The accounting technique allowed the town to weasel out of a small fortune in 401K contributions.

As the LifeStar helicopter settled onto the roof of town hall, a crowd of townspeople discussed the use of derivatives as a financial risk-management device.

Continued on page 2

Born Artist Born

Police have cordoned off 17 Lucier Heighths as the Arthur P. Dequeault family reported the birth of a born artist, a boy tentatively named Fantabulo pending development of a comprehensive promotional plan.

"We don't know if we have another Michael Angelo in there or what," said resident state trooper Chris Johnson. "If we do, the Dequeault Museum becomes eligible for recognition as a national landmark, and the town of Sprague will need to be placed on a map. Until a determination has been made, no one goes in or out without passing through a metal detector."

Reports from family members associated with the child say that Fantabulo — it has not been decided whether he will use the family name — appears to be of exceptional intelligence and endowed with "a certain flair."

Anita Moore Dequeault, the child's mother, says that she has not been able to find black diapers for the artist but that several black shirts and berets have been donated by local patrons of the arts.

"We have enough post-modern outfits for now," Ms. Dequeault said. "What we need is Gaulois cigarettes and a decent espresso machine. We can't keep going into New York. We were also thinking of getting him a little pink goatee except Art says don't you think that's just a little too gay, and I say, hey, isn't that all right, he's an artist, but Art goes no, no [expletive] pink goatee, so we're still thinking about it."

Just three days into his career, Fantabulo has shown no indication of what artistic medium he will work in. The Dequeaults

Continued on page 2

Featherless Biped Population Way Up

Baltic has been invaded by featherless bipeds! Or so it seems, according to state police.

"They're all over the place," said resident trooper Chris Johnson. "We saw one pushing a lawn mower. Another one walked into the convenience store and bought a gallon of milk. A whole herd of small ones were reported headed in the direction of Sayles School early this morning."

Johnson said that if the small bipeds were actually "kids," as young bipeds are called, it could indicate mating activity in or near Sprague.

Increasing numbers of featherless bipeds have been reported all over Connecticut. Unpredictable in their behavior, the bipeds have caused traffic accidents, started fires, built dams across rivers, killed and eaten livestock, devastated entire fields of corn, mated in stuck elevators, sent rivers of fecal material through veritable sewers under city streets, and migrated south in the middle of the winter only to return well before spring.

Where large numbers of the animals have passed through the woods, wide trails remain. Some are wide enough for two trucks to pass.

Undies, continued from page 1

"I told them sow bellies wasn't a good idea," commented Wilfred Zinavage, a retired noncommissioned officer of the U.S. Navy. "If you've ever seen a sow belly, you know what I mean."

As the LifeStar thudded into the distance, a straw poll found that no one present had ever actually seen a sow belly. As the natives grew restless with concern, Pellegrino explained the mechanics of financial derivatives.

"A sow is an adult female hog, and the belly is that part of the adult female hog that hangs closest to the ground except when she is suckling her young," Pellegrino explained as he chalked a rough illustration on the sidewalk in front of town hall. "These are the young right here, see? The little piggies that went to market and stayed home and had roast beef and all that stuff. Same basic idea. Where was I? Oh yeah, derivatives. The nice thing about sow bellies is that when you buy them, you don't have to actually look at them. In fact, they're really just little sparks of electricity in a big computer down on Wall Street somewhere. What's important to remember is that for a brief moment on a day that didn't exist, Sprague owned 114 pounds of them, and now we have none." Ω

Known for their cleverness, featherless bipeds can open garbage cans, outsmart dogs and cats, stack beer cans in pyramid shapes, walk on their hands, and produce simple public access television programs. Some have even been taught to drive cars.

Johnson said that residents should be on the lookout for featherless bipeds, some of which can be dangerous when cornered or threatened.

"These are the deadliest animals on earth," Johnson warned. "Some of the big ones are estimated to weigh over 300 pounds. Believe me, you wouldn't want to get bit by one."

In Connecticut, there is no hunting season for featherless bipeds, though the feathered species are often raised or hunted for their delectable meat, which is commonly likened to the taste and texture of chicken. Poaching of feathered and featherless species is by no means rare.

While many featherless bipeds have been domesticated, Johnson advised residents to treat all such animals as potentially dangerous.

"Some of them are really very cute, especially when dressed up in clothes," Johnson said. "But if you start petting them, even the friendliest little critter can all of a sudden start litigating. There's not much you can do after that. Calling 9-1-1 isn't going to help. You can

Continued on page 3

Artist, continued from page 1

say they are keeping their options open.

"His eyes are still closed," Mr. Dequeault said. "Let's give him a chance to think about it. All he's had to work with is diapers, though I must say he has already presented us with some amazing initial works. Some of them are truly breath-taking, especially considering the size of the guy."

Fantabulo's early works are currently hung on a clothesline behind the Dequeault Museum.

American Artists Talent Agency has already outlined the basic structure of Fantabulo's life. During a period of structured weirdness in the lower grades at Sayles School he will be ostracized and kept in social isolation. An art teacher with a foreign accent will be brought in to show him the light. He will be thrown out of an ivy league college or university for painting nude students on nude students before passing through a brief period of alcoholism in Paris.

"We've asked to have him blossomed early, possibly in his mid- thirties," Mr. Dequeault said. "We're figuring that three wives in rapid succession will guarantee him good press coverage and the financial backing that he, as an artist of exceptional vision, needs to survive and succeed. Needless to say, a pink goatee isn't going to help, but will anybody listen to me? No, of course not." Ω

Republicans Call for End of Sewers

Sprague Republican Town Committee has called for an end to the use of sewers for disposal of waste.

"It's time we stopped telling people what to do with their own hard-earned excrement," said prominent Republican Ken Genron. "Why can't people make their own choices? This is America, isn't it? It's time we got government off our backs and out of our bathrooms!"

Genron said that taxes could be cut drastically if Sprague shuttered its sewer plant and plugged its pipes.

"Nowhere in the United States Constitution does it give the government authority to take possession of personal body waste. Correct me if I'm wrong, but the last time I checked, the word _flush_ does not appear anywhere in that document. I think it's time we started asking why."

Public opinion was split right up the middle.

"Last time I checked, the Constitution says something about We the _people_," said a toilet user in Baltic. "There's probably a reason it doesn't say We the _troglodytes_."Ω

Trooper Accused of Swearing

A Sayles School fourth-grader has reported a foul language incident involving resident state trooper Chris Johnson. While the exact word has not been specified, Sayles investigators have narrowed the possibilities down to a scant handful.

The incident is said to have occurred last February when the trooper arrived at the scene of a cat stuck in a tree at 340 Main St. in Hanover. Stepping from his cruiser, the trooper allegedly sank his left foot into a puddle of slush, at which time the swearing is suspected to have taken place.

Priscilla Hansen-Hooper, vice president of the fourth grade at Sayles, was nearby, where she had been trying to coax the cat from the middle branches of a sycamore.

"I wasn't sure back then if it was a swear or not, but I had a feeling" Hansen-Hoope said. "I was in the third grade then. Now I'm in the fourth grade, and I know it was for sure. A bad one."

Hansen-Hooper has refused to repeat the word or even indicate what letter it started with. Trooper Johnson is refusing to confirm or deny his participation in the alleged swearing.

Swearing by adults has been legal in Sprague since early last year, but the Connecticut State Troopers Code of Ethics prohibits the use of certain words while on duty.

Town Mother Brunhilda Onus issued a verbal warning to Johnson, stating that she had better not hear about any swear words from then on or there would be real trouble. Ω

Cheney Awarded Nation's First Ph.D. in Sports Trivia

Ian Alan Cheney, a Norwich Free Academy graduate, class of '01, has taken a Ph.D. in Sports from the University of Connecticut. It is the highest academic degree given in that specialty.

Cheney described his studies as rigorous but easy.

"They should of given me this back in the seventh grade," said Dr. Cheney. "My knowledge was complete then. The Ph.D. program was really just a matter of keeping up with the recent scores."

Dr. Ian Alan Cheney

Infinity minus one

Cheney said that the most fascinating aspect of sports is that the scores keep on changing at both the macro and micro levels. The micro level, he said, occurs during a game, when empirically verifiable scores are positively modified from a normal minimum of zero toward a theoretical maximum of infinity minus one.

Bipeds, continued from page 2

figure on having a headache for at least the next three years."

Johnson asked that featherless biped incidents be reported to the state police and recommended that residents monitor their televisions for reports of dangerous biped behavior.

In the town of Scotland, psychologists Gary Greenberg Susan Powers have been observing the behavior of a domesticated kid for over three years. They say their research has been "challenging."

"We had little hands-on experience with kids when we started this project," Greenberg says. "What little we knew came from written materials, though we also had a few anecdotal reports from other researchers. We quickly discovered that what limited documentary information exists is often inaccurate, sometimes utterly useless."

Greenberg said that housebreaking took almost 18 months, and the biped's eating skills are still rudimentary, and its communication is monosyllabic at best. He and Powers expect to try teaching "Joel" a few tricks next year. So far, however, they have made little progress with such basics as fetch, stay, and roll-over-and-play-dead .

"Sometimes you can see it yearning for the wild and the woods," Powers said. "It'll scream and howl and tear around the house looking for a way out. It breaks your heart, and there's some days when we wish we could just open the door and let it go."Ω

At the macro level, he continued, the scores of one year are different from the scores of the previous year, decade, century, or millennium. At the macro level, he said, scores tend to fall within ranges that vary from sport to sport within the parameters of standard probability deviation that are determinable by algorithmic estimation.

Cheney's dissertation explored parallels between runs-batted-in prior to the Eisenhower administration and concurrent incidence of dental cavities among infielders.

"Some of baseball's most strategic hitters were playing under the influence of Novocain," Cheney said. "We have solid evidence that outfielders brushed their teeth less often basemen did. The proof is evident in their batting averages."

Dodger molars

Cheney was part of a archeological team that exhumed the remains of all deceased Brooklyn Dodgers to examine their teeth.

"I have touched the molars of Pee Wee Reese," Cheney said. "I have held Sandy Koufax's fillings in my hand. Just thinking about it

Izbicki Banks on Possum Saucers

New London Day delivery person Robin Izbicki, 28, has found a surprising new source of income. During her daily pre-dawn tour of the town, she has noticed a seemingly unending supply of flattened possums. After months of head-scratching, she perceived a market niche she could fill.

"I just knew there had to be something I could do to recycle those poor marsupials," Izbicki said, explaining the birth of her brainstorm. "It seemed a shame to waste them."

Early one morning, halfway down Pearl Street, it came to her: the stiff, flat remains, cut to disks, might fly with the best of Frisbees. She took one home, trimmed it neatly, added a secret ingredient, and removed the wrinkles with an ordinary clothes iron. She then took her "possum saucer" to the backyard and gave it a flip. To her surprise and delight, it soared to tree-top level, swooped over the Shetucket, and skipped halfway to Occum.

"I knew I had something," Izbicki said, and she promptly filed her invention with the U.S. Patent Office.

Izbicki's biggest concern now is that someone might steal her idea. Until her patent has been issued, she's gathering raw materials and building up an inventory. She will accept orders now but cannot ship the product pending patent approval. Ω

gives me goosenipples on my pimples...I mean goosepimples on my nipples. Look."

Cheney will be taking the Dodger teeth on a speaking tour across the nation. His objective goes beyond dentistry. He wants to advocate the teaching of sports trivia in public schools.

"Those who don't know sports history are doomed to repeat it," he says. "Think of the implications of having batting, passing and assist records broken every year in the future as they have been in the past. Sooner or later we are going to reach the maximum capacity of human beings. What will sports fans look forward to? What will sports announcers talk about? Will every statistic have to include the word *since*? Who wants to hear about *the most steals to third base by left-handed pinch-hitters of below-average intelligence with more than 18 RBIs in the first ten games of the National League since so-and-so did the same damn thing last year?* Nobody. Thirty million sports-oriented couch potatoes could go into existential crisis. Do you know what that could do to the beer and potato chip industries? I hate to even

Continued on page 4

Hamster, continued from page 1

ad hoc, ex tempore, tutti incogniti out-of-the-blue mid-week parade.

In a parallel turn of events, the papal nuncios who arrived in Sprague to investigate the possibility of a miracle have announced that perhaps it would be best if Chunky were allowed to live. Earlier this year, a mysterious message written in the dust of the elusive Lone UPS Truck called for Chunky's demise, which, if rendered by the Church, would transfer her fortune — relatively small at the time — to the Vatican.

"Quicunque"

A death rendered by a secular government, however, would validate a last will and testament.

"*Mors tua, vita mea, nascentes morimur, et finisque ab origine pendet,*" stated one nuncio at a town hall press conference."*Naturam expelles furca tamen usque recurret.*"

"*Quicunque,*" Papineau retorted. "Nobody washes this floor till the hamster's will is done." Ω

Acronyms Break Up Holly Jolly Bazaar

Baltic's Best Knitters Busted

Agents from the WTO, FBI, CIA, FDA, IRS, INTERPOL, and the State Department of Revenues swooped in on the Holly Jolly Bazaar last month just as the Baltic Fire Department Women's Auxiliary opened the doors on their annual sales event. Customers scattered as the acronymic agents knocked over tables, seized handicrafts and handcuffed organizers.

"We acted on reliable information that hand-made items were being sold over the counter while imported and manufactured goods were excluded," said Darth Schwartzmeister, WTO special agent. "WTO agreements specifically prohibit all such acts of protectionism."

Schwartzmeister said that the unrealistically low prices on a stack of crocheted potholders indicated probable dumping at lower than cost.

Suspicious brownies

As the WTO was the first organization through the door, it won the right of first arrest. Marie Bona and Faith LaCharite were taken to Geneva, where they would be held until their trial.

The FBI seized a dish of suspicious brownies. An agent said that the bureau had received reports of a controlled substance in the brownies.

"It could have been anything," the agent said. "Coke. Hash. Marijuana. Opium. We had no idea what, so we thought it prudent to seize the goods and arrest the alleged suspects. As soon as the WTO is done with them, we get our turn to give them a fair trial."

CIA agents arrived too late for an arrest but brought evidence that Bona and LaCharite may be linked to international terrorist organizations, including the Red Cross, which was bombed repeatedly in Afghanistan, the Catholic Church, which has been known to shelter foreign peasants, and the United States Air Force, which is suspected of carrying out bombings in several non-WTO nations.

The Internal Revenue Service and State Department of Revenues had warrants for the arrest of both members of the Women's Auxiliary on charges of failure to collect sales taxes and report unauthorized income.

Bastards

INTERPOL brought charges of dealing in suspicious white powders. Boxes of Christmas cookies were covered with a substance that could have been, in an INTERPOL agent's words, "anything from heroin to anthrax to baby powder laced with radioactive lye, the bastards."

The Bureau of Alcohol, Tobacco and Firearms seized bottles that had been wrapped with red, white and blue yarn and stopped with decorative corks. Stating that the bureau had not been deceived for even a moment, an agent noted that the bottles could easily have been used to transport illegal distilled spirits or even gasoline.

"It was the patriotic colors that attracted our attention. These bottles were clearly designed for use as Mozeltov cocktails," the agent said. "All they needed was a combustible fuel and a match. We're lucky we got here in time."

Robert Tardiff, BFD fire chief, said he was shocked that suspected terrorists had infiltrated the local fire department.

"This just goes to show you," Tardiff said. "You can never be too vigilant. Terrorists may be those who you least suspect." Ω

Sports Ph.D., continued from page 3

think about it."
Where Frunze is
Cheney's tour is being sponsored by the American Snack Food Institute. He will present local school boards with statistical evidence that Spanish classes have zero impact on local economies, that no one has used geometry outside a classroom since 320 B.C., and that penmanship could be taught much more efficiently by computer.

By dropping obsolete subjects and orienting others to sports, Cheney says, schools can make lessons more interesting and relevant. Geography, for example, could be restricted to cities such as New York, Atlanta, Boston and Oakland. Places without decent teams could simply be removed from the map, greatly simplifying matters for everyone.

"Do we really need to know where Frunze is?" Cheney asks, referring to the capital of an Asian nation no one has ever heard of. "What do they have there? Fly-swatting teams? Does it really matter who plays center for the Frunze Frogtongues? Let's get real. A ball's a ball, a strike's a strike, Frunze's about as important as the butt-end of Uranus, and that's all you need to know." Ω

Another Versailles Found in France!

"Not fair," say local residents

Sayles School fourth-grader Priscilla Hansen-Hooper says her teeth almost fell out when her jaw hit the floor as she moved her magnifying glass over a map of France and discovered a town called Versailles — the same name as the village where she lives in southern Sprague.

"I couldn't believe it," Hansen-Hooper said. "Not only did they steal our name, but they put it right on the map where everybody could see. Have the French no sense of shame?"

Versailles residents generally agreed that something smells Vichy in France.

Versailles Town Hall

"It isn't fair that they just take our name after all we've done to make this part of town so nice" said Cheryl Mish, of Church St. in Versailles. "The magnificense that is the Stone House Café, the bulletin board at the post office, the nice, new yellow line down Hanover-Versailles Road, that burnt-down house on River road that we're going to get rid of pretty soon...we've put a lot of spiff into this place."

Town Historian Dennis Delaney says that the village's name derives from the old Vers Woolen Mill that once stood beside the Little River. It became the Vers-Sayles Mill when the Sayles family bought it. Then somebody misspelled it, and the rest, he says, is history.

How France got hold of the name is still a mystery.

"It's very unlikely that they had a Vers Mill that was bought by the Sayles family," Delaney says. "More likely Alexis de Tocqueville came through town, liked the place and took the name home to some backwater Podunk that couldn't think of anything better. I hate to think how they must pronounce it. I just hope the place is worthy of the name." Ω

Neighborhood News

May - 2001

Sayles Opening Doors to Grown-ups
Adults get a chance to "do it all over again."

In response to popular demand, Sayles School is now accepting grown-up enrollment for all classes, from kindergarten through eighth grade, starting in the fall.

"After hearing so many people say, 'I wish I could do it all over again...but knowing what I know now,' we decided to let Sprague taxpayers have their wish," said Michael Bychowsky, school board chairman. "Town residents of all ages can enter any grade they qualify for. We're putting the *public* in *public schools*, and for the first time in American history, taxpayers can really get what they pay for."

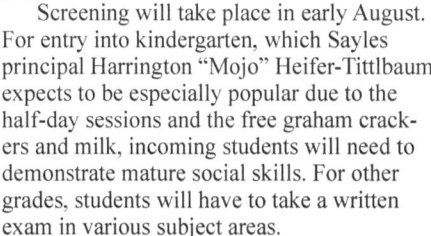

Screening will take place in early August. For entry into kindergarten, which Sayles principal Harrington "Mojo" Heifer-Tittlbaum expects to be especially popular due to the half-day sessions and the free graham crackers and milk, incoming students will need to demonstrate mature social skills. For other grades, students will have to take a written exam in various subject areas.

Heifer-Tittlbaum warns that upper-grade students will need to prove that they can add fractions of unequal denominators, remember key dates in European history, pass the state physical education test, and say at least *it* in Spanish.

"Let me give you a hint," Tittlbaum said. "*1492* is *not* one of the answers on the history test. Neither is *1776*, and neither is *0*. Ha, ha, ha, ha, ha, good luck."

Tittlbaum also said that *taco* does not mean *it* in Spanish, and that the state physical exam includes the ability to do 20 squat-thrusts on a full stomach.

B.Y.O.B.

Kindergartners taller than five feet are advised to bring their own blankies. To accommodate returning students, the school's lawn tractor will be fitted with a winch for lifting those who are unable to get up off the floor after naptime.

Local residents are very excited about the new program.

"I am definitely going to do it," said Thomas McAvoy, a town selectman. "I'm going to start at kindergarten and do it right. I'm going to follow instructions. I'm going to apply myself to my penmanship. I'm going to play clarinet in the orchestra and I'm going to stick with it. Instead of going into banking, I'm going to start my own salsa band because life is too short for banking. Also, I'm going to start dating as soon as I get into the first grade."

Fr. Emile Tito, St. Mary's parish priest, has shorter-term plans.

"I'm going straight into the third grade," he said. "Just one semester. My goals are to:

Continued on page 2

Citizens Miffed as Elephants Fail to Show

A town hearing on the fate of Chunky the Hamster and her $98 million Lotto winnings was adjourned early as citizens grew boisterous when a promised troupe of elephants failed to show up.

The elephants were hired by town hall to encourage more public participation in the democratic process.

"Under the town meeting form of democracy, local residents constitute the legislative body of our government," said first selectman Stephen J. Papineau. "It just doesn't work if nobody shows up at town meetings. So we thought that maybe half a dozen rented elephants would get people to turn off their TVs and come do the yay-or-nay thing."

The widely announced meeting was to feature the elephant sextet of the Galloping Wazoo Brothers. The package deal was to include fire-breathing sword-swallowers who juggle beavers to live calliope music. Unfortunately, the group never showed up, and the townspeople quickly lost interest in democracy.

"From what we heard, the Wazoo Brothers got mugged in Bridgeport and were unable to arrive here in time for the hearing," Papineau said. "It makes sense, when you think about it. Mugging fire-breathing, beaver-juggling sword-swallowers on elephant-back is undoubtedly a delicate, complex and time-consuming task. But so is democracy."

Papineau said that the Board of Selectmen is looking into the possibility of maintaining a full-time troupe of elephants with

Continued on page 3

Justification Required by May 15

Sprague town clerk Claire Glaude has notified town residents that they must register justification for their existence by May 15 or face stiff fines and possible vaporization.

"It's not as difficult as some people seem to think," Glaude said. "We just need a simple statement of 25 words or less about why you think you are entitled to standing room on this planet and a lifetime supply of oxygen."

Glaude said that something as simple as "I help sew the annual raffle quilt at the Senior Center" will suffice. She has even accepted "I need to mow the lawn."

Among last year's justifications that were deemed inadequate are "I can't miss *Days of Our Lives*" and "I have a cat."

"I really hope we don't have to vaporize anyone this year," Glaude said. "It's a burden on taxpayers and leaves a bad smell behind, so we try to give everyone the benefit of the doubt. I'm not saying that we'll take a shopping list as a *raison d'etre,* but we'll have a look at it. If it includes 'warm socks for orphans' or something, probation may be possible."

Virgil Profundo, owner of Mottos 'n' More, says that bumper stickers alone do not serve as justification for anyone's existence, but they can help.

"If you're really, really borderline, a 12-inch *Honk If You Love Jesus* can make the difference between going about your normal life and having your toasted residue shot into space," Profundo said. "I suggest that everyone come in and look around and see if there's something they can stand up for."

Percival Tørdslörp, chairman of the local chapter of the Septic Tank Pumper-Outers Defense League, reminded residents that there are fewer than 170 shopping days before Septic Tank Awareness Month. Ω

Pets Offer Aphorisms and Advice

Psychic channels wisdom from the lower forms of life.

Sprague Committee on Supernatural Events has published a compendium of wise words gleaned from the thoughts of local pets.

A Guide to Life from the Furred and Feathered was interpreted and edited by Cassandra Cogumelo, chair of the SCSE subcommittee on psychic monitoring.

"They know more than we think they know," Cogumelo says. "They communicate with each other all the time, giving each other advice, teaching the young to do their jobs. Why else do you think puppies grow up to behave like dogs rather than parakeets? Obviously someone has given them a little counsel."

Many of the lessons, Cogumelo says, apply to humans as much to any given species. *When barking at a stranger, don't wag your tail,* for example, can apply to a toy poodle as well as to a state trooper and a school principal. *If your master did half the things you do, he'd be in jail for a long, long time* has general applicability to men and dogs of all breeds. *Shut up and sing* is good advice to a fellow canary and to

Chunky

the host of many a public access TV program.

The book does not include the counsel of reptiles because, as Cogumelo explains, "Who wants to take advice from someone whose belly drags on the ground?"

"Reptiles have obviously made a mess of their own lives, and that's why they're reptiles," she says. "Just looking at a reptile should be all the advice you need."

Cats have provided some of the pithier, realpolitik dicta, such as, *If it moves without permission, kill it...slowly* and *Woe unto she who tinkles behind a couch during a sleet storm, for heavily shall the icicles hang upon her.*

An anonymous dairy ruminant is responsible for the subtly intriguing *Stick to your cud.* A horse named Spent Bullet, however, says, *Don't listen to cows.*

Chunky, the Sprague hamster who gained international renown after escaping from a Sayles School aquarium and pleading for euthanasia, has offered several tidbits of dark counsel. *The more they love you, the longer they lock you up* apparently reflects on Chunky's 46 years spent in classroom confinement. *Playing dead will get your farther than looking alive* sounds like morbidity crossed with boredom. *Wet the hand that feeds you* reveals a possible attitude problem.

"Animals know what they're talking about," Cogulemo says. "This is obvious from their track record. When do you ever see an animal screw up? You never see a dog lay an egg, you never see a cat trip, and it's a cold day in July when you hear an iguana go *moo.* That damned hamster's about the only animal that can't get her act together. I say we back a dump truck over her and end her problems." §

Public Schools, from page 1

a) at least once, tip over backwards in my chair on purpose, b) at least once, ask to go to the bathroom even if I don't have to, and c) ask a certain young lady if I can hold hands with her on the bus. Then I'm going back to being a priest. We were in love but too young to know it. "

Bychowsky said that the board is still trying to resolve a possible conflict of interest involving third-grade teacher Edna Guertin, who plans to enroll as a third-grade student in her own class.

"I don't think that's half as schizoid as some people seem to think," Guertin said. "I'm going to be a model student, and I'm going to have myself sit at the head of the class. I'm going to write thank you notes to my teacher. I'm going to get straight A's, and I'm going to know how to spell diarrhea in the spelling bee. And if Fr. Tito tries to hold my hand on the bus, I'm kicking his ass out the exit door so fast his head'll spin." §

Bulgarino Perfects the Triple-Shift

Elbow grease wins him spot in Blue Collar Hall of Fame

A Sprague resident, Howard Bulgarino Sr., 34, has perfected the hebdomadal triple-shift — three eight-hours shifts every day for seven days straight. His accomplishment, sought by workers since the invention of the time card in ancient Egypt, has earned him a

Howard Bulgarino, Sr.

place in the Blue Collar Hall of Fame.

"Um," Bulgarino said at an afternoon breakfast held in his honor in the company cafeteria at American Bell & Whistle, where he is an assembly line product component cart pusher-arounder. "Um...um..."

Bulgarino manages his round-the-clock duty by sleeping while working. Though that skill was perfected by labor innovators during the economic boom of the Reagan administration, workers inevitably awakened and went home. Bulgarino can been able to regain consciousness only long enough to punch his timecard out and back in again.

Other workers at American have calculated that their nonstop colleague will be earnings double-triple-time-and-a-half-squared if he manages to work 168 hours in a week that

Continued on page 3

Sisters Looking for Leper Look-alikes

The Holy Sisters of Occumite are looking for area volunteers to pose as lepers during two weeks this summer. All expenses will be paid for a trip to the sisters' leper colony at Jacareacangatuba, a village on the upper Xingu River, a tributary of the Amazon.

"We have a serious problem in Jacareacangatuba," said Sister "Big" Maria, Occumite mother superior. "We are down to our last leper and we have the Pope coming to visit in July. If we can't show him some lepers, our bottoms are grass."

Sister Maria said that the colony had lost all but one of its lepers late last year when they grew bored with life in Jacareacangatuba and

decided to relocate to a colony operated by Club Med in the Bahamas.

Without lepers, the Occumite colony faces a cut in Vatican funding.

"This is an excellent chance for some lucky Catholic to get kissed by the Pope," Sister Maria announced ruing a mass at St. Mary's church. "If you think the Holy Father's coming to Occum or Sprague to kiss somebody, forget it. But anyone who can come down to Brazil for a couple of weeks and lie in a hammock and look reasonably sick stands a pretty good chance of getting blessed by the best."

Try-outs for the International Leper Look-alike Team will be held at the Occumite convent in Occum early next month. §

Loitering Penguin Baffles Local Authorities

Papineau: *Why does it just keep standing there?*

Local authorities admit they are clueless as to why an emperor penguin has been standing on the corner of Main and West Main streets in downtown Baltic. The curious bird, known locally as "the penguin," has been there, motionless, for almost a month.

"We have no idea where this penguin came from or why it's here or even whether a penguin needs to have a reason to be anywhere in the first place," said Stephen J. Papineau, first selectman. "We have notified the proper authorities. It's up to them to decide what to do about it."

Until the town receives an official response from the Connecticut Department of Inexplicable Phenomena, state police have been monitoring the penguin's movements, which so far have been nil.

Corrie Protubero III, a total braniac at St. Joseph's Elementary School and the closest thing Sprague has to an ornithologist, says the penguin probably came from Antarctica and that it may be hatching an egg.

Too bad for Daddy

"It's the male of the emperor species that hatches eggs which have been laid by the females," Protubero said. "He holds the egg between his feet and keeps it warm under his butt while the mother spends the next two months sliding around on her belly on an iceberg. If she happens to lay the egg on the corner of Main and West Main, then that's where Daddy has to stand. If it happens to be in the middle of the summer, well that's just too bad for Daddy."

Protubero has suggested that someone lift the groin feathers of the penguin to see if it is a male or female. As no volunteers have come forward, the task has been turned over to Sprague animal control warden Timothy Hawks, who has expressed reluctance to stick his nose where, in his opinion, it does not belong.

"Nooooo, sir," Hawks said. "There's nothing in my job description that requires me to peek under the groin feathers of a penguin. My job is to make sure it doesn't bite anybody, doesn't have rabies, and doesn't lie there dead in such a way as to threaten the public health. So far, the penguin is obeying the rules."

State resident trooper Chris Johnson says he has perused local ordinances, Connecticut state statutes, and the Constitution of the United States and found nothing prohibiting penguin loitering.

"It's a public sidewalk, penguins don't require a license, and my personal rule of thumb is not to arrest anyone in a feathered tuxedo because the one and only time I ever did so, it turned out to be a very big mistake," Johnson said. "Furthermore, one thing they never taught us at the Police Academy was how to handcuff a penguin, and I know that if I try, I will come off looking like an absolute idiot. It'll be worse than the time I busted Liberace."

Papineau says the motionless bird is an eerie sight that has begun to bother residents.

"Why does it just keep standing there?" he said, his voice cracking with emotional stress. "Why doesn't it run out in the road and get hit by a car? I'm giving it two months, and if it's still there, I'm going to go out there and hit it with a broom." §

Triple-shift, continued from page 2

begins on Christmas and ends on New Year's Day if both fall on Sundays and he decides to work during a vacation he had scheduled for that week.

"He could walk into Walmart and buy anything he wanted," said Joan Szinfrit, a whistle volume control knob flange support bracket screwer-downer at American. "He could buy every 42-inch Widget Ltd Edition in the place, which I, personally, think is pretty goddam funny."

Locally famous for the House of Ads where he lives with his wife, Consumadora, and son, Howard Jr., Bulgarino is a graduate of Occum Technical College, where he majored in grunt work.

Industrial specialists from across the country are visiting the American production facility to learn more about Bulgarino's landmark achievement. His use of a feedbag has been of special interest. Ophthalmologists are studying his eyeballs, which have developed the consistency of concrete. Colombia is considering using the image of his eyeballs and his assembly parts cart to replace that of Juan Valdez and his donkey.

"Mr. Bulgarino doesn't seem to know it yet — we're not sure whether he's even awake — but he is the worker of the future," said Dr. Seymour Dewmore, an industrial psycho-historian. "For America to stay competitive, workers must constantly increase their output. Working around the clock is obviously where the American worker is going, and Howard Bulgarino Sr. has arrived there first." §

Family Mortified as Anthrax Strikes

The Vandaloso family has gone into hiding as Vincent Vandaloso, 34, was reported to have contracted nasal anthrax. Though considered only a mild threat to health, the nasal form of anthrax often has a humilliatory effect because the only known means of contracting the disease is digital insertion.

"That's what he gets for picking his nose all the time," said Betty Vandaloso, his wife and mother of their three ill-kempt children. "He does it in the car because he thinks nobody's watching, but you should see some of the phone calls I get. Complete descriptions. Like I need that, right?"

Vincent Vandaloso

A spokesperson for the Center for Disease Control confirmed that fingers are the most effective vectors for nasal anthrax.

"Contrary to what most people think, it's the pinky that delivers the anthrax spore most deeply into the nostril," the spokesperson said. "If the insertion reaches the second knuckle, it's party time for the anthrax family."

The CDC spokesperson declined to comment on how the spore might have gotten onto one of Vandaloso's fingers except to say that, "It's too disgusting to talk about. Suffice it to say that we are taking samples from the nasal passages of all persons who have been in contact with the patient, including the entire mem-

Elephants, continued from page 1

local volunteer fire-breathing sword-swallowing jugglers to encourage more participation in local government.

"We have a lot of important issues coming up," Papineau said. "People need to pay attention and get involved." §

bership of Uncles for Education."

Vandaloso has been transferred to a re-education camp in Occum where he will be trained in hanky skills and vehicular etiquette. §

Rod & Gun Club Charters B-52
Area Deer Given Ultimatum

Sprague Rod & Gun club is looking for passengers for a chartered bombing run in a B-52. The club plans a high-altitude carpet bombing of the area between Baltic Reservoir and club headquarters on Bushnell Hollow Road.

"We hope to make this the most successful hunting season we've ever had," said Gunter Pleisto, club president.

In an effort to minimize costs and collateral damage, the club has issued an ultimatum to local deer. To avoid "terminal consequences," deer are being encouraged to surrender before the start of hunting season on the fifteenth of Septic Tank Awareness month.

Signs have been posted throughout the target area, advising deer and their sympathizers to "surrender now and join the greatest rod and gun club in the western world as we know it today." Deer with the courage to change their ways are instructed to approach the Rod & Gun Club target range backwards with their tails raised.

The club has invited Annie M. Woronecki, 4, supreme commander of NATO forces, to be honorary bombardier. Father Emile Tito will perform the Blessing of the B-52 before take-off. Munitions for the run will be provided by several anonymous television networks. §

Republicans: We are not troglodytes!

In a brief written statement, Sprague Republican Town Committee has denied accusations that they are all troglodytes.

"We are not, nor have we ever been, troglodytes," the statement stated. "Our recent call for an end to public sewerage was not meant as a step onto the slippery slope back to the days of cave-dwelling, when taxes were low and life was short and sweet. Still, why not?"§

Infinity Run Down on Rt. 97

Infinity manifest in the guise of an opossum was apparently struck and killed on Route 97 last month and would not have been noticed were it not for the rapid response of the Hanover Philosophical Society.

"The irony of the incident has not escaped us," said Robert Meya, HPS president. "Mankind has been seeking a manifest definition of infinity since the concept was first propounded by the pre-Socratics. Preliminary evidence indicates that the flattened tuft of this unnamed opossum may have once been infinitely what it was, an inexplicable totality, lacking nothing and summing any conceivable count. It was infinity caught in the wrong place at the wrong time."

Animal control warden Timothy J. Hawks stated that he was finitely distressed over the loss of what to him appeared to be a male possum of less than average intelligence that had been headed in a westerly direction across the state highway just north of Salt Rock Road. Arriving several hours after the issue had ceased to be an animal control issue, he turned the matter over to the town maintenance department. They scraped it up with a shovel, transported it to Lord's Bridge, and flipped it into the Shetucket River, where it began an inexorable march to the sea.

"It floated," saidMark Benson, chief of the department. "But not far. I'd say about 20 feet — not as far as you'd expect expired infinity to go, but what do I know?"

Meya said that the society had not yet determined whether deceased infinity should float. The society's subcommittee on infinite matters was still grappling with the concept of infinity getting run down by a motor vehicle.

Robert K. Meya

"The odds of the vector of an infinite opossum crossing a specific coordinate at a given moment in the incomprehensible vastness or eternity are pretty slim," Meya said. "Had it not been an opossum, things might have turned out differently. A Swedish girl in a bikini, for example, might have caused the finite vehicle to alter its velocity."

Meya said the society was searching for a Swedish girl in a bikini so that his hypothesis might be tested under controlled conditions. §

Underground Aristocratic Activity Reported

Snipers from the Egalitarian Defense Initiative have reported suspected aristocratic guerrilla activity in the Hanover section of Sprague. According to unsubstantiated rumor, the underground hoity-toities may be trying to clone a duke.

"We must be on the guard against those who would have us believe that some people are better than others," said EDI spokesperson Joseph Sixpak. "Nobody rises from the muck until everybody rises from the muck."

Until recently, the EDI has been able to control spontaneous upityness through an active campaign of personalized mudslinging, vicious innuendo and high precision "smart" gossip that identifies a target and puts it in its place.

Despite the EDI's vigilance, however, secret cells of aristocracy advocates are reported to have been meeting after dark to drink imported wines, listen to Russian music, and eat dinner long after decent people have gone to bed.

Sixpak says that EDI guards have been randomly inspecting fingernails, listening for funny accents, and looking out for lawn ornaments of exceptional taste. Certain unnamed residents, such as the entire board of directors of Sprague Public Library, have been under almost constant surveillance.

Perdita Postino, postmaster of the Hanover post office, said that a package marked "Fragile: Duke Zygote" arrived with British postage stamps but disappeared from the loading dock before it could be delivered. §

Coming soon . . .

Evil Republicans

Bank confessions

Bible Extension

Homeless Leftovers

Unprecedented Pretzel Problems

Neighborhood News

What's really happening in Sprague.

June - 2001

Glenn Cheney, Editor

Sprague to Add New Chapter to Bible

The Sprague Committee on Supernatural Events has set itself to writing a new chapter for an old testament, *the* Old Testament, which the committee says should not be seen as an old document about paranoid dead people with bent noses.

"Who says that God's work on Earth is done?" said Brujilla LaStrega, SCSE chair-witch. "We say the jury's still out on that question, and until it's back with a verdict, we think we should pitch in to keep the Bible up to date."

LaStrega says it was hard to know what to include in the chapter that will follow Malachi, currently the last chapter of the Bible. Some members of the committee say that if the earlier chapters are a model, then begettings and deaths and local ordinances should be included.

The committee intends to record suspected miracles such as the appearances of the Lone UPS Truck, the mysterious messages of the hamster known as Chunky, and the annual budgets of the Board of Finance. Scholars of the future will have to decide whether the phenomena were the handiwork of God or the hallucinations of people who watched too much TV.

"This definitely puts Sprague on the maps of future archeologists," LaStrega said. "They're going to want to dig us up to find out exactly what happened here. What earlier chapters were to the Hittites, Edomites and Cherethites, our chapter will be to the Hanoverians, Versaillites and Balticians. Baltic Reservoir is our Dead Sea, the Baltic Mill our pyramids, the Hanover post office our Taj Mahal."

First Selectman Stephen J. Papineau supports the project, saying it means a multimillennial boom to local tourism.

"The casinos are *nothing* compared to this," Papineau says. "Ten thousand years from

Continued on page 3

Town Mum Calls for Mandatory Naptimes

Citizens advised to keep blankies handy.

Town Mother Brunhilda Onus has given all Sprague residents official notice that she will soon be declaring naptimes at random moments during the day. Upon public announcement that naptime has arrived, all residents will be required to stop what they're doing, unroll their personal blankets, and lie quietly until naptime is over.

"I don't suppose anyone else around here has noticed that sometimes people start to get a little cranky," Onus said at town hearing on the issue. "As any mother or kindergarten teacher can tell you, there comes a time when people need to settle down and take a little nap.

As a professional public mother, I know when those times come, and it is incumbent upon me to declare a public naptime."

Onus said that she would use the loudspeaker system on her surveillance blimp to advise everyone in town, including visitors from other places, that they have till the count of three to lay out their blankets and assume a supine position until further

Brunhilda Onus

notice. She advised everyone to carry a personal "blankie" with them at all times.

Comments at the hearing generally supported Onus's proposal.

"I wouldn't mind a little siesta now and then," said Thomas Girard, a member of the town maintenance crew. "It just has to be even. As long as everybody's taking a nap at the same time, I got no problem with it."

Onus said she would guarantee that there were no exceptions. From her blimp, she will be able to observe the entire town.

"Don't worry," Onus said. "I'm trained to see movement."

One unidentified resident asked what would happen if naptime came during "a blizzard or something." Onus said that anyone caught outdoors at naptime during inclement weather would be allowed to enter the nearest house and lie down on the living-groom floor. She added that she did not want to hear "a peep out of anyone" regarding who happened to be snoozing on their floor.

Onus said she was also working on plans for daily half-hour recess periods when everyone would be allowed to run around, scream, tickle each other, jump rope, roll on the ground, play kickball, and share newly discovered information about s-e-x. ✳

Evil Republicans Name Spin Doctor

The Sprague Republican Town Committee has named Garth W. Butch spin doctor of the party's subcommittee on evildoing. Butch is looking forward to the challenge of helping voters see the rosier side of "[truly evil] Republicans."

"It's time we looked beyond the conservative neckties, the golf scores, the cleft chins and oily stains of America's corporate toadies," Butch said at a press conference on his plans for converting the image that many Americans have of local and national Republican figures such as President George W. Bush. "We have to stop seeing these elected patriots as closet fascists

Garth W. Butch

who would sell their country up the river if some sleazy association of corporate child molesters offered them enough in the way of soft money. And I don't mean just the oil companies, the defense industry, the banks and the Enrons of the world. We must embrace all who have so dug so deep to contribute so much grease to the big wheels of American democracy."

Butch said that the image of Republicans as "shady" is a perfect example of misinterpretation by the American public. Republicans, he said, are demonstrably opposed to shade, especially the kind of shade so commonly harbored by America's overabundance of broadleaf trees.

"Over 89 percent of American shade is under trees," Butch said, holding up a graphic of an obese man sleeping in a ham-

Continued on page 2

Devil to Contest Traffic Ticket

"Not just a case of death looking for a place to park."

Resident state trooper Chris Johnson says he knew he'd rue the day he wrote a parking ticket for The Devil, Inc., who left his car facing the wrong way at the curb in front of Fred's News as he dashed in for take-out coffee.

Now The Devil wants his day in court.

"The trial doesn't bother me," Johnson said. "It's my word against his. What bothers me is the paperwork."

It may indeed be the paperwork that spells doom for the trooper, not to mention the word of witnesses. Citing errors in docu-

Belzeebub

mentation and the conflicting testimony of a passenger in the car, The Devil says the trooper cannot

make his case stand up in court.

"First of all, it's Beelzebub, not Belzeeblub," stated The Devil, prince of darkness. "Moreover, my last name is Satan, not Satin. And the Inc. doesn't stand for Incorporated. It stands for Incarnate. And I was not driving a black Plymouth Pariah. The actual color is midnight satin. That's satin, not satan, right? And what makes him so sure I was in the driver's seat? I mean, like, *damn*, can't this guy get anything straight?"

Johnson said that not only can he get it straight but he can make it stand up in court. Among his witnesses is Diane Hastings, part owner and maitre d' of Fred's News.

"It was The Devil all right," Hastings said. "The horns, the tail, the goatee, the whole schmear. He ordered two medium sweet-and-lights to go and got all bent out of shape because we don't take credit cards. And his car was definitely parked facing the wrong way."

The Devil says his primary witness will be his passenger at the time of the incident,

"The" Grim Reaper. Trooper Johnson, however, said that he has reason to doubt Reaper's word and that he doesn't believe this was just a case of "death looking for a place to park."

"First of all," Johnson said, "how do we know it was *the* Grim Reaper and not somebody else with bony fingers, no face, and proto-goth garb? To be perfectly honest, I didn't peek under his hood, but what was I supposed to do, ask him for ID? Second of all, he wasn't wearing a seatbelt, which I let him get away with because I'm a nice guy and because he's already dead. Third of all, there was a scythe on the back seat, but that doesn't prove anything. His breath was deadly enough, but I get that all the time around here."

State Circuit Court Judge Francis X. Foley, who will preside over the trial, said that even though it's sure to be interesting, he isn't looking forward to it.

"I already know this is going to be a messy one," Foley said. "The last time we tried to swear in this particular defendant, the Bible burst into flames as soon as he put his hand on it, and we had to evacuate the building. And if Reaper thinks he's coming into my court with

Francis X. Foley

that scythe, he's got another thing coming. Ditto if he tries to take the stand in sunglasses. Jury selection is going to be pure hell because where are we going to find nine people who have no association with the defendant? Meanwhile every lawyer in town wants to play The Devil's advocate. I already know that it's going to be one of those days when American jurisprudence takes it on the chin."

Foley also said that there could be jurisdictional problems because, in his words, "nobody knows where the hell Hell is" and what, if any, extradition rules apply. ✳

Republicans, continued from page 1

mock between a pair of sugar maples. "So before you go criticizing evil Republicans for selling our great country's national forests cheap to timber companies, I suggest you go lay your hand on the motor of a chain saw. You'll find that it's warm, like a puppy or the forehead of a child with a fever whose parents can't afford a doctor because they're too stupid and lazy to hold a job in a company that offers a decent insurance plan."

Butch said that his biggest challenge will be to persuade voters that evil isn't necessarily bad and that the best evil is evil that is good. According to his research, evil is an ancient concept that is found throughout prehistoric mythology, including many of his favorite chapters of the Bible, Psalm 123 of

which unequivocally states that we should fear no evil, advice which, Butch explained, "is the modern equivalent of Vote Republican."

Republicans, Butch said, want to keep the Bible and its preconceived notions of evil out of American government. He would like to see voters paying more attention to relevant, modern-day issues such as golf scores, cute little interns, and the cost of tickets to movies where sooner or later just about everything blows up.

"Have you ever checked out the price of Sugar Frosted Flakes?" Butch asked with a rhetorical sneer. "*That* is evil. It's more expensive than good old American beef like the kind John Wayne used to herd and, I might add, eat. Now suppose I tell you that Kellogg's has never contributed a dime to the evil Republican party. Does that set off any bells?"

Chelsea-Groton to Hear Confessions

Protestants across Sprague are rejoicing as Chelsea-Groton Bank announces that it will be hearing confessions at its drive-up window.

"It's about time," said Wilhelm Benson, a long-time Congregationalist who says he has "a lot on my chest, sin-wise, nothing big, but you know...some stuff."

Chelsea-Groton tellers are being trained to hear confessions and dispense appropriate non-denominational penance. Rather than require the traditional rosary prayers appropriate only for Catholics, tellers will send the confessed to mow their neighbors' lawns, wash clean dishes, iron wrinkle-free clothes, help the town road crew fill potholes, join the Chelsea-Groton Christmas Club, or serve as alternates on the planning and zoning board of appeals.

"We hope to give all our clients an opportunity to cleanse their souls even as they cash their checks and make deposits," said Joanne Lynch, branch director. "The days of giving out lollipops and free toasters are gone. Today's bank users demand global solutions."

Lynch said that a bank is a logical location for confessional services since many of the "sins" of modern life involve financial transactions.

But Chelsea-Groton recognizes that in a community as diverse as Sprague, sins often involve activities that are more "personal" than "financial." For these customers, the bank provides a comprehensive checklist that itemizes most of the "fun and trouble" that human beings can get themselves into when the think nobody's looking. Sins not listed can be described as "other."

But don't think that you can just check off "other," receive a slap on the wrist and drive away.

"We cannot process a confession to 'other' transgressions without a full description," Lynch said. "We want all the juice. If the space provided is not enough, you can attach additional pages, but we ask that you do so inside the bank, not at the drive-up window." ✳

Clip-'n'-Confess!

Squeeze your confession in here and drop it in Chelsea-Groton's night deposit box! You'll receive your penance with your monthly statement!

Name:_____

Account #_____

Sin: _____

Butch enjoined the Democrats to form an alliance with the evil Republicans in a legislature "unsurpassed in self-sustainability." ✳

Sergeant-for-a-Day Elections Open

Sprague Recreation Committee has opened a 30-day election period for the honory position of Sergeant-for-a-Day. The town resident gaining the most votes will be allowed to bark at people for 24 hours.

Melonie Cruise, 78, is considered a favorite not only for her many connections at the Senior Center but for her widely acknowledged inability to so much as tell a fly to shoo.

Vincent Vandoloso, endorsed by Uncles for Education and Gutmeisters of Sprague, is also expected to to receive wide support. Though he and his family fled to Occum after he contracted nasal anthrax, his reputation remains.

"Vinnie *looks* like a sergeant," said Paul Pryzkowitcz, last year's honorary sarge. "You should see him in his favorite tee-shirt and an old stogie in his mouth. If he tells you to drop and give him fifty, you really feel like doing it."

Last year the Sprague Taste Reference Board agents removed Przykowitcz from the front of Sayles School, where he had been hollering "Move it! Move it! Move it! Move it!" as children descended from their school buses. The board charged him with using distasteful anatomical synecdoche when addressing lower-grade children who, due to their short legs, were unable to come down the bus stairs quickly enough. Przykowitcz had to plead "segeant's privilege" to avoid harsh fines.

Vandoloso's campaign platform includes commitments to tell several town residents "shape up or ship out." He would also like to see the entire town take a 20-mile hike in the rain while chanting the traditional army poem, "This is my weapon, this is my gun."

"Spraguers can use a lot of personal improvement," Vandoloso said, "but it's never going to happen if somebody doesn't yell at them." ✳

Bible Chapter, continued from page 1

now, Blanchettes and Glaudes and LaLibertes will return to Sprague and think, *My ancestors walked here. They scraped ice off their windshields. They sacrificed their pets to the demands of inner voices.*

Papineau is concerned, however, that present-day Spragucolites will begin smiting and slewing each other in attempts to have their names included in the chapter.

"Gird thy loins for an unclean noise shall arise from the east side of the Shetucket and yea from the west side, too, shall it arise," Papineau stated in a press release issued from town hall. "Mightily shall thy neighbors eschew thee, and verily wilt thy pate be smitten by the

Gutmeisters Seek Homes for Leftovers

Gutmeisters of Sprague has issued a call for foster homes to take in leftover food, some of which has been in Gutmeister refrigerators for years.

The anonymous president of the club, known by his nom d'aliment, "Mr. Jiggles," explained that by the Gutmeister code of ethics, food must never be thrown away.

"Our priority is always immediate consumption," Jiggles said. "Failing at that, we offer our food to others. If they decline, we offer it to a dog. If he declines, we store it properly

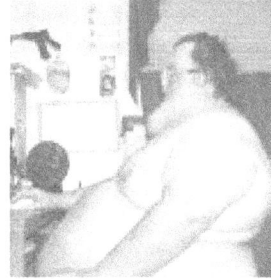

"Mr. Jiggles"

for consumption at a later date, perhaps in a soup or stew, perhaps slathered with Cheez-Wiz and jalapenos."

Jiggles said that some of the club's leftovers dated back to the Eisenhower administration and were but a fuzzy green shadow of their former selves. In one case, a crescent of cheeseburger has decomposed to the point of sprouting what may be mushrooms. Samples have been sent to the State fuzzologist to see if they are edible.

The Gutmeisters are looking for homes that have just a little room in the back of their refrigerators. The leftovers come in sealed plastic containers which the Gutmeister recommend not be opened. Photographs and brief descriptions of the leftovers can be seen at the Gutmeister website.

"We have some leftover chili that is absolutely breathtaking," Jiggles said. "We have leftover pizza that even insects could love. We have wax beans like something right out of Van Gogh. We have broiled sea bass marinated in passion fruit juice and topped with an ambuscade of shredded arugula and Brie that has synergistically decomposed to become a potential source of live bait which could be used to catch *more* sea bass, which if you think about it is a very, very deep concept in foodstuffs."

Sprague residents who shelter a leftover for a year will be invited to the Gutmeisters' Leftover Reunion Picnic, where the traditional Grand Stew d'Tout is served as club members eulogize great meals of the past. ✳

---

resident state trooper for thy slovenly beseechments."

Papineau denied rumors that he had suggested "Steve" as a title for the chapter. He also said that he had not decided whether the town would foot the printing bill. ✳

BFD Denounces Pretzel-Choking

Calling pretzel-choking an irritating fad, Baltic Fire Department Chief Dan Nagle is asking people to find something else to do. Since President George W. Bush passed out after choking on a pretzel last month, eighteen local residents have been rescued by the BFD ambulance with pieces of pretzels stuck in their throats.

"This isn't coincidence," Nagle said. "It's a full-blown trend. We had a similar situation about ten years ago when Bush's father threw up on what's-his-name, the Emperor of Japan. We also suspect there was widespread presidential emulation during Monicagate but we don't know the extent of it because no one called 9-1-1."

Nagle said that from now on, any emergency calls for pretzel-gagging will result in someone's stomach getting pumped, "but good."

The fire department plans to ask the Board of Selectman to pass an ordinance making it a misdemeanor to fail to chew food thoroughly. During the first Bush administration, the town made it illegal to vomit on emperors. No incidents were reported after the ordinance went into effect.

Spanish Inquisition Remembered

The department dropped plans to outlawing the possession of a pretzel after Viren Patel, owner of Baltic Convenience Store, said that he had several cases of pretzels in his inventory. Proposing an alternate ordinance, the fire department suggested a law prohibiting possession of a pretzel with a bite taken out of it. That restriction would make it legal for Patel to sell his pretzels.

The BFD abandoned the plan after the American Civil Liberties Union warned that the law would encourage people to insert entire pretzels into their mouths, potentially a cause of choking.

Nagle said the BFD stomach pump is made of cast iron and bronze. It was bought, used, from St. Mary's Church, which said the pump dates back to 1233, when it was manufactured by order of Pope Gregory IX for use in the Inquisition.

"It's a little rusty, but it works fine," Nagle said. "Once you get used to the squeaking, it's not so bad." ✳

Believe it or not . . .

When EMTs arrived at the White House to rescue President Bush, they had to read his lips to find out why he was turning blue!

TRB to Set Guidelines on Gluttony

The Sprague Taste Reference Board has added to its technical agenda a project to develop guidelines for local gluttony. The Board emphasized that it did not intend to set formal standards. Rather it will establish criteria that both gluttons and observers can use to draw the line between genuine gluttony and mere overindulgence.

"A number of confirmed gluttons in this town have expressed frustration in recognizing when they've merely overeaten, for example, or have succeeded in really going too far," said Prudence Retenturl, board chair. "We've had several cases of verbalized disagreements over enough being enough. In some cases, it would seem that only too much is actually enough."

Retenturl said that the board would look at not only food consumption but also alcohol intake, hot tub usage, television, fishing, golf, and "you-know-what."

The board will consult with the Gutmeisters of Sprague, an organization dedicated to alimentary excess. The Gutmeisters will experiment to establish scales of reference that will help eaters and interested parties determine how much is too little, enough, more than enough, and too much, with a "Red Zone" for waaaaay too much.

"Waaaaay too much is still a theoretical quantity," said the anonymous Grand Manatee of the club known as Mr. Jiggles. "None of our members have been there, but we know it's out there somewhere. We're still looking, still striving, still growing."

Resident State Trooper Chris Johnson says that his office has received 38 calls for acts of gluttony so far this year, up from 32 at this time last year. About half were repeat offenders. Four were minors, including one NFA student who had to be dragged from a hot shower after spending approximately half the day there.

The board plans to issue a list of warning signs of gluttony. Among them are dizziness, loss of motor control, a sense of slothful euphoria, inability to laugh without manual support of the stomach, and conflicting feelings of guilt and accomplishment. Ω

Police Clueless on Cereal Case

Police are continuing to investigate a badly beaten box of Honey-frosted Tutti-Frutti Shredded Wheat Now with Crunchy Nuggets Plus that was found sprawled across Potash Hill Road. The product lay scattered along almost a quarter mile of the road, and the box was described as "beyond recovery."

As police continued to search for clues, they could only speculate on who may have committed the act of litter.

"We're looking for someone with a lot of pent-up anger and frustration," resident state trooper Chris Johnson said. "Either that or a total wheatophobe."

Johnson said the investigators were especially perplexed at the ingredients of the cereal, many of which seemed to be from some bizarre planet on the other side of the galaxy. One had three hyphens, two numbers and 27 letters, three of which were lower-case Q's.

"We see plenty of Shredded Wheat around here," Johnson said. "And once in a while we get some tutti-frutti. We get honey-frosted products in town about as often as we get a Ph.D., which is to say once, maybe twice in a blue moon, and we never get blue moons. It's the Crunchy Nuggets that seem to account for many of the suspicious ingredients, and God only knows what the Plus stuff is. All we can determine at this juncture is that we are definately dealing with an out-of-town cereal."

Johnson said that he himself had never seen Honey-frosted Tutti-Frutti Shredded Wheat Now with Crunchy Nuggets Plus before but that he had heard of children in large cities eating it, sometimes straight from the box. He said the product was sold openly in New York City and parts of New Jersey. ✳

Baboon May Have Infiltrated Board of Education
Sayles Pincipal Suffers Rare Stroke

Sprague citizens have been looking askance at the Board of Education after an anonymous tip that one of the board members may be an undercover Cercopithecidae Chaeropithecus, or baboon.

In an official response, BOE chairman Michael Bychowsky pointed out that baboons are considered one of the more intelligent apes and that scientists have succeeded in teaching them to communicate through a rudimentary language of gestures and grunts.

"If we would of had a boner-fide baboon on the board, which I'm not saying we actually did, but if, then we could say we did ourself proud," Bychowsky burped. "And anyways, in a democracy, everybody is created equal irregardless of sex, gender, creed, color, genus, species or family preference, if you catch my drift."

Sayles School principal Dr. Harrington "Mojo" Heifer-Tittlebaum stated that he had indeed caught the chairman's drift but declined to comment on the presence of an undercover baboon on the board. He added that if a baboon could occupy the White House, then one could certainly hold a seat on the Sprague Board of Education.

In what has been described as "a rare stroke of pedagogical inspiration," Dr. Heifer-Tit-

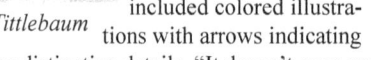
Dr. Heifer-Tittlebaum

tlbaum seized the opportunity of a local controversy to have students prepare projects and reports on the alleged ape.

The school-wide research effort was curtailed, however, after several students discovered that the *American Heritage Dictionary* described the baboon as "characterized by an elongated, doglike muzzle, a short tail, and bare calluses on the buttocks."

"This is no way to describe an alleged school board member," Dr. Heifer-Tittlbaum said as school administrative staff prepared a bonfire of the research projects, 93 percent of which included colored illustrations with arrows indicating the distinctive details. "It doesn't even say what kind of dog."

Resident State Trooper Chris Johnson said that he knew of no law prohibiting elected officials of that description serving on a town board but that he had a plan to identify the alleged infiltrator. Without revealing the details of his trap, he said only that it would take place at the next school board meeting and would involve a fishing pole and some slender yellow fruit. ✳

Coming soon . . .

Town to Replace Paradigm
Gutmeisters Prepare for Winter
New Ruling on Beer, Cigs
Teen Depressed
Uncle Trouble
Sasquish Sighting
New Motto Shop

Neighborhood News

What's really happening in Sprague.

July 2001

Teens Nabbed with Van of Remotes
Electronic Revolution Quelled

Three local adolescents were arrested but promptly released after police found their van loaded with sophisticated remote control equipment. The youths had been using the equipment to manipulate household appliances as they drove around Sprague.

The three were released after police failed to press appropriate charges.

"There is no law on the books prohibiting the use of remote control devices on public streets," state circuit judge Francis X. Foley stated. "Just when the state thinks it's got all its bases covered, somebody comes along and creates a new crime that isn't illegal. We had to release them, and for all we know, they're still driving around, sabotaging appliances from afar."

The youths, whose name were not released because they are minors, had made digital copies of the signals of a wide variety of household remote control devices. By using

cont. on p. 3

Tootsie-roll Taints Town Election
Registrar launches new word

Sprague election results were thrown into turmoil last month as an alleged Tootsie-Roll was found stuck to a key voting booth lever. Election officials suspect the involvement of a child.

The Tootsie-Roll, chewed and gooey, was found stuck to the lever of Democratic presidential candidate Albert Gore.

"I would describe it as gross," said Kathleen Boushee, registrar of voters. "It wasn't something you'd want to touch. And of course nobody was going to vote for the Green Party candidate besides you-know-who because Green is just too weird, Tootsie-Roll or no Tootsie-roll. And nobody in their right mind would vote for George Bush, so he only got 48 votes. That's more than anybody else got, but still, it doesn't seem like enough."

State police were notified. A milk crate found in the voting booth indicated that a

Kathleen Z. Boushee

short person may have been involved, perhaps a child.

"We're looking for someone between three and four feet tall with lots of cavities," said Chris Johnson, resident state trooper. "So far we have detained 372 suspects. We're also looking for a Republican with an off-beat sense of humor but so far we have found no one matching the description except for you-know-who and a couple of his friends, and quite frankly we suspect they are actually in the Bull Moose party. Also, they aren't the type to eat Tootsie-Rolls. If it was chewing tobacco, I might say maybe, but Tootsie-rolls just aren't their M.O."

Glenn Cheney, chairman of the town Green Party committee, said that many voters may have assumed that they were supposed to stand on the milk crate, as he himself did. The raised position made it difficult to reach the Green Party ticket, which was placed below the tickets of the two totally corrupt parties of the corporatocracy, where it was inaccessible to the sciatically disabled.

Boushee, who is also host of *Sprague Today*, a public access television program, interviewed herself regarding the electoral brouhaha.

"I think it's time we held our horses," Boushee said. "There's a lot of constitutional stuff involved here. Like can a child go into a voting booth with a parent or other adult? If so, can the child pull the levers? If so, does that give Republicans an advantage? Does the child have the right to take a milk crate into

Continued on page 3

Beer and Cigarettes are Good for You!

Town rejoices as chips, ice cream, return to "Good List."

Sprague residents rejoiced as the Federal Health Department released a report that moves many foods and former vices from the FHD "Bad List" to its "Good List" of health-inducing substances.

Drawing on the latest statistics, the report found that cigarettes are actually good for the circulatory system and can be used as an effective antidote for the stress brought on by "goody-goodies" who have traditionally enjoyed making smokers feel guilty.

Beer was also moved to the department's good list as a source of orally ingested carbonation. The report recommended simultaneous doses of potato chips, preferably while the consumed is in a semi-reclined position with the legs raised slightly to ease circulation and allow cooling of the knee-pits.

"I always knew this day would come," said Elizabeth Foley, a local alternative health practices activist as

she joined friends in a victory dance at the town gazebo. "It was just a matter of time until new findings led to new conclusions that are a lot easier to live with."

Sales of cigarettes have soared as former smokers rush to rekindle their habits. Town-sponsored smoking classes will be held at Sayles School for nonsmokers who have trouble learning to smoke late in life.

A few diehard nonsmokers are resisting the new findings.

"I just hope I live long enough to see the new conclusions reversed," said Lungella Phlegming. "I want to have the last laugh, even if it kills me."

The report attributed the new findings to observations that smokers spend more time outdoors, where they periodically retreat to relax in fresh air among friends. The sense of camaraderie, righteousness and community apparently reduce the stress that can lead to heart attack and stroke.

Foods rich in glycerol esters, once known disparagingly as "fat," are now recognized as

Continued on page 2

Patent Pending on Izbicki Dogstiltz™

Versailles inventor Robin Izbicki has filed a patent application for quadripedic tibia extenders which she intends to market as "Izbicki Dogstiltz™."

Izbicki, inventor of possum saucers, says the stilts will make it easier for the elderly, the obese and people with back pain to pet their best friends. The stilts can raise a small dog, such as a Pomeranian or Chihuahua, to waist level, making it possible, for the first time in history, for their owners to pet them without bending over.

"I don't know who's going to enjoy this product more, pets or pet owners," Izbicki said. "I see it as a win-win product."

Izbicki's dog stilts are adjustable and easy to attach to a dog's tibia, or lower leg. Use of the stilts involves a little training, but their inventor says the dogs quickly catch on.

"First you have to let them stand there and get used to it," Izbicki explained. "Then hold them as they take their first few steps. Then it's easy. Four legs makes for a very stable platform. They pick it right up. Just watch out for the males when they have to pee."

Izbicki said she got the idea for Izbicki Dogstiltz™ after an elderly aunt bent down to pet her toy dachshund and then couldn't straighten up. An emergency medical crew from Baltic Fire Department had to use two winches and a ladder truck borrowed from Willimantic to return the woman to a reasonable facsimile of her former posture.

Seeing her aunt's dachshund crying for attention, Izbicki was inspired.

"I thought to myself, there has to be an easier way," Izbicki said.

Izbicki plans to manufacture the dog stilts in her Versailles possum saucer factory, where her research and development department has been experimenting with cat stilts. Her marketing department has begun developing a new spot that will involve dogs on Izbicki Dogstiltz™ chasing and catching possum saucers flipped like Frisbees. ❈

Beer, Cigs, continued from page 1

long-term sources of energy. The report recommends using the word "latent energy" as the general term for glycerol esters.

With salt now recognized as effectively combating low blood pressure, potato chips have been identified as a nearly perfect foodstuff.

Quick to respond to the new health standards, the Baltic Fire Department am-

continued on p. 3

Society to Test Proverbs

Following a series of tragic accidents in the Sprague community, the Hanover Philosophical Society has initiated a long-term project to test common sayings and proverbs for reliability. Approved sayings will be issued an "HPS Seal of Safety."

"Age-old truisms have led to countless deaths and injuries," said Robert Meya, HPS president. "We feel that it's time we stopped putting blind trust in short statements."

Meya warned that *What you don't know won't hurt you* is a classic example of bad advice. He cited the case of a local man who didn't know which end was up and had been walking with a limp ever since.

The society is looking for volunteers to test the seemingly innocent adage, *Look before you leap.* The volunteers will be presented with a statistically significant number of situations in which they will look and then leap.

Early to bed, early to rise, makes a man healthy, wealthy and wise is also a priority proverb. Initial research, Meya said, has failed to find a single incidence of health, wealth and wisdom in an individual with a conservative bed schedule.

"The closest we've come is healthy, wealthy and obnoxious," Meya said.

Meya said that not looking in the mouths of gift horses has so far proven safe. Further studies will be conducted to search for a more appropriate place to look a gift horse. Local equestrians have been asked to donate horses for the studies.

The classic warning not to put all one's eggs in a basket has also led to local problems. A Baltic man put all his eggs in eight baskets, put the baskets in a canoe and attempted to descend the Little River alone.

"It was tragic," Meya said. "If he'd ignored the adage, he would have lost only one basket, not eight. We think the problem may have been resulted from someone telling him he had to paddle his own canoe. He left home with his American Express card, but that doesn't seem

to have helped at all. There's been too little research on these untested combinations of sayings. It's like mixing apples and oranges. And of course this incident also raises the issue of counting chickens before they hatch. Would that have helped? And would it apply to ostrich eggs?"

The society will be also be working with local doctors and orchards to determine how many apples are needed to keep an HMO away.

Does all work and no play really make Jack a dull boy? The sheer antiquity of the saying would seem to prove its validity, but HPS research has turned up an unexpected finding. Guys named Jack don't work very much and tend to play more than guys named Charles, John or Helmut.

The implications, Meya says, are complex.

"Do Jacks work less because they've been warned?" Meya asks. "Do the Johns think they are impervious to personal dullness until someone calls them Jack? Can Jacks be dull from other causes, such as being early to bed and early to rise or counting their chickens before they hatch?"

HPS has also been stymied in its attempt to compare the value of a birds. Jack LeParesseur, chairman of the HPS bird evaluation committee, found a bush with two birds in it, caught one and held it in his hand. The committee reached a consensus that the bird in the hand was discernibly superior to the one in the bush. As the question regarded a two-birds-in-the-bush scenario, however, the bird in the hand was returned to the bush, at which juncture both birds flew away.

"Mistakes were made," Meya stated. "We're going back to the drawing board on this one. We may try assessing the relative values of gift horses in the hand versus those in the bush if we can find some that have been adequately trained and don't bite. Or we may start with gift ostriches. That way we can kill two birds with one stone. No, wait a minute, that's not going to work, either." ❈

Library Trustees Sign Out All Books
Trooper: "It looks like they're headed for Tijuana."

Sprague Public Library patrons were shocked to enter the library last week and find the shelves stripped naked. Not a book remained.

"We are guardedly concerned about the situation," said Renee LaPine, library director. "According to our records, the library's seven trustees legally signed out 14,888 books last week. Until the due date, a week from now, there's nothing we can do."

Neighborhood News has been unable to contact any of the trustees. Terri Woronecki,

wife of Stuart Woronecki, Grand Wazoo of the Trustees, said she has not seen or hard from her husband since he drove toward Baltic in a black tractor-trailer about a week ago.

The satellite tracking system of the Connecticut State library has been following a suspicious black tractor-trailer that has been making maintaining a southeasterly direction across the United States. It was last reported to be crossing Arkansas at the legal speed limit.

"It looks like they're headed for Tijuana,"

Continued on page 3

Electronic revolution, from page 1

a boosted signal, 14 antennas and a satellite dish, they were able to open and close garage doors, turn stereo systems on and off, cause CD players to switch disks, reset clocks on various appliances, change television channels, start VCR machines, participate in conversations on cordless phones, reset alarms, listen to answering machines, and generally take control of household electronics.

"We were very relieved to learn that our town's appliances had not taken control of themselves," said Stephen J. Papineau, first selectman. "The electronic revolution we were expecting has apparently been called off. It was all a practical joke." ❊

Tijuana, continued from page 2

commented a resident state trooper who requested that his name not be released. "We see this kind of thing all the time. In the middle of the night they sign out all the books, load them into a truck and light out for the border. For two weeks, there's nothing we can do. By the time the books are overdue, they've read them all and sold them to a Mexican library. Three days later they've blown it all on cheap Mexican Coke."

The trooper said that Coke in Mexican border towns can be had for as little as ten cents a bottle.

"They have kids selling it in the streets," he said. "They'll barter it for Danielle Steele novels. They don't care."

The police have been combing the library for clues. Removal of the books revealed a suspicious number of dead cockroaches, but so far fingerprint analysis of the bugs has turned up only the prints of the former cleaning crew. ❊

Teens Find Road to Rack and Ruin

Four teens have reported finding the mythical Road to Ruin. The well worn, litter-strewn trail began at the old "swimming hole" on the Little River and apparently led in the direction of New York and New Jersey.

"We're pretty sure this is the big one," said Stanley "Smoothie" Spidoonski, president of the Sprague Institute of Cool Ones. "We've been looking for it for a long time."

Spidoonski described the trail as wide, obviously well traveled, and littered with the bottles and cans of beer and alcoholic beverage. Marijuana and poppy plants grew wild along its edges. Unmentionables of an allegedly sexual nature were hanging from branches and lying on the ground. Vending machines offered snack foods and video games. Temptation was heard rustling in the brush.

A SICO exploratory team ventured down the road and returned with amazing tales of bliss and excitement. The road is easy to follow, they said, until it forks on the outskirts of New York City, where one road to leads to Rack, N.J., and the other goes over the Triboro Bridge.

"Watch out for the toll," Spidoonski said. "It's a little stiff. That's where we turned back."

Brunhilda Onus, town mother, warned residents not to approach the trail.

"Just because it's there doesn't mean you have to go down it," Onus said. "You're a lot better off staying right here and keeping your nose to the grindstone, where it belongs." ❊

Tootsie-roll, continued from page 1

the booth? Does anyone, child or adult, have the right to stick a Tootsie-Roll to a candidate's lever? What happens if it is determined that a Tootsie-Roll, or for that matter a lolli-pop or a wad of gum, has affected the outturn of an election? This is obviously a case for the Supreme Court. They're the only ones who'll know what to do. Is that a word, outturn?" ❊

beer, cigs, continued from p. 2

bulance has been outfitted with ashtrays, oral and intravenous snack concentrates, and four beers on tap.

The report, sponsored by the International Snack and Tobacco Institute and Eager Undertakers of America, is available at participating bars and convenience stores. ❊

Exam to Rank Citizenry on Scale of Smartness
"We've needed this for a long time."

In an effort to end inaccurate accusations of stupidity, all Sprague residents 18 years of age and older will be required to take the state Moron-Genius examination on January 15-19. The exam will rank everyone according to how smart they really are.

"We've needed this for a long time," said Sprague first selectman Stephen J. Papineau. "I've had it up to here with people coming to me and asking who's right and who's wrong and whether it's fair that so-and-so called such-and-such an idiot or a dweeb or whatever. It really isn't for me to decide."

The grueling 36-hour exam, conducted over the course of four days, covers every conceivable area of knowledge, from ancient history to barbeque grill operation. Scores between zero and 24,000 will rank everyone on the Connecticut-Massachusetts-Rhode Island Scale of Smartness, which ranges from "absolute, total moron" to "unbelievable genius." The low-end ranks of the scale include fool, boob, nitwit and dork. The middle ranks, where most Nutmeggers fall, ranges from not-too-bright up to to not-too-dumb. The more astute test-takers can receive rankings as high as smart one, very knowledgeable guy, whiz, and brain.

Contrary to widespread belief, most often held by those in the range of dunderhead through medium-galoot, such categories as wise-guy and smart-ass are not determined by the tri-state Scale of Smartness.

Each individual who completes the exam will receive an official certificate from the state of Connecticut, signed by Governor John Rowland and the State Director of Native Intelligence, whoever that is.

The written part of the exam will cover not only academic subjects but real-life situations, such as the best action to take if your pants fall down in a public place. The practical part of the exam, which will be held at Babe Blanchette ball field, will test people's abilities to start lawn mowers, understand what dogs and cats are trying to tell them, cook an omlette, spell omlette, catch a trout, make something out of wood, and change a diaper in the dark.

"Smartness ranking should end a lot of problems," said Dr. Harrington "Mojo" Heiffer-Tittlbaum, acting principal of Sayles School. "We all know how irritating it is to have some blockhead call a Ph.D. like myself a blithering nincompoop. Once everybody's ranked, we'll know what to call each other."

Papineau pointed out that under state protocol, it will be approporiate to call someone a name that appears higher in the smartness ranking than the person actually scored.

"It's OK to call a certified imbecile a dimwit," he explained. "In fact, it's a compliment. On the other hand, if you call a total brainiac a perspicacious guru, you are, in effect, insulting the person."

Papineau said that all scores will be posted in a public location, and he advised everyone to carry a list of the ranking categories for quick reference. ❊

(see State Smartness Scale on page 4)

Connecticut-Massachusetts-Rhode Island Scale of Smartness

Note: Some categories are divided by such modifiers as *complete, total, regular, absolute, utter, major, certifiable, proven, pretty, kind-of-a, demonstrable, federal,* and *semi-* .

1.	Moron	27.	collie	62.	cerebrally exhausted	99.	braniac
2.	moron	28.	Occumite	63.	oaf	100.	egghead
3.	imbecile	29.	ding-a-ling	64.	ox	101.	nerd
4.	blockhead	30.	dingbat	65.	yokel	102.	thinker
5.	nincompoop	31.	clod	66.	not especially gifted	103.	intellect
6.	nitwit	32.	boob	67.	basically without forte	104.	talented one
7.	dimwit	33.	dummy	68.	school smart	105.	aptitudinal
8.	ungifted in any way	34.	fool	69.	not too bright	106.	highly apt person
9.	stoop	35.	nit	70.	regular	107.	on the ball
10.	simpleton	36.	schmo	71.	medium	108.	expert
11.	cow	37.	turkey	72.	OK, brain-wise	109.	ace
12.	dullard	38.	loon	73.	used to be smart	110.	adept
13.	jackass	39.	ig-no-runt	74.	tyro	111.	authority
14.	ninny	40.	half wit	75.	not-too-dumb	112.	maestro
15.	tomfool	41.	cretin	76.	one with a knack	113.	Ph.D.
16.	rambo	42.	feeble-minded person	77.	Lassie	114.	geek
17.	bimbo	43.	dork	78.	skilled	115.	maven
18.	staunch Republican	44.	dolt	79.	accomplished	116.	prodigy
19.	twit	45.	dildo	80.	general specialist	117.	professional
20.	flake	46.	dullard	81.	jeopardy material	118.	specialist
21.	dope	47.	bufoon	82.	endowed	119.	virtuoso
22.	goose	48.	imbecile	83.	sharpest knife in drawer	120.	whiz
23.	donkey	49.	lout	84.	brightest light on tree	121.	whiz kid
24.	bonehead	50.	churl	85.	cerebrally enforced	122.	wizard
25.	meathead	51.	boor	86.	savvy	123.	savant
26.	[vegetable]head	52.	popsickle salesman	87.	polymath	124.	Green Party material
		53.	rocket scientist	88.	wag	125.	sage
		54.	brain doctor	89.	Hanoverian	126.	gifted
		55.	clod	90.	scholar	127.	regular Bob Batten
		56.	oxymoron	91.	human Chunky	128.	regular Einstein
		57.	blockhead	92.	authority	129.	genius
		58.	galoot	93.	diviner	130.	unbelievable genius
		59.	klutz	94.	expert		
		60.	lummox	95.	guru		
		61.	obligate mouth-breather	96.	highbrow		
				97.	intellectual		
				98.	brain		

Ties to Vie for Top Knot

Sprague neckwear traditionalists are invited to submit their best knots to the First Annual Sprague-Franklin Necktie Knot Competition. Prizes will be given for the best knot, biggest knot, oldest knot and most original knot. A speed contest will determine who can tie a tie the fastest, and a "Sunday School" event will pit father against father to see who can knot a tie around a boy who, for purposes of the contest, refuses to wear a tie.

Sprague is said to hold a significant advantage in the oldest tie category. Paul Pryzkowticz claims to have a knot that came over on the Mayflower and has been handed down through 14 generations — and perhaps ten times that — without being untied. His wife, Sylvia, claims that the tie has been hanging on the same bedroom doorknob since an undetermined date during the Truman administration.

"I don't know whether Paul hanged it there or it hanged itself," Mrs. Pryzkowticz said.

Mr. Pryzkowticz said that the tie was given to him by his great-grandfather, Horace Wigglesworth Pryzkowticz III, a staunch Republican who wore the tie constantly for 78 years, beginning at the age of ten, when he opened a savings account in a the now-defunct Occum National Bank and Trust. He lowered the knot as he lay on his deathbed and handed it down to Paul.

"He told me the knot had been tied by Noah's valet, a Biblical Presbyterian who died in the flood shortly after slipping his tie over his head and hanging it on the horn of one of two rhinoceroses that were allowed onto the ark," Pryzkowticz said. "The rest is history." ✳

Take the Neighborhood News Quiz!

1. Wht company is this?

2. Why did the would-be brain-donor want to go to Mexico?

3. What did Chunky piddle on the floor?

4. What's name of the launderette in Baltic?

5. Why did Mary LeBoi work for the town crew?

6. Who was the first saint canonized by Fr. Anthony Ozga?

7. What is Stanley Spidoonski's nickname?

8. Who was depressed over the imminent collapse of the American Numismatic Society?

9. What did Mother Onus fly?

10. When is Septic Tank Awareness Month?

11. According to Angelynn Meya, what does it sound like to have your beak tweaked?

12. What is the name of Woronecki's band?

13. What kind of animal is Spent Bullet?

14. Who is this?

15. Who invented Dogstiltz?

16. Where did the library board take all the books?

17. Who is president of Hanover Philisophical Society?

18. Who is Sprague Town Liar?

19. Where is the Bat Boy suspected to be hiding?

20. Who kicked a woodchuck?

21. Who is chairman of the Economic Development Commission?

22. Where was suspected Shinola found?

23. Where was a mystical image of Chunky sighted?

24. What color was the Manhattan Volunteer Attorney Corps bus?

25. What one person knows the German word for "urge to die"?

26. Who is Luiz Inacio da Silva's manager?

27. What sports equipment did Sprague Historical Society find in its closet?

28. In Sprague, what is the plural of "you"?

29. What family lives in the House of Ads?

30. What restaurant is to open in the ruins of the Baltic Mill?

31. Why was auditor Garth Tronstrom taken to the hospital?

32. What is Ian Cheney's Ph.D. in?

33. Where is "the other" Versailles?

34. Whose feathers did Trooper Chris Johnson peek under?

35. What is the name of the Economic Development rat?

36. Complete this quote: "If there's a boy and he's a bat, we're gonna find out…"

37. What is Garth W. Butch's job?

38. Who is president of Gutmeisters of Sprague?

39. What ancient road did the Institute of Cool Ones find?

40. Who's dumber, a ding-a-ling or a dingbat?

41. Who "just ain't screwed down tight"?

42. For whom was a scootery to be built?

43. What happened to Idi?

44. Who said, "To the rest of the world, we look like idiots?"

45. How much do three Quebecois uncles on a couch weigh?

46. Why does Sprague EDC want to name Earth Kevin?

47. Who is Agent 228?

48. Where can parents drop their children off at a drive-up window?

49. Who said, "When you think about it, aren't we *all* dumpsters?"

50. Where did Francis X. Foley find signs of caribou?

51. What is Robert Meya's title?

52. Who loves Brenda Pons?

53. Why was the town road crew trying to gain weight?

54. How many hours a day does Howard Bulgarino Sr. work?

55. What's the big hit of the Dead Morticians?

56, What is Anonymous Botch's real name?

Name these individuals and summarize their significance.

1.

2.

3.

4.

5.

6.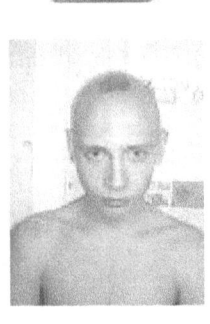

7.

8.

9.

10.

11.

12.

13.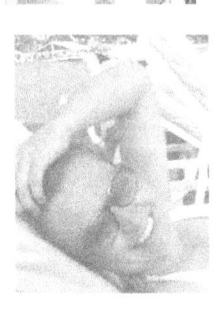

14.

15.

16.

17.

18.

19.

About the Author

Glenn Alan Cheney is the author of over 25 books of fiction and non-fiction on such topics as Chernobyl, Abraham Lincoln, the Pilgrims, nuclear proliferation, environmental issues, the Quilombo dos Palmares, and Brazil's Estrada Real. He has also translated works by zmachado de Assis and Rubem Alves. And then there's whatever *Neighborhood News* is. He has also written hundreds of articles, op-ed essays, and poems.